About the Author

Roger Tessier is the author of six motion picture screenplays that have won numerous awards in a variety of scriptwriting competitions; two of which have been optioned by motion picture producers, and one that garnered his first screenwriting agent. He has also written, produced, and directed a Music Bio Documentary Film, DEAD MAN ROCKIN', which was accepted at eleven film festivals in the US and has directed a number of short films. An avid musician and collector of vintage guitars, this is his first fiction novel.

The Van Gogh Incident

Roger Tessier

The Van Gogh Incident

Vanguard Press

VANGUARD PAPERBACK

© Copyright 2023
Roger Tessier

The right of Roger Tessier to be identified as author of
this work has been asserted by him in accordance with the
Copyright, Designs and Patents Act 1988.

All Rights Reserved

No reproduction, copy or transmission of this publication
may be made without written permission.
No paragraph of this publication may be reproduced,
copied or transmitted save with the written permission of the publisher, or in accordance
with the provisions
of the Copyright Act 1956 (as amended).

Any person who commits any unauthorised act in relation to
this publication may be liable to criminal
prosecution and civil claims for damages.

A CIP catalogue record for this title is
available from the British Library.

ISBN 978 1 83794 204 6

This is a work of fiction. Names, characters, businesses, places, events and incidents are either the product of the author's imagination or used in a fictitious manner. Any resemblance to actual persons, living or dead, or actual events is purely coincidental.

*Vanguard Press is an imprint of
Pegasus Elliot Mackenzie Publishers Ltd.*
www.pegasuspublishers.com

First Published in 2023

**Vanguard Press
Sheraton House Castle Park
Cambridge England**

Printed & Bound in Great Britain

To my wonderful wife, Janice, whose support and encouragement made this novel – like all my crazy schemes – a reality!

Thanks to Cara Lockwood for her initial editing and commentary. Thanks to my writing group for their support of my endeavors. Special thanks to Dale Reynolds who has been a mentor and supporter of my writing from the beginning.

INTRODUCTION

In Cambodia lie the ruins of the once magnificent ancient city of Koh Ker. The city is surrounded by numerous mountain ranges in North Central Cambodia that rendered it inaccessible to casual travelers in ancient times. With its perilous swampy grounds teeming with ravenous wildlife, miles of sunburned unprotected plains, and sheer hillsides concealed by thick almost impassable jungle, travel to and from was a terrifying journey – corridors of exotic and hungry wild animals threatened all who ventured there.

King Jayavarman IV ruled the country from 928 to 941 AD from his home at Koh Ker. Under Jayavarman IV's reign, art, sculpture, and architecture ascended to levels unknown in the Southeast Asian world. Little remains today of these great works due to the subsequent civil and territorial wars, lootings, and illegal acquisitions by the many so-call explorers who, in that name of preserving culture, pilfered the many indigenous treasures.

One work of art was never uncovered by outsiders and still lies buried deep below a seven-tiered pyramid called Prang. Thought to be the state temple and seat of power, the pyramid today lies in total ruin, secreting a millenniums old secret. Buried a hundred meters below the temple are the deteriorating remains of an alien spacecraft.

The spacecraft arrived over three thousand years before the reign of Jayavarman IV. Adrift for over eighty thousand years, the spacecraft had suffered a malfunction of cataclysmic proportions during a journey of discovery in the solar system of Proxima Centauri. Its mission was to discover if any of the three closest planets in their system were suitable for colonization. Finding no other hospitable worlds, the ship endeavored to return home – but catastrophic mechanical failure doomed the craft.

Cast adrift and subject to the whims of its massive engines that eventually burned out, then ultimately surrendering to solar winds, the spacecraft became an interstellar ghost ship, traveling to the outer reaches of the system and finally breaking free from the diminishing gravitational holds. Subjected to relentless solar rays, intergalactic matter, space debris, and tens of thousands of years of collisions with meteorites that fused onto the craft like barnacles attached to a sea vessel, the craft in its waning years no longer resembled its maiden form.

Seven hundred years before Tutankhamen was interred in the Great Pyramid of Giza in 1324 B.C., the spacecraft plunged to earth and landed in the valley of Koh Ker. It burrowed deep in the earth and the resultant eruption was possibly noted only by the distant Khmer tribes huddled in their huts. In the following three millennium, the depression in the valley caused by the spacecraft was subjected to backfill by the incessant rains, quakes, erosion, and shifting plates. The crater was rapidly engulfed and quickly grew over. No trace of the craft was discovered until the site was excavated to build the temple. The sheer size of the planned project demanded a deep and wide foundation. Utilizing manual labor by thousands of slave workers, the digging began under the supervision of Jayaraman's finest engineers. In a little over five years, a crude base was dug out of the original depression area. The first indication that something unusual was buried under the ground was the discovery of an engine exhaust port. The massive exhaust was forty feet wide and partially disengaged from the craft itself, leaving a hidden entryway into the body of the ship. The engineers were at a loss to explain the presence of the strange foreign object. After much handwringing and supplication to his god, Jayavarman IV himself visited the site accompanied by his council of elders to investigate. Time had destroyed and distorted the structure beyond recognition and surviving parts of the structure had been subject to the continued ground shifting and cave-ins. With nothing in existence as a reference, the tenth century elders and wise shamans declined to enter the ruins but declared it a gift from the gods that would serve as a holy foundation for the construction of the temple.

Jayavarman IV, a wholly self-possessed individual, considered himself, in what later centuries would be called, a Renaissance Man. His interest in the arts, architecture, science, and math separated him from his contemporaries. Much to the protest of his executive staff, Jayavarman IV himself undertook the perilous task of investigating the interior of the spacecraft – numerous times. It was during one of his many trips inside the craft that he came upon a set of capsules – all broken and destroyed, the contents turning to dust when disturbed – save for one. The intact capsule was roughly the size of a human torso and Jayavarman IV was able to lift it up from its base. Upon touching it, the capsule became translucent and lit up brightly. Alarmed, Jayavarman IV dropped the capsule, cracking it, but the light inside continued to glow and transform into a series of virtual images. The images and sounds presented incredibly vivid scenes from the home planet of the craft. Fertile valleys and thick jungles, massive spire topped structures, all attended to and inhabited by a race of sentient beings, not unlike humans, but larger, leaner, and more graceful – they referred to themselves as the N'Ghap. Alongside the N'Ghap in this charming Eden were many beautiful and mysterious creatures – but one extraordinary species appeared to exist in a separate class between the animals and their masters. These were the N'Khal – creatures most closely resembling an earth-like feline species, but extraordinarily built and amazingly dexterous. Images of their close relationship, history, bonds, and the powers that existed between the two were imprinted upon Jayavarman IV's memory. The N'Khal were inseparable companions with amazing powers. They were healers and communicated telepathically with the N'Ghap.

When the presentation finished, the globe extinguished itself and broke apart. Nevertheless, the knowledge of the home world of the N'Ghap and their wondrous N'Khal was imprinted upon Jayavarman IV's memory.

Jayavarman IV analyzed what he had witnessed and concluded he was bequeathed with a guide map for the future of his people and humanity. Not for one second did he consider that he was given a glimpse of an alien world. Rather, he resolved that the gift was his template for a future world to be built and handed to his ancestors. He commissioned his scribes and most trusted artists to render what he had witnessed only of the N'Khal, and thus a myth was born.

Jayavarman IV ordered the entrance to the ship be sealed, and never revealed what he learned of the N'Ghap race – he selfishly credited himself as the forebearer and architect of the future of mankind. Indeed, already possessing an uncommonly lithe and graceful physique, Jayavarman IV convinced himself that he was the first of this new race of man.

The new race never materialized but the myth of the N'Khal lived on.

CHAPTER 1

6:00 p.m. Thursday

The creature waited patiently for her master's daily visit. The tranquility of her concealed nest was soothing and comforting. Soon, the mechanical grindings of the elevator lowering her masters to the basement would start.

She cocked her head – alerted by the ring of the doorbell. It was a rare sound in this household. Her eyes fixated on the door to her sanctuary in anticipation.

#

Charles Reynolds finished pouring his wife Dana's pomegranate martini – her drink of choice these days – and stood quietly in appreciation of her as she glanced up from the book she was reading and smiled. The aroma of fresh baked chocolate chip cookies drifted in from the nearby kitchen. Charles was not only a great bartender, but he had also recently discovered the joys of cooking. Gazing at her, he felt he was the luckiest man on earth. The couple both worked out of the Beverly Hills home they owned going on some twenty years now and liked it that way. The unending traffic jam that was Los Angeles held little appeal to either of them. They ferociously guarded their privacy and lifestyle and had truly found no better company than each other. Charles strode across the den as Dana closed the book and offered her the glass. His gaze had not escaped her.

"Thank you, dear. Now what *was* that look for?" she asked.

Charles grinned ever so slyly. He was about to tell her what she no doubt already knew when their video doorbell announced a visitor at the front door.

"I'll get back to you on that. Are you expecting anything today?" he asked, as he returned to the bar and reached for a bottle of Glenfiddich to fill his tumbler.

Dana reflected momentarily. "Nothing that I know of," she replied. Charles already knew she was conducting a quick mental inventory of her recent online shopping as she sipped. "Pretty sure I'm up to date, dear."

Charles spoke to a mounted LCD screen at the bar. "Alexa, show the front door." The screen changed abruptly from the latest headline news to a live video shot from the front of the house. A young man with a trim Van Dyke beard and sporting a Viking style haircut – *so typical these days,* thought Charles – stood surveying the artisan carved wooden door to the home. Nothing otherwise about his appearance particularly alarmed Charles. He touched the screen.

"Hello, may I help you?" he asked in an unusually authoritative voice. *Maybe it'll scare them off.*

The young man onscreen seemed nervous as he focused on the mounted doorbell device. "Hello. Yes! Is this the, uh," he glanced down at something he was holding in his hand, "the Reynolds residence?"

Resigned to the evening cocktail hour intrusion, Charles sighed. "Yes, yes, it is. May I help you?" he repeated. He quickly gave Dana a side glance, shaking his head in a wide-eyed cartoon disgust. Dana circled the rim of her martini glass with her ring finger, raised an eyebrow and motioned a familiar *I agree.*

"I have a package for you, sir," replied the young man.

"Just leave it please. The porch is very secure. No one—"

"I'm sorry, but I can't do that, sir. A signature is required," he insisted.

Charles' business dealings with art and music collectibles required the occasional sales contract or notarized document of a confidential nature so this was not unheard of.

"Hold on," he replied. Dana had now turned on their wall mounted TV and was scrolling through the cable guide.

"Find that doctor show," he said.

"Which one? There's about ninety!" She giggled.

He broke into a grin at that. She was right – the couple were occasional TV watchers but each had a few guilty pleasures – doctor/hospital shows were Dana's weakness while Charles caught his beloved Los Angeles

Dodgers broadcasts whenever he could. He staunchly defended his sports show by proclaiming it was *'not really TV'*, but Dana caught him loitering in the den more often than not when one of her medical dramas were on.

"I think it's the one where he's underground. In England. I'll be right back."

Charles walked briskly down the hall towards his front door in cadence to the ice cubes clinking in his glass in hand.

As he reached the door, he heard Dana reply, "Found it! It's called *Temple*."

Charles turned back and shouted, "That's it!" Then, he opened the door and swiveled back to greet his visitor.

What greeted Charles was the business end of a sawed-off 30-30 shotgun aimed squarely at his face.

#

At an even six feet tall with a moderately athletic build, Charles was rarely intimidated. He could easily overpower this slight figure, but at sixty-five years of age, this ex-Marine was also wise enough to know when to weigh the odds. Now was that time. Focused on the polished barrel, Charles peripherally noted two other figures emerge from the side of his porch. Another man, this one older, and a young woman. *Odds definitely not in my favor*, he decided.

The oldest of the trio broke into a wide sardonic grin. "Forgive us for the intrusion, Mr. Reynolds. I'll take that glass if you don't mind. Back up into the house please. We have some business to discuss."

#

Charles and Dana were instructed to sit together on their oversized burgundy leather sofa in the media room as the older man leaned against a standalone bar facing them. The younger man inspected the bar's varied liquor offerings while the girl joined them from the kitchen area balancing a plate of Charles's fresh cookies. She had one in her mouth already as the younger man grabbed a bottle of Tito's Handmade Vodka and took a generous swig, then handed it to the girl. The older man studied the couple;

Charles doubted that his rugged All-American good looks impressed the fellow much, but Dana's darker Mediterranean complexion and striking petite figure was definitely a draw. It was not the kind of attention Charles was comfortable with.

"You're not at all what I thought," he said and snorted as he lifted the glass he took from Charles to his lips. "I expected a little more fight." He drained the tumbler. "I do commend you on your choice of whiskey, however." He rolled the glass in his hand. "Was that a twelve-year-old?"

Charles' eyes darted back and forth at the offending trio. He started to speak, then hesitated to correct him and tell him it was an eighteen-year-old scotch, not a whiskey, but decided *it's not worth it*. "What do you want? We have money. I can take you to my safe."

Dana added, "Please." She looked at the two younger thugs. "No one needs to get hurt."

Charles immediately understood Dana was not referring to themselves, but an encounter like this could go off the rails at any moment and he was fiercely protective of their safety, to the point of violence if necessary.

The older man chuckled and turned to his accomplices. "Wow. You hear that, Ben? Allison? I guess I didn't need you two after all. No one needs to get hurt!"

Charles quickly memorized the names of the two assistants to the boss automatically.

Ben picked up a crystal glass. "That's a shame," he mumbled as he theatrically dropped the glass to the tiled floor. It shattered. Dana winced. Charles knew it was one of the good pieces she used for company. *But not the unwelcome sort.*

"I was expectin' some hurt," Ben continued. "That's where the fun is." Ben stomped onto the glass and ground it into the floor. The grinding of the crystal shards by well-worn red Doc Martins added insult to the couple.

"Bring it down a notch, fun boy," the older man said.

Crash. Another glass hit the floor – a red wine goblet this time – and Allison offered a sardonic "Oops! My bad!"

The older man turned to her and winced. "You too, Ali!" He looked back to his captives. "Cripes! What do they teach the kids in school these days? I hate that fuckin' expression," he submitted to Charles and Dana with a shrug. "This generation."

"Jeez, sorry, Mark. I forget you're so sensitive," Allison responded with a giggle. The older man flipped Allison off with his middle finger.

Now knowing the older man's name, Charles used it as an opening. "Mark," he said, "This business you mentioned. Can we talk?"

Mark leaned back and shrugged. "I do the talking, pal. We'll start by you telling me where you keep it."

"It?" Charles offered.

Mark cocked his head. "Don't be coy. We've done our homework on you." He motioned around the house. Charles wondered who the 'we' were that the man was referring to. Mark and these two dunces? Probably not.

"This place," Mark continued. "You. Big shot art dealer. Massive collection. Fifteen million dollars cash for that newly discovered Van Gogh last month. That's a lot of scratch! I've got a buyer who'll pay me double. Just tell me where it is and we'll be out of your hair."

An insistent cell phone buzzing interrupted the interrogation. Mark reached into his pocket and held it up to his ear. He listed intently. He held a finger up in the air as if to say, *Quiet, please!*

Charles stared intently at the three. The one called Ben – he of the Van Dyke beard – appeared mid-twenties, thin, anxious, and nursing a runny nose. Probably a meth head. A thrift store Army fatigue jacket hung on his frame. Charles was offended that the chevron stripes were clearly store bought – not earned. Allison was young also but presented calmer. Her outfit was straight from Forever 21 – the five finger bins. Too much makeup on her hardened face did little to soften it. At her feet was a large grey gym bag she lugged in – he presumed it was to carry their bounty out. Charles imagined the two of them plotting a life of crime interrupted only by the occasional drug or sex orgy. Or both. The older man was obviously the brains of the outfit and would discard the two younger ones at a moment's notice.

"Yeah. Yeah, I know," Mark said after a bit of head bobbing. "We'll get it. It's under control." Mark clicked off. "Asshole," he muttered.

"Your buyer?" Charles asked.

"Again, the Van Gogh?"

Charles and Dana remained silent. The Van Gogh was not in a place this group would be welcome.

"I suppose I could just find it myself without your conscious assistance," Mark continued.

"Emphasis on conscious, of course."

"You're free to get it," Charles said. "I won't stop you."

"Of course, you won't. Just tell me where."

Charles and Dana exchanged glances.

"Oh, what is this, hide and seek? I'm in no mood for games and my pals here probably can't count to one-hundred. Ben, tie Mister I've-Got-a-Secret up." He motioned to Dana. "We'll take you as our tour guide."

Charles jumped up. "No, take me. No one needs to get hurt."

Ben stepped forward and struck Charles in the head with the butt of his shotgun, knocking him unconscious to the floor. "Too late, mister."

CHAPTER 2

7:00 p.m.

The young hothead Ben was charged with restraining Charles and keeping watch on the main floor as Dana was instructed to lead the other two to the treasure. Allison was ordered to handcuff Dana, a task she undertook with zeal as she tightly snapped on a pair of regulation police cuffs in front of her. The sight of Charles lying on the floor helpless with a bleeding head wound sickened Dana but anticipating their entry to the gallery with these strangers worried her more. She led them through a giant hallway and into an elevator. Once inside, Dana raised her cuffed hands to reach for the 'B' button, but Mark stopped her.

"No fucking games, lady," he sternly admonished her. "I'll do it."

Dana started to speak, but instead sighed and retreated as Mark pressed the button and the doors closed. The elevator shook slightly, then started its descent. Dana shook too, but not in cadence with the elevator.

#

Mark thought of himself as a decent planner, but already this was going way too easy. He knew that all plans went awry so he was guarded. The rich broad was understandably fidgety but there was something unsettling about her. He could swear that he was getting a very bad signal from her; her eyes darted back and forth fearfully, her breathing quickened. You would think she was being led to a certain death. What was she hiding? Maybe she was just being clever. He figured these one-percenters always had an out or an escape plan – he would tune up his radar. He'd let the little shithead girl take the lead and see where this was going. As the elevator hit bottom, he grabbed Dana roughly and held her in front of him. The doors opened onto yet another a long hallway.

"Down to the end door," Dana said.

He motioned for Allison to take point. Allison gave him an *are you serious* look but complied. Automatic overhead lights flickered on as she started walking down the long hallway. The fluorescent lighting buzzed irritatingly. One light dimmed, then went out. Mark halted, listening intently for anything amiss, then resumed the march.

Mark relaxed a little, then allowed himself the indulgence of staring at Allison's rear. He liked the way Allison walked, especially from behind. His pulse quickened slightly as he thought maybe when this was over, he'd off Ben in some spectacular fashion and take Allison somewhere private. In his wildest dreams he knew he could never hook up with a girl like Allison – unless he paid, naturally – but that just added to his desire. Beyond that he had no real use for her. He looked forward to it.

#

Allison sensed – no, she knew – that Mark watched her walk slowly down the hallway. It was that walk at the Flight Line Bar in San Bernardino that fired up his interest in her in the first place. She knew the effect she had on a certain type of man, and she resolved to work it to her advantage. Getting men to do her bidding was never a problem. The real problem was that the men always ended up being real shits. They always drank too much, they all eventually cheated on her, even occasionally hitting her. *But only when she couldn't keep her mouth shut*, she convinced herself. Ben seemed different – finally. Once his divorce was settled, he told her he had big plans. Mark and his little caper here was just a steppingstone. She and Ben had discussed what they would do to Mark when this was over. She looked forward to it.

The trio arrived at the door and Dana was allowed to punch in a code on a stainless-steel wall fixture. The door slid open to reveal a darkened room. They walked a few feet in and Mark stopped the group. Dana flipped on a nearby wall switch. The basement gallery came to life. The two intruders stood in awe.

"Holy shit," Mark whispered.

They found themselves in a huge private gallery of sculptures and paintings affixed to walls and freestanding kiosks. Concealed overhead

LED lighting illuminated each piece to its fullest viewing advantage. In the center of the room stood the largest kiosk with the newly acquired Van Gogh. It was a heretofore unknown self portrait of the artist done in his trademark vivid colors with unusual swatches of thick paint. His face a pale representation of his own once vibrant personality that had been solidly beaten down by years of rejection, yet with a stare so intense one could not look away.

Dana watched the two gawk in wonder. Her heart beat steadily against her chest, propelled by a disconcerting fear the two would soon regret their decision to pursue this particular theft. She felt assured the Van Gogh would remain unmolested – but she could not guarantee the outcome would end to anyone's satisfaction. For the briefest moment, she imagined these two could not be that far removed from a chance at some sort of a redemptive life. She felt the need to warn them without revealing any of the room's secrets. Maybe if she sweetened the pot they would listen to reason.

Dana turned to her captor. "If you leave now, I promise I won't call the police. Charles and I will forget this ever happened. I have a hundred thousand dollars in cash you can have. I can take you to it. And jewelry. You just have to leave this room now!"

Allison's eyes grew larger as she looked at Mark with raised eyebrows – Mark only laughed at the offer. "Lady, I'm going to take that piece of crap Van Gogh and whatever else I want down here – and there's a lot I want – and then I'm going to take that hundred K as a bonus for my trouble. And there's nothing you can do about it."

Dana had only a millisecond to rethink her take on the two as Mark produced a 9mm Glock pistol from behind his waist and shot Dana point blank in her chest.

#

Something above, unseen by the intruders, watched intently with fiery eyes as Dana collapsed to the floor. Already alerted by the recent sound of the elevator descending to the basement, she anticipated visitors – but something was now very wrong. The reverberation of the pistol's angry discharge was a call to action. She rapidly unfolded her neatly tucked legs and arms and uncoiled her tail. She arose gracefully and stealthily padded towards the gallery entrance through a maze of mezzanine supports overhead. The two human forms standing over her beloved master's still body were immediately identified as unwanted interlopers and she instinctually resolved to deal with them as needed.

ONE YEAR AGO

Charles and Dana were enjoying an Asian Discovery Trip that took them to Thailand. Thailand was a compromise – Charles had served as a Marine in Vietnam in 1972 and even though that country had opened up to normalized relations and tourism, he staunchly refused to return. There were so many terrible memories there that Charles wanted to forget – memories he tried hard for years to erase. He often denied that the war and his experiences there had affected him, but Dana recognized moments. PTSD was not discussed freely back then, but Dana knew when a loud noise would stiffen him, or a police helicopter passing overhead made him uneasy.

Dana had always been intrigued by the region and wanted to visit so Thailand was agreed upon. It was a satisfying trip. Charles fell in love with the countryside, and he and Dana embraced the peoples, the food, and the history of the country formerly known as Siam.

It was in a small visitor's suite at the outskirts of the Chanthaburi Park Preserve across from the Cambodian border that Dana was startled to see a pair of tiny green eyes in the corner of their hootch.

"Hon! Come quickly," Dana called out as Charles was shaking off the dust of the day's jeep adventure.

"What is it, dear?" He joined Dana, now in a crouch by a corner cabinet.

"Look!" she said, as she pointed towards a small furry moving form with two green eyes ablaze.

"What the…?" Charles whispered. They both looked at each other as the small creature issued a plaintive squeal.

Dana had rescued and fostered several dogs and cats in the past and had a soft place in her heart for helpless creatures unable to care for themselves, but what she now saw was neither a dog – nor despite first glance similarities – certainly not a cat she knew of. A small tightly wound down covered stretch-your-imagination cat-like animal with fully articulated arms and legs and an expressive feline face comically snarled as Dana got closer to look. Dana reached out.

"Wait!" Charles implored her, taken aback by its appearance.

Dana ignored him. She reached out her hand and gently touched the small creature. A barely perceptible thrum – eerily like a purring – issued from it. The thrum grew louder into an audible drone that rose and fell with each probing but gentle stroke of Dana's hand. It was both soothing and mesmerizing. Charles sighed in relief and gave Dana a quick glance.

"Please, do not tell me…" he trailed off as he recognized the look in Dana's moist eyes. It was a look he had seen before that was simply a glimpse into her compassion for any vulnerability. Dana picked up and cradled the small helpless baby. Dana's medical training took over. Retired now, Dana spent twenty-four years at UCLA as chief medical research biologist. Writing and reviewing for medical and scientific journals part time was her avocation and left her with abundant time to spend with Charles in their home – a home she felt was too big at times. Dana was ready to leave the hills and settle down in less ostentatious digs but she knew Charles wasn't ready yet. Someday, maybe.

She inspected the discovery and assured herself that the creature was in good physical condition. Using a small syringe from her ever-present medical kit, she fed it milk and water which it hungrily devoured. Charles knew there was no changing her mind – the determination to rescue this creature was just one facet of Dana's personality he fell in love with.

Getting it back to the US was a simple matter – it settled into Dana's suitcase as a newborn to a swaddled crib and seemed to understand her reassuring command to remain still and disappear into its recesses. To their utter amazement, it did disappear. Its skin or fur consisted of a fine downy covering. Each individual graft of fur or hair had concealed micro scales that reacted to the light so that it rippled and shifted – becoming invisible. It was there one moment and then swallowed up by its surroundings a second later. Dana speculated this was an unexplained evolutionary response to the creature's environment whereas Charles, being pragmatic, just scratched his head in wonder.

"What have we found?" he asked.

One evening over drinks they both briefly posited a wild theory that Eve was of alien origin – a theory they quickly dismissed as impossible when the veracity of life on other planets and what it would take to get to earth created insurmountable problems. Eve couldn't operate a go-kart much less man a starship.

In the ensuing months back home, Dana and Charles dug into volumes of reference material determined to unmask what they had discovered. No luck. There was no known creature like this referenced or cataloged. The creature exhibited a fondness for the two immediately as if it was a well-trained ten-year-old German Shepard or fully adapted housecat. Dana readily and expertly pronounced it a female and so it became a 'she' for their reference. She named her *Eve* for obvious reasons – although Charles protested it was too 'on-the-nose-Hollywood' for him.

Dana just shook him off. "Eve it is!"

Eve rapidly grew to become extremely agile and powerful. Eve was decidedly feline with nods to her species ranging from panthers to lionesses, but Eve's fur coat and her double-jointed extremities that allowed her to fold in on herself were heretofore unknown. She crawled stealthily and ran easily and was extremely adept in climbing and rapid movement. She used her oversized prehensile tail to balance and assist in grasping the overhead railings of the basement gallery. She was most comfortable when perched high above the floor where she could observe her playground below.

"She's maturing," Dana told Charles after an afternoon of watching Eve swooping around in abandon, chasing a basketball. "What do we do when she's fully grown? We can't just release her like a tiger into the wild. She knows only us and this place."

"I'm not sure. She appears content so maybe this is all she needs."

"She certainly wouldn't be accepted anywhere else."

"Anywhere we know of," Charles added.

Dana grew silent. "Are we doing the right thing?"

"I don't know. We'll figure it out. Somehow."

Dana watched as Eve chased a large ground squirrel across the lawn, captured it easily, and took it off into the wooded area abutting their expansive lawn. She was alarmed by a squeal and a growl from the woods that made her shift uneasily in her lawn chair.

"Are we in any danger?" she asked.

Charles had also noted Eve entering the woods. "I won't let anything happen to you, if that's your concern."

#

Charles installed a metal cage above the gallery floor on the mezzanine framework. It was built out of iron piping and eighth inch thick steel frames. It was above a small equipment room in the corner and hidden from casual view. Eve quickly made it into her own adorning it with toys she loved and her colorful blankets. Amazingly, she was able to cover the cage with discarded shimmering scales that would become invisible upon her different moods. The cage door was left unlocked as the couple saw no reason to keep Eve from any appointed rounds she felt responsible for. Dana kidded that they had their very own Cheshire Cat.

Eve became a de facto family member, and the Reynolds became her sole provider and protectors from the outside world. Eve, in turn, became protective of them. At a year old, she appeared fully mature, and the humidity-controlled environment suited her well. She knew this room was special to its owners. She could not comprehend why, only that it was the place her masters came to sit and admire the many contents of the room. She felt wanted and loved and in return, in service to Charles and Dana. Their touch was gentle against her now full fur that reacted to their very touch. It shimmered and rippled like an autumn wheat field caressed by an undulating breeze. Her fur would inexplicably at once turn golden brown to silver and gold and then become transparent. At year one, she was waist high to Charles and could easily crush a human with a single blow or swift slashing but that thought never entered her mind. She loved their visits and learned to share their joy when they came down.

Recently, they spent more time at one of the newest walls – a new man on the wall. She sensed they loved the man on the wall. She in turn, then, would protect the man on the wall. Since the man had arrived, though, Eve sensed a growing change. A fleeting faraway voice had begun a dialogue with her – one she could not yet understand – but knew it demanded a response.

CHAPTER 3

In the media room, Ben jumped at the crack of a pistol. "Fuck," he said. He rose from his recliner. "The fun starts and here I am babysitting you, you old prick."

Charles was tied to a chair, his head bleeding and lolling to his side. He slowly opened his eyes and focused on Ben through the thickening blood trailing from his wound. *It's started*, he thought. "You're. A. Dead. Man, kid," he slurred.

Ben laughed in reply. "We're all dead men, dude. Some just dead sooner than others. Go back to sleep."

Charles spit blood out of his mouth and with some effort, chuckled and said, "You got that right, sport. Maybe you'd better go check on your buddies."

Another *crack* of the Glock from down below sounded.

Ben paced the room and stared at Charles. "Fuck!" Ben grabbed the shotgun.

#

Allison crouched down to look at Dana, then back up to Mark.

"Damn, man," she laughed nervously. "Did you have to do that? She was going to take us to a shitload of money, and we could have just split."

Mark stood over the two with his Glock still in hand.

"Little darlin', that money is a drop. You look around this place yet? There's gotta be millions of dollars' worth of goodies here. Now let's go grab some."

"Jeez, man. That's a lot of blood," she said, rising.

"Hey, omelets and eggs! It's business. C'mon."

Eve silently traversed the landing platforms above and over to where Dana's body lay still. She sensed Dana was mortally wounded.

The two left Dana and walked straight to the middle of the room to the kiosk that held the Van Gogh. They both stood before the painting. Allison tilted her head sideways and back like a curious dog listening to its master's voice.

"We're getting fifty grand for this piece of crap? That dude looks wasted," she offered.

Mark glanced sideways at her and shook his head. He turned back to the painting and grabbed the frame to pull it off the kiosk. It wouldn't budge. It was bolted in place.

"Fuck!" he shouted. Glancing around, he reached into his pocket and pulled out a hunting knife and crudely cut the canvas out of the frame. He rolled up the painting and handed it to Allison, then busied himself cutting another canvas from its' frame. *Bonus!* he thought. Allison placed the Van Gogh in the gym bag next to the gallery door.

Eve unwound herself from the rigging, dropped down, and landed with a loud heavy thud next to Dana's body.

Mark and Allison both turned at the sound as Eve's blazing eyes glared at them. She had never seen these two before, but Eve immediately sensed that Dana did not like these new visitors and the man on the wall did not like them either – *but where was he*? She instinctively placed her clawed paw on Dana. She felt for life, but none was detected. She looked at the intruders and bellowed out an ear-splitting roar.

"What the hell?" Mark said as he shakily raised his Glock and aimed at the strange animal.

"Fuckin' A, man, shoot it!" Allison shouted.

Mark squeezed the trigger. The aim was wild, but the round caught Eve in the shoulder. Eve was knocked back on her haunches. She looked at her shoulder joint where the bullet penetrated. She felt warm sticky blood oozing, but she sloughed it off. Allison screamed and backed up slowly, stumbled and fell down, then scrambled on all fours looking for shelter but could only slip behind the Van Gogh kiosk. Mark fired wildly, emptying the clip. No other shot found Eve. She slowly rose from Dana's body. Her regal chest heaved as she took in great gulps of air and focused in on the intruder. Eve's tail swept from side to side, then stopped. Mark slowly backed up.

With the ferocity of a trapped mountain lion, Eve sprang from Dana and was on Mark instantly. Her talon-like claws ripped through fabric and flesh with ease. Allison clasped her hands over her ears and watched in horror as Mark was reduced to a bloody pile in seconds. When she was satisfied that this being no longer threatened her space, she turned towards Allison. She felt the rush of her blood racing through her veins that served to double her strength. As she took a step towards the girl, she sensed movement from behind and turned quickly towards the entrance to the gallery. Ben stood in the doorway, shotgun at the ready. Eve faced him fearlessly.

Allison screamed, "Ben! Kill it."

Ben fired on Eve, but the buckshot fell on her harmlessly. She simply shook them off. Ben felt his pockets for extra shells but found none. He threw the shotgun down on the floor towards the big cat. He frantically searched the gym bag near his feet in case anything was there he could use – it only held the canvas. The shotgun clattered on the floor and landed just short of Eve as she looked back and forth between the two, a deep growl escaping her throat – deciding where to strike next. Urine drizzled down Allison's leg as she started to cry in great gulping sobs. Ben reached down carefully to pick up the bag containing the Van Gogh and backed up towards the gallery door. Allison was disbelieving.

She screamed through her tears. "Ben, what the hell?"

Ben continued cautiously backing through the door. "Sorry, babe," he said. "Daddy didn't sign up for this shit." Ben fumbled with the wall fixture and the door slid closed.

"Ben, you fuck!" Allison sobbed through a flood of tears.

Now the choice was clear. Eve turned, exhaled ferociously, and immediately sprang upon her. Time stood still for Allison and her whole body felt as if it had expanded three times its size – she saw red and then she saw nothing.

Ben ran to the elevator and pressed the buttons frantically, babbling to himself. Behind him, the door to the gallery exploded outward and Eve barreled towards him. The elevator door opened, and he scrambled in. Again, he wildly searched for and found the *close* button. He pounded it, commanding it to comply, then fell back as he saw the doors close with the creature still halfway down the hall. When the doors shut with a loud satisfying *thud*, he finally exhaled – his terror subsiding slightly.

Ben stood still waiting for the elevator to start its ascent. A series of clicks and whirrs sounded but nothing moved. With a gear stripping squeal, it finally did, but just as quickly ground to a jarring halt. He held his breath. A loud scraping on the exterior door jolted Ben into a greater panic – he felt his heart on the verge of bursting. He retreated back against the elevator wall as sweat dripped from his brow – obscuring his view. A small split appeared between the two doors accompanied by a nails-on-a-chalkboard grating. The split grew larger and then the doors flew open.

There was nothing there!

Shivering from fear and shock, Ben thought his eyes must be playing tricks on him. He pushed a lock of hair from his eyes and focused. He opened his mouth but nothing came out as he witnessed a shimmer of silver light materialize in the doorway. Ben slowly rose to his feet. Then the silver just as quickly transformed into gold, then a blur of movement and finally, Eve presented herself. She issued a low growl, followed by a slow display of her razor-sharp teeth, then rose on her hind legs. Ben shrank back again in terror.

"No. No. Please…" he pleaded.

Even as his plea fell on deaf ears, Eve cocked her head and froze. She detected a small groan from the gallery – Dana! She turned to look back, gave out a deep throaty roar, then shimmered and disappeared. Still shaking, Ben crawled to the control panel and shut the door. The elevator haltingly but slowly started its ascent.

8:00 p.m.

Through the searing throb in his head, Charles heard a muffled cacophony of sounds emanating from the basement. Gunshots mixed with raised voices – both emboldened in defiance and pleading in terror – brought him back to Vietnam. Nights of explosions and screams from long ago swirled in this head mixed with what he knew was the immediacy of events happening now below him. He struggled hard to separate the past from the present. Just as quickly as the commotion erupted it ceased. Charles knew Dana was below, but what was happening? The thought of Eve being assaulted by the two below filled him with dread. Could she protect Dana and herself against the gunfire she heard? The smell of cordite filled his nose and overpowered the stench of the filthy river he was mired in and unable to escape. Was that a helicopter he was hearing? He saw three young marines in battle gear walking through the jungle, M-16 rifles held in defense of any incursion. One of the Marines had a chiseled face and a faraway stare. He sported a bandage on his head covering his ear. Had it been cut off? Had the Viet Cong saved it as a souvenir? The three Marines became his invaders, the trio below triumphantly returning with their precious cargo and one last confrontation with him, lying in the mud.

Instead, breath held, utter silence – nothing.

The amount of blood on the floor had Charles worried as he struggled with the duct tape holding him in his overturned chair. The blood ran in rivulets down his face. He thought he heard the plaintive cry of a peacock and realized it was his own voice crying for help. Unable to free himself, Charles took stock of his surroundings. No knife or weapon was in his immediate reach. The girl, Allison, had taken their cellphones and placed them in an oversized brandy snifter on a serving cart next to the bar. Charles jokingly referred to it as his tip jar. Maybe he could get to it and indeed, tip it. Tied to the chair, on his side on the floor, Charles pushed against the rough Mexican tile that adorned the bar/media room. The chosen Terracotta had enough irregularities that Charles was able to get a purchase on the flooring with his legs and propel himself towards the bar. Once his pantlegs mixed with his blood on the floor it was a slower and slipperier go. Bits of previously broken glass dug into his arms and legs – each shard a brief flame in him that kept burning like a small ember.

Straining at his bindings, pulling himself and the heavy chair, he quickly tired. He recognized himself losing consciousness with mere feet to go. He roused himself with the thought of Dana and what was happening – or had happened – in the gallery. With renewed willpower, he continued his push and made it to the sidebar. With his head and chairback firmly in place against the cart, he pushed against it in an effort to dislodge the snifter. His push managed to tip the jar over onto the bar surface. Charles realized he needed to leverage the cart to upend it. He pushed himself in a half circle until his arms and the chair arms were positioned under the cart. He immediately rolled over onto his side and the cart raised itself off the floor, sending the tip jar crashing to the floor – a good ten feet away. Exhausted and out of breath, Charles closed his eyes and rested. Through an oncoming foggy haze, he thought he heard footsteps. Dana? The intruders? Overwhelmed by the loss of blood and exhaustion, Charles passed out.

8:30 p.m.

Eve returned to the gallery. The room reeked of spent gunpowder, stale waste, and copper. She slowly padded over to the bodies of Mark and then Allison – sniffing them in curiosity. She pawed at Allison's corpse as if to make sure this thing was unmoving. She went to Mark's remains and sniffed. Satisfied that these two posed no further threat, she sat and considered her recent experience. She recognized that she had prevented the visitors from doing any additional damage to Dana, but she did not understand 'death'. She knew, though, that she felt strangely satisfied with the actions. Turning quickly to Dana, she went to her side and laid her head on Dana's chest. She detected a weakened heartbeat.

It was then that she clearly heard the cry that had been recently intruding her thoughts. She trembled slightly in exhilaration. At first, she dismissed the call as nothing and as it steadily grew stronger it was still only a half-formed embryo of jagged visions. Now it was a clearer revelation.

There was another. An other like her. Calling.

She turned and focused on the kiosk that had held the man on the wall. He was no longer there. A deep rumble escaped her throat. She would search the room later for him.

After a bit, she licked and cleaned her shoulder wound where Mark's bullet had entered. She dug in with her incisors, impervious to any pain and pulled out the offending lead. Continuing her licking, the wound subtly started to close and knit itself together. The damage below the surface was mending itself also. She felt stronger immediately. A fleeting vison entered her head – it was at that moment she knew she could mother and protect Dana.

9:30 p.m.

Randall 'Red' Heard was a patient man, but it had been almost three hours since his call to Mark Catalina at the Reynolds residence. By now, Mark should have gotten his hands on the Van Gogh and called back confirmation. The two of them along with Mark's rookie goons were then to meet him at the Santa Monica Yacht Club and exchange the canvas for the agreed upon fifty thousand dollars.

Red had a twenty-five-footer docked at the club that he used for cruising down to Dana Point where his lover lived. Whenever her husband was out of town – he had a place in Cabo, so it was quite often – he would call his captain and make the trip. Dinner at The Drake in Laguna. Excellent bourbons and diver scallops. An hour in the sack with her and then back up the coast for a nightcap. A pleasant enough diversion.

He drummed his fingertips on a finely figured African Mahogany desktop in his home office. Red straightened his desk blotter in alignment with his notepad and phone. It was nothing more than busy work, but Red was not the kind to stare at a blue screen and play solitaire all evening– he needed to be doing something. Anything. He punched in Mark's cell and waited for him to pick up. It rang four times then Mark's phone responded with a curt, "Hello. Leave a message." Then a pause.

"What the fuck, Mark?" Red barked. "Call me! Now!"

Red clicked off. Feeling the weight of his iPhone in his hand, he hurled it at the wall of his office. The military grade holder that encased Apple's finest bounced bizarrely and plopped onto a plush sofa. So unsatisfying compared to slamming a receiver onto its cradle. *Phone receivers in a cradle. Ah, the Eighties*, thought Red.

In the eighties, Red was a student at UCLA and a big man on campus. The frat life, the boozing, the women, all suited him. Visiting his friends' homes in the environs of the Hollywood, Brentwood, and Holmby Hills estates suited him, too. He quickly found out he had an eye for luxury and a knack for burgling the unsuspected. He had gotten in and out of a dozen homes with cash, jewelry, and other easy to fence items by graduation. He set up a talent agency on Sunset Boulevard by 1990 as a front for the necessary money laundering. He needed to look legit and although his client list was made up exclusively of young starlets, he rarely found work for any of them. He wasn't a greedy man by any means, but by the turn of the century he had amassed a nice bank account of over twenty million. He was selective in his work and had assembled a list of 'contractors' he could rely on to do the actual donkey work now. Mark Catalina was one of his contractors – not his first choice for this art heist – but he was reliable and available on the spot. Red was not known as an art thief. He cared little for paintings, but he had met a buyer on a trip to Spain and it was apparent that 'art as an investment' was the coming thing. Delivering this new painting would net him a cool ten million. This was an opportunity he couldn't pass up. He did a little research on the Reynolds and found no red flags. A quiet elderly retired couple with a nice home. A long winding driveway set back from Mulholland Drive. If someone got hurt, no big loss to Red. People were there for his use, not the other way around.

Red rose from his chair and walked to his mahogany sideboard. He grabbed a rocks tumbler and a half-empty bottle of eighteen-year-old Oban Scotch and walked to his floor-to-ceiling bulletproof window overlooking Los Angeles. The city lights sparkled. It was the rare kind of night when the day's earlier stiff Santa Anas had grabbed the smoke and the smog and detritus of the city by the ears and escorted it all out into the Pacific Ocean. The wind was a great garbageman. *Let the fish choke*. He poured himself half a glass and drank it down in one gulp. The burn was heavenly. He knew his gut would resent it later but *later was later*.

Goddammit, Mark, he thought. *I'm going to kick your ass if you don't call me soon.*

He poured himself a second glass and as if he had willed it, his cell rang. Without even looking at the caller ID, he punched in the green 'accept' button, downed his scotch, and steeled himself for the ass-chewing he was going to lay on.

"It's about fucking time, Mark," he growled.

Heavy breathing and a momentary silence troubled Red. Then the caller spoke. His voice cracked and shaky – restrained.

"Mark's dead," the caller stated.

"Who is this?" Red asked.

"I'm the guy Mark hired to help steal that painting you want. Me and… some girl."

"What do you mean 'Mark's dead'?"

"He's fucking dead, man. Gone. Some, some *thing* tore him to shreds down there!" He paused, voice breaking. "The girl, too."

Red's mind raced. This thing had now gone three ways sideways but if this cocksucker had the painting, then it might still be salvageable.

"A *thing* killed Mark? But you have the painting?"

"Jeez! Thanks for your concern! Yeah, I got the Goddam painting." he replied.

"You know the marina?"

"No. No. Not there. Fuck that shit. I'll tell you where and when. I'll get back to you. In the morning. But the price just doubled."

Red weighed his options. Knew what he had to do.

"I'll be waiting. And yeah, I can do the one hundred thousand dollars."

CHAPTER 4

1.00 a.m.

Charles roused. Five hours had passed. Lying on his side he could see the shattered snifter and two cell phones. Charles held his breath. The house was dead silent. He resolved to continue his task and reach one of the cell phones. He started the slow crawl through blood and broken glass that had become his personal minefield. His mind was consumed by thoughts of Dana and what had happened down below. The thoughts turned dark and a terrible scenario formed in his mind. What did the gunshots below signify? How could he have been so cavalier about Eve? Even the most well-trained police dog could turn – he had seen it before. The glass shards on the floor easily worked their way into the fabric of his clothes and bit into his skin.

    He heard a scream. Ear-piercing and troubled. Was it Dana? One of the intruders? With the first cell phone almost in reach, he halted his crawl to concentrate on the source. Nothing. He started across the floor and the scream sounded once again. His fingers were within inches of the cell when the realization hit him – the scream was his. Reality had been fleeting the past few hours but he was instantly thrust into lucidity. He broke into a maniacal laugh that quickly turned to tears as his hand clutched the phone. It was all he could do to bring the phone up to his line of vision and focus to insure it was on and dial 911.

2:30 a.m. FRIDAY

Senior Detective First Grade John Fox was roused out of a sound sleep by the discordant vocals of some British heavy metal rock group from the '70s. The song was the chosen ringtone of the fifty-six-year-old and never failed to get an arched eyebrow and dirty look from his chief when it rang – usually at any inopportune moment. Fox reached over and picked up the phone as the tune trailed off. He looked at the hour – two-thirty a.m. – and scrolled his missed calls to see who dared interrupt this night off.

"Yep, I'm here, Rocky."

He dialed back.

The watch commander on duty that night was Lieutenant Rick Davis – everyone called him Rocky – a transplant from New Jersey who came from a good cop family and was a 'joisy boy' through and through but whose partner was a gorgeous former beauty queen with stars in her eyes who dreamed of making in in Hollywood. So, the 'joisy boy' obliged her wish for stardom and moved to LA. Apparently, not 'making it' in Sinatra's 'New York, New York', meant that you could still give Tinseltown a shot. Davis braced himself for the return call.

"This better be good, champ," the detective said and yawned.

"John, it is. I mean it's not, but… oh… hell."

Something about the lieutenant's voice grabbed Fox by the gut. Being the senior detective usually meant that he was only called in on the most important cases. Cases that usually made front page headlines and a whole lot of rear end pain.

"Gimme an address."

Davis spit out a street number on winding Mulholland Drive.

"God damn, L.T."

"Yeah. Black card territory, but… I'm… hell, just get here."

The detective waited for a beat. "I can be there in thirty." He hung up quickly. He couldn't remember if he ever heard the lieutenant so subdued.

Detective Fox was a fourteen-year veteran of the BHPD. After doing twenty in the United States Navy as an NCIS, he opted for yet another policing job only with better food. Being raised in suburban Ventura County, Fox was no stranger to the environs of the LA basin and his love of surfing and boating brought him to all the beaches and towns up and down the coast. A permanent bachelor, he was fit and lean. He abided by the strict grooming standards of the police department and wore his full head of hair short and neatly combed – all the better to show off a perpetually tanned and clean-shaven face. He had an easy smile that could be quite infectious. He was often mistaken for 'that guy in that movie' when out on the street but had never been in front of the camera – although he had been a technical adviser on a short-lived television series that contributed mightily to his 401K.

He resided in Venice Beach presently – a haven for liberal activists and do-gooders that occasionally chaffed at his conservative bent, but the bars were fun, the restaurants kitschy and the house he had purchased in the mid-nineties was worth sevenfold his buying price. What was not to like? Crime in Beverly Hills was normally a quiet, soft-spoken affair. The ultra-rich and do-anything-for-publicity crowd was usually treated with kid gloves. This was not South LA or Compton, but Fox had seen it all.

3:00 a.m.

Exactly twenty-five minutes after he hung up, Detective John Fox wheeled his unmarked black Ford LTD onto Mulholland Drive in Beverly Hills. The winding road brought him past high-dollar gated communities, multi-million-dollar mansions, ranch style houses, and cute bungalows tucked into crevices of the hillsides – some with long sweeping driveways and others mere yards from the road. He glanced down at his GPS to insure he was nearing his destination. Looking back up, he slammed on his brakes for a coyote crossing the street; a reminder this was still hill country in this city of seven million. The coyote stopped in its tracks and stared at Fox.

"C'mon, buddy. Get moving," Fox muttered, then chuckled at the image of a *fox* telling a coyote what to do. The coyote sniffed at the wind, then moved on. Minutes later, his cruiser pulled into the Reynolds driveway. Two marked police cruisers, an EMS ambulance and a coroner's van was parked in the spacious apron that skirted the home front. A young police officer was stringing yellow crime scene tape around the property. The coroner's van was never a good sign and usually signaled a very long morning ahead. He looked around the front of the house and immediately noted the absence of any media presence – that temporarily lifted his spirits but at the same time raised a red flag. He exited his ride and was immediately struck by how quiet his surroundings were. Not a breeze stirred or bird chirped. *Unusual*, he mused.

Detective Fox was led into the Reynolds's house by yet another young Officer and met immediately by Lt. Davis in the foyer. Davis swayed from foot to foot nervously.

"I'm sorry I had to bring you out here, John."

Fox glanced around at the home – high ceilings, Italian tile on floors and columns, exotic plants adorned the hall, tasteful designer colors and accent lighting.

"Waddya we got here, Rick?" he asked as he wrangled on some latex gloves – he knew the procedure. "I'm thinking this is not a simple B&E to drag my ass outta bed at two a.m. Right?"

"John, you remember that Van Gogh that sold for a cool fifteen mil a month or so ago?"

"I think I heard something?"

"Yeah. Newly discovered. This house belongs to the guy that bought it."

"Shit. So instead of installing it at the Huntington or Getty – this guy hangs it over his fireplace mantel, huh? It doesn't look like he needs to impress anyone. He here?"

"He was. Follow me. Take a look."

Lt. Davis turned and walked down a hallway that opened into the Reynold's combination bar/media room. Two crime scene investigators were taking photographs and marking the floor with numbered cones for any debris or items that were possible clues to a crime.

"Damn," muttered Fox as he eyed the trail of blood from the den to the bar, noting the overturned chair, discarded duct tape, and broken glass. He immediately noted the two cellphones lying on the ground where the blood trail ended. Folded paper markers were marked with the numbers thirty-four and thirty-five. That's a lot of damn evidence, Fox thought. Davis consulted his notepad.

"We received a 911 call approximately two hours ago from Charles Reynolds, the owner. He had been assaulted and tied up. We figure he somehow crawled over to the phone – it was identified as his by the caller ID – and made the call."

"Where is Reynolds now?"

"At Cedars. First patrolman on the scene found him unresponsive. Nasty head wound. Big gash. That's when I was called. EMS triaged and transported him."

Thirty-four and thirty-five markers. Fox had an uneasy feeling already that there was more than meets the eye. Davis was being too terse and kept looking around as if whatever caused the mess was still present. He knew he'd get to it.

"Is this Reynolds going to be okay?"

Davis glanced off into the secondary hall leading to the elevator.

"Lieutenant?"

Davis turned back. "What? Oh, I guess. It looked bad. We'll know more later today. There's more. Follow me."

"Wait," Fox said. "There were two cells on the floor – do we know who the other one belonged to? The wife? Was Reynolds married?"

Davis started down the secondary hall, turned, and stopped.

"Yeah, it's the wife's phone. She's not here, though. We're trying to locate her now. The techs will get it to IT ASAP."

"Suspect rule number one. Always look at the spouse. Done deal."

Davis started to respond but just stared blankly, turned, and continued down the hall.

"Did I say something wrong, Rick?"

Fox shrugged and followed. He noted the highly polished hall ended at opened elevator doors. A patrolman stood by. Davis nodded at the officer. The two walked in. Davis pressed the down button. The door closed. Fox noticed deep scratch marks on the inside of the door. He reached out to touch them. He traced a finger across one of the longest scratches.

"Jesus. What the hell did that?" Fox asked.

"I doubt it was his wife."

Fox smiled grimly. "Touché."

"We don't know for sure. Animal, maybe?"

Fox looked closer at the gouges. He rubbed his unshaven jaw and shook his head. The elevator settled and the two exited. The detective turned and waited for the basement exterior doors to close. There were additional scratch marks on the stainless steel – these more and deeper. Davis started down the hallway to the gallery door. He turned to Fox.

"Bring your booties?" he asked.

"Aw, hell," Fox replied.

"Watch your step, there's trace blood leading from the gallery."

"Of course there is," he mumbled to himself.

A CSI technician was marking the hallway for clues. Davis and Fox stopped to watch as the tech gingerly picked up something from the floor. Davis cleared his throat and the tech looked at him.

"Lieutenant, Detective, look at this." The tech showed the two of them a single strand of what appeared to be a brown hair held in his tweezers.

"Hair? They have a dog?" Fox asked.

The tech took a deep breath and looked at Davis and the Detective "Well, that was my thought, but look at this."

The two of them watched the tech rotate the tweezers as the strand shimmered silver, then gold, then disappeared, only to reappear moments later. Then disappear again.

"What the heck?" Fox growled.

"Ah, yup. No dog hair I know of can do that," replied the technician. "These are all over the inside of the gallery, too."

"There's more, huh?"

The technician glanced at Lieutenant Davis then back at Detective Fox.

"You haven't been in there yet?" he asked the detective.

Fox shook his head. He was starting to get a very uneasy vibe now.

"Bring your booties?" the tech asked.

"Aw, hell," he replied.

With the door to the gallery already open on its battered hinges, Fox was the first to enter and survey the scene. A mere two steps in, he halted.

The gallery was an abattoir.

"What the fuck is *that?*" he asked loudly, to no one in particular.

That was the bloody remains of what appeared to be two human torsos with various limbs missing. Torn clothing and a dismantled shotgun rested in and by the strewn mess. Fox had witnessed his fair share of blown off arms and mangled legs and scattered remains in his years on the force, but this took it to a new level. The detective tasted sour garlic in his throat – remnants of a Greek chicken dinner last night – and fought to push it back down.

"We're trying to figure that out, John." Davis cleared his throat. "This is just so…"

"So Manson?" Fox interjected as he surveyed the scene. "Where's the 'Kill the Pigs' graffiti?" The body in the middle of the floor was clearly male. He bent to look closer.

"Animal? Not human, that's for sure. But if it was, it was a pretty pissed-off human."

Fox took out a pen from his coat pocket and prodded the corpse. A rib protruded from the carnage; the last five inches snapped clean like a twig. He stood up quickly and glanced at the other body – the woman. Cautiously, his training in full alert not to disturb this hurricane of gore, he walked to the second corpse. He bent down and prodded at her also. Fox mused that this was one fucked-up mess smack dab in the middle of the priciest real estate in California. Not since Tate-LaBianca had something this evil taken possession of a seemingly safe, secure, and serene environment.

"What happened here?" he whispered to himself.

#

High above the slaughter, Eve held her breath and silently watched the figures on the ground. Motionless, she was shielded from the prying eyes of the new intruders by her nest – an invisible stronghold that housed Dana and herself – safe from any harm. Light could not penetrate the meshwork she had made by shedding her micro-scales. Scales that regenerated on her within minutes. Observing the many humans below, a calm filled her as she detected no malice from them – unlike the earlier intruders – they moved slowly, touched little, and showed respect for the room. This place was a haven of calm and quietude – the new beings below exuded concern and a caring – not the caring that Charles or Dana bestowed upon her – but a caring, nonetheless. She exhaled, relaxed, and clasped Dana ever tighter, feeling the weakening heartbeat retreating rapidly to stasis. She knew that soon Dana would be completely still – requiring no nourishment or stimulation except the healing which Eve could give.

#

Detective Fox and Lieutenant Davis stood surveying the kiosk that had contained the Van Gogh. The frame remained in place upon the wall with some ragged remnants of colored canvas – canvas that had been sliced with a knife that lie discarded and at their feet. Fox pointed at the knife, keeping his distance as if it were a slithering snake rearing its head in readiness to attack.

"We'll need prints off of that, the sooner the better."

"Yes," Davis agreed.

Fox put his hands on his hips and turned to survey the entire gallery. His experience had taught him that any scenario he could imagine standing in this room at this moment would only be guesswork. He closed his eyes and breathed deeply into the air. He imagined the gunshots and the ripping of canvas and then…then what? His mind was racing, but he knew the actual puzzle would need to be assembled bit by bit from the various parts and pieces available to them before a true picture could be arrived at. Still, that didn't stop him from sharing his first thoughts with Lieutenant Davis.

"How did these two gain access? I don't think they just stumbled upon the room. They knew the painting was in the house, but did they know its location? Did Reynolds bring them here? You say the wife is missing. Were they brought here by her? If they were, where is she now and where is the Van Gogh?"

"Neither are in the house," Davis responded.

Fox snorted. "Well, the painting didn't just walk off by itself."

Davis nodded tacitly.

"Yeah, there were more that these two involved. This smells fishy. We're going to need to know who had access to this house. Workers, gardeners, meal delivery services. We'll need the Reynold's social calendar. Was the mister and the missus having any trouble? What do we know of these two?"

Fox left Davis and walked slowly through the gallery. He was no art expert but he knew enough to recognize a Pollock and a LeRoy Neiman – several others he thought he knew but couldn't place the artists. *I will not take art for five hundred dollars, Alex.* He continued the circuit and arrived in front of the Van Gogh kiosk once again.

"Jeez, what a shitshow," he said to a sullen Davis.

Fox's cell phone went off. He looked at the caller ID. It was from the Beverly Hills chief of police, Stan Hellman.

"Now it begins," he muttered as he accepted the call. "Yeah, Chief?"

4:30 a.m.

Thirty minutes later, Fox and Chief Hellman were seated in a booth at Norms on La Cienega in West Hollywood. The smell of sizzling bacon and too-strong coffee that lingered in the air mixed improbably with disinfectant religiously sprayed on tables after each dining party ate at this 'always open' family restaurant chain in Southern California. Norms – it proudly advertised – *Where Life Happens 24/7*. Hellman was a big man. Balding, rubber faced with a ruddy complexion that confirmed years of alcohol abuse he proudly claimed to have recently conquered. Usually a verbose man, he was quietly digging into Norm's Lumberjack Breakfast – three eggs, three bacon strips, three sausages, hashbrowns, and three giant buttermilk pancakes. Fox wondered when last the chief swung an axe. Or had a salad.

Fox had coffee – black. He currently had no stomach for anything after witnessing the scene on Mulholland. Hellman gulped down a diet soda. Fox mused that the chief must have felt it sufficiently complimented his morning meal. He pushed his plate away and dabbed at the corners of his mouth with his napkin.

"Look, John, we got bare bones on this. An apparent home invasion robbery, a missing fifteen million dollar Van Gogh, the homeowner in the hospital, his wife missing, and two dead bodies in the basement. You got anything to add to that list?"

Fox weighed whether to add in the strange hair that the CSI tech found but decided against it. It would only muddy up already opaque waters.

"No, I don't, Stan."

"So where do we go from here and what do you need? The *Times* will run with a priceless art heist and Reynolds in the hospital. Wife being questioned. That's a lie, but Jansen at city desk will agree to keep it low key. It'll hit the afternoon edition, of course. But it's online as we speak. Need I remind you the fucking Golden Globes are in two weeks."

Fox nodded. "I appreciated the lack of any newshounds at the scene."

Hellman leaned back. Clasped his hands together. "What don't I know?"

Fox deliberated for a moment. Hellman was cagey and knew there was more to it than he was being fed, but the less he knew the better to deny any speculation from the press, city, and especially the mayor. The mayor was an ex-Hollywood 'D' player has-been who loved to stick his nose into every headline making event. Fox rapped his knuckles on the table, pointing at the Chief.

"You know it all."

"Good. That what I want to hear."

"Until we find the wife or talk to Reynolds, we're hamstrung. Once the remains are identified we can start digging deeper."

Hellman nodded in agreement.

Fox added, "Just keep the lookie-loos away from the property and we're good."

Hellman belched loudly as he picked up the bill from the end of the table and looked it over. He tossed it Fox's way.

CHAPTER 5

11:15 a.m.

Ben slept fitfully. The Hotel East Inn on North Cahuenga situated between Sunset and Hollywood Boulevards was a dump. For a paltry sixty dollars a night one could get a lumpy bed and a tiny bath with an annoying dripping faucet but little else. Ben had shared that bed with Allison the past three nights but was alone now.

With the stolen canvas safe in the gym bag under one arm and a Burger King chicken sandwich in hand, he snuck in earlier under the not-so-very-watchful eye of the night clerk – a pimply faced adolescent more interested in his Tik Tok videos than whomever came and went. Ben was understandably freaked out over the goings on last evening. A quarter-full bottle of the cheapest whiskey he could find lay on the floor amidst fast food wrappers, half used ketchup packets, and an ashtray full of unfiltered cigarette butts. Three shots of that whiskey calmed him before his call to 'Red' Heard, then the rest was to dull him enough to sleep.

Ben awoke and stared at the water-stained ceiling. If the air outside was cleansed by the breezes the night before, the air he inhaled inside was stale and heavy with grease and sweat. He was justifiably shaken up by the events witnessed the night before, but a big payday loomed, and he was going to mourn Allison later – a hundred thousand dollars later. That kind of money could buy a lot of Allisons and a much better room to enjoy her in. He eased out of bed and grabbed the whiskey – putting it to his lips, he laughed to himself and drained it. He grimaced at the burn as he studied the label. Bottom of the shelf generic store brand whiskey. He chucked the bottle across the room.

"No more cheap crap for me," he told himself aloud.

He searched his stained bed sheets and found his phone. He dialed the buyer's number. While waiting for the call to pick up, he recalled that he had met Red briefly once before.

Ben had assisted Mark on a small-time collection job. He was the designated muscle that Mark expected to use while collecting a couple of grand from a classic car body shop worker for Red. The shop guy was a greasy little Chicano gang member wannabe who fancied himself a poker player. The would-be Amarillo Slim was a dumbass hot head who bet all-in on triple-fours during his last chance hand of Texas Hold'em at an illegal poker room only to lose to a ridiculous trip-nines. He'd been dodging Red for a couple of weeks and Red had had enough. Ben went to the body shop with Mark and got his money. Or rather he got the shop's money – the owner ponied up the two Gs after Ben had destroyed two newly installed windshields on a 1969 Mach I and a '63 LeMans and was headed in the direction of a two-tone blue 1952 Bel Air. The Chicano was left 'almost' unharmed. He suffered a couple of broken ribs – no sense in losing future business – but Ben mused he was probably no friend of the owner any more. The meeting was at the marina where Red docked his boat, and Ben stood shivering on a cold pier as Mark passed on the cash to Red. From the deck of his craft, Red made eye contact and gave a head nod. That was the extent of their 'meet and greet'. Ben had already decided that an invite onto that boat and a harbor cruise with a hundred G on the line was not going to happen.

Red picked up. "Yeah?"

"This is Ben. I…"

"I know who you are," Red interrupted. "How you wanna do this?"

"You got the money? Cash?"

"Yes, I have the money. Do not waste my day, Mister Benjamin."

Ben panicked as he realized he still had no plan or clue where to meet Red and make the exchange. He thought a daytime meet would be safe enough, so he snapped off the first dive bar that entered his mind that was not touristy.

"You know the Overtime on Sunset, east of the 101?"

"Near all the crappy hotels? Yeah, I know it."

"I'll be there at three this afternoon. We can have a drink and do our business."

"Sounds good," he agreed.

Ben thought he picked a good spot, and the handoff would be easy-peasy.

"Get us a booth in the back if they have one," Red added. "We'll need a little privacy."

"Can do. See you there, Red," Ben signed off. He did a little fist pump. He felt large and in charge – *Screw this,* he thought. *Put yesterday behind, my friend! Clear sailing ahead!*

Ben stood up and walked in front of a full-length mirror on that wall. The mirror was cracked and missing some of the reflective silver behind it. He fancied himself a young DeNiro.

He crossed his arms across his chest. "You talking to me?" he asked his reflection. "You talking to me? Ha!"

He walked over to the sole battered dresser in the room and opened the top drawer. He opened the gym bag and took out the rolled-up canvas. He brushed the crumbs away from his bed sheet and laid it on the stained mattress cover. He unrolled the canvas and looked at the self portrait of Vincent Van Gogh.

"You one ugly dude man, but you're my ship finally sailin' in!"

He rolled up the Van Gogh tightly then picked up his phone again and scrolled through his contacts and punched a name. Neil Bravo was a small-time drug dealer he knew he could trust to watch his back at the bar. Ben presumed this Red guy was not a hard-core thug but better to be safe than sorry, he thought. An extra set of eyes and a little backup wouldn't hurt.

#

Red knew the Overtime only because he drove by it on occasion – it was not on anyone's radar of places to enjoy a cocktail, so it was perfect. Red laughed to himself – this jackass was obviously under the impression that they were going to form a warm interpersonal working relationship. Red had other ideas. He had watched the *KXLA Morning News* show earlier and there was no mention of any art heist in Los Angeles that day or before. He took that as a good sign. If indeed Mark was dead as well as another accomplice, chances were the homeowner and his wife were also dead or otherwise indisposed. If that was the case, the sun that day broke through the San Gabriel haze on a peaceful valley void of any extraordinary police action. Still, the loose end of this Ben person needed to be dealt with. If this Ben guy had any brains, he assumed he would protect his interests in some half-assed way so Red would play it straight until after the meet.

12:00 p.m.

Eve watched through her veil of invisibility as the last beings left the gallery. She had watched with curiosity and a degree of amusement as the bodies of her victims had been removed. All that remained was the bloodstains on the marble floors.

After an hour, satisfied that Dana had achieved stasis, she dropped down to the floor. She padded to the area where she had attacked Mark, sniffed the ground quickly then moved to survey where Allison had met her fate. Eve had no remorse for her actions. She was threatened and she reacted. Remorse or guilt was not in her nature. She went to the kiosk that held the Van Gogh and looked for the portrait of the Man on the Wall with the staring eyes. He was gone. She was, expectedly, anxious. Her Man and her other master were nowhere. She was anxious to see her master. She missed him and his voice and touch. She made her way to the gallery door. The door was hanging by a single hinge and bent permanently half open – the result of her chase the night before. She looked at the lazily fluttering remnants of yellow police tape hanging loosely, pushed by the ever-present flow of air cooling the room. She turned her head back and up to the scaffolded mezzanine to assure herself that Dana was safe and healing in her cocoon. Eve slid through the doorway and guardedly continued down the hall to the elevator doors. When she arrived, she sniffed curiously at them, detecting the still lingering scent of Ben's fear. She sneezed loudly, shook her head, then sat on her haunches to wait for Charles to return.

2:00 p.m.

Detective John Fox had been at his desk for little over an hour typing up his preliminary report of the incident on Mulholland.

Following his early morning meet with Chief Hellman, he returned home for a quick shower and change of outfits. He may have been a plainclothes detective, but he had his own style that was definitely not plain. He donned a pair of slim tan Kenneth Cole Reaction slacks and a Robert Graham shocking blue long sleeve shirt with a paisley collar and sleeves. No tie, but a pair of Yates Oxfords from Beckett Simonon completed his ensemble. He was kidded a lot by his cohorts about his clothing but had a standard reply: *This ain't Bakersfield*.

Putting some time and distance between him and the crime scene, he was surprised to find himself more than a little hungry. He put on half a pot of Maxwell House coffee. He recalled reading that none other than Tom Petty considered it the pinnacle of brewed drinks. After twenty in the service of Uncle Sam and as many in the service of the good folk of Beverly Hills, he had to agree. He was no fan of Starbucks or any of those places that junked up a perfectly good cup of java with sugary sweet condiments. He deftly cracked a couple of extra-large eggs into his trusty old cast iron-skillet. As the eggs bubbled, he added some chopped scallions and cherry tomatoes, then forked the ingredients into a fluffy scramble. He slid them onto a paper plate then added a handful of shredded cheddar jack cheese. Thirty seconds in the microwave was all it needed to melt the cheese, then he added a generous scoop of Hatch chili salsa.

He ate his scramble over the kitchen sink, careful not to spill any onto his shirt or shoes. Then it was on to his cubicle at the police station on North Rexford Drive.

He had called Cedars Sinai upon arrival earlier to ask after Charles Reynolds. Reynolds, he was informed, had been treated for the head trauma and was in ICU, still unconscious but in stable condition. Fox asked for notification as soon as Reynolds was awake and able to talk. Lieutenant Davis had left a message that a BOLO had been ordered for Dana Reynolds and was underway but there was no update yet. The coroner's office reported that the autopsies and identification of the two bodies were to be conducted later in the day as time and availability permitted. LA always had a backlog. Rich or poor, famous or unknown, there was always a waiting queue. Fox was no closer to any answers than he was almost ten hours ago. It was a waiting game now. Any update would trigger movement on the case but for now all he could do is wait and begin the process of assembling background information on the victim and his world.

3:00 p.m.

At precisely three p.m., Red Heard's black Tesla Model S Plaid eased itself into a parking space next to the Overtime Bar and Grill. Exiting the car, Red smelled the grease exhauster on the rooftop expelling the odors of cooking hamburgers and cheap paper-thin ribeye steaks. He would definitely have a robust bone-in ribeye later that night when this messy business was done, but at a more acceptable place – maybe Mastros or Flemings. He had his own wine locker at both places and a standing reserved private table. He thought he may even call on one of his clients to join him. That would qualify as a business dinner. He carried a leather satchel containing the agreed upon monies.

Entering the dimly lit bar, he scanned the place quickly. The layout was typical of most local dives. Long bar to the left, blinking neon signage extolling the most popular brands of beer, red leather booths to the right, a few countertop tables in the middle of the floor and a well-used pool table at the rear. Red noted a Hispanic couple seated at the first booth having a late lunch, two elderly ladies dressed in a fashion twenty years too young enjoying Lemon Drops at the bar, and the Bartender refilling the shot glass of a Johnny Depp look-alike. Ben sat in the last booth and raised his hand in greeting. Red nodded and worked his way over to him. It was hard not to miss the stare of the Depp guy through the mirror behind the bar tracking Red's stroll to Ben's booth.

Red slid into the booth and placed the satchel on the tabletop.

"Whoa!" Ben said staring at the bag. "You get right down to business, dontcha? You wanna drink or something?"

"I'll have whatever you're having,"

Ben raised his glass and nodded to the bartender. "Another and one for my friend, Dean."

Ben reached to his side and brought the edge of the canvas, wrapped in newspaper, above the table and into Red's line of sight.

"We good?" he asked.

"Yeah. We good."

"You want me to slide it under the table or…?"

Red was amused. "Jesus, kid, just hand me the damn thing."

"Oh, okay."

Ben handed the canvas over and Red pushed the satchel towards Ben. The bartender walked over and put two scotch on the rocks on the table without a word.

Red took a drink, looked at the glass. "Well whiskey?" he asked.

"Yeah. Good shit, huh?"

"If you say so." Red paused; he had no intention of forming a secret buddies club with the kid. "What the hell happened to Mark? Just give me the *Reader's Digest* version please."

Ben lifted his glass and emptied three-quarters of it in one long gulp.

"The Reader's what?"

"Just make it short and sweet, please."

"Okay. Mark and Allison – the chick I told you about – them two went down to the basement place with the lady – the wife – where they had the painting. I stayed upstairs. The old guy was coughing and shit like that – making a real fuss – when I heard some gunshots all of a sudden from downstairs, so I kicked him in his shoulder a couple times to shut him up and then I headed on down."

Ben shook the ice around in his glass and took another swig, draining it. He continued, slowly.

"When I got to the room, Mark was like in pieces on the floor with some animal over him that had just ripped him to shreds. Dude, I don't know what kind of animal it was. I never seen anything like it before. Like a big ass shiny mountain lion or something. Only weirder."

"A big ass shiny lion," Ben mockingly reiterated.

"Yeah, only weirder. You know those rich dudes. I mean they keep all these foreign animals and crap around. I wasn't about ready to ask questions that's for sure."

"Where was the girl?"

Ben paused for a second before answering and Red figured the kid was fixing to lie, so *whatever*.

Sure enough, Ben lied. "She was, like she was dead already too, so I just – you know – I grabbed the painting and I split. The damn thing started chasing me but I got to the elevators and then it was there and then it wasn't and… and that's all I remember. I don't really, I don't know.

Red considered his story. Nodded. "The wife. Where was she?"

Ben paused, trying to remember. "I think she was dead, too. Yeah, she was lying on the ground all crumpled up with blood and stuff."

Ben's eyes were shifting back and forth between Red and the bar area. Red could see the kid was uncomfortable and wanted an end to this inquisition. Red wasn't done yet. He had one more.

"No one saw you leave?"

"Nope."

"Where's Mark's car?"

"Mark had a rental. I left it at LAX."

"Good."

Red finished his drink and gathered up the painting.

"Thanks for the drink, kid. And the goodies."

Red got up and looked around quickly. He noted that the bar was filling up; a waitress had come on shift and Ben's wingman was still sitting on his stool pretending to be interested in the hockey game on a big screen TV. He slowly walked out. The spring sky was darkening as Red opened his trunk, tossed the Van Gogh in, then climbed into the Tesla and pulled out of the parking lot. Heading west on Sunset, he checked his rear-view mirror to insure he wasn't being followed, then pulled into the parking lot of the Sun Motel a block away. He parked on the side of the lot nearest a cross street that afforded him both a clear view of anyone leaving the Overtime and quick access to the exit connecting Sunset.

#

At the Overtime, Ben gave his pal at the bar a nod. Two seconds later the Johnny Depp look-alike joined him at the table. He brushed his hair to the side.

"Everything cool?" he asked Ben.

"Yep. Piece of cake. You got some of those Scooby Snacks I asked for?"

Faux-Johnny smiled and nodded.

Life is good, thought Ben.

CHAPTER 6

5:00 p.m.

Eve continued her vigil at the elevator door. The doors did not budge. She padded back to her invisible nest to look after Dana. Instinctually she knew Dana was healing rapidly from her trauma and would remain safe as the wounds closed and her tissues mended themselves. Once started the process would continue. In less than twenty-four hours, Dana would be completely healed and able to fend for herself. This knowledge was comforting as the other continued its persistent call. The voice in her head was now a permanent presence. Eve left her nest – restless – and began her rounds of the gallery. She stopped in front of the kiosk that had held the Man on the Wall; it was still missing. She was confused. Until Charles returned and the Man on the Wall was it its rightful place, she was lost. Maybe the other would have answers.

    She had been out of the gallery several times but always with Charles and Dana, never alone. The estate was sufficiently large and allowed her room to roam where she enjoyed the discovery of the trees, the flowers, and the grasses that fascinated her, but she was still most comfortable in her basement.

    She knew every inch of the basement and found herself headed towards the equipment room – a room she rarely spent any time in. The equipment room housed the air conditioning and heating, the boiler, and all the necessary plumbing, mechanical, and electrical devices that the dwelling needed. Once inside the room she sat motionless. After a bit she detected a slight breeze across her fur – her eyes traced it up to an opening in the ceiling. An aluminum grille covered the opening. She hopped up on top of the adjacent maze of steel ducting exiting from the furnace just below the grille and felt the breeze even stronger as the air from the room was being exhausted through this opening. She listened intently to the sounds from the other side. A chirping she recognized as belonging to the winged creatures she saw darting from tree to tree. Other noises were heard – foreign to her, especially the faint rumbling of machines in the distance. She quickly determined the opening would offer access to the outside and did not hesitate to reach up and pull the grille from the ceiling.

Moments later she emerged from a louvered opening that easily gave way at the backside of the house. Her grasses and flowers and trees were here for her, but the other was not – it was still some distance away. Eve decided it was time to find the source.

7:00 p.m.

Ben was feeling it. After the meet he returned to his hotel room, tossed the satchel on a tattered excuse for a desk, and snorted the meth he got from his pal at the bar. *Yeah, life was good*, he mused. He congratulated himself on the score and the balls to pull it off. This could be a new beginning. He decided a little company was in order. He picked up his cell and scrolled through until he found the number he wanted. He dialed and waited. A tired female voice answered. A child was crying loudly in the background amongst a din of noise emanating from a television.

"This Cherie?" Ben asked.

"Yeah. Who's this? *Shut the fuck up.* Sorry, babysittin'."

"Ben Walsh. From Tony's place last month?"

A pause on the line. "Yeah, okay. I remember. You looking for a date?"

"You know the Hotel East?"

"Yeah, can you gimme an hour?"

"I'm in Room 112."

"It's two large, ya know. Three for two pops. I got no driver, so I got no time limit. I'm independent."

"Sounds good. Maybe we'll see about the three. See you soon."

As Cherie hung up, Ben could hear something crashing in the background. "Kids," he muttered to himself. He flipped on the television and started scrolling through the guide.

An hour later, Cherie knocked on his door. Ben looked through the peep hole to assure himself it was his expected guest. A gap-toothed smiling face filled his vision. He smiled and quickly opened the door. Cherie stood in the doorway with a gloved and masked man behind her. The masked man pushed Cherie violently towards Ben and aimed a 9mm Glock equipped with a long silencer at him. Ben raised his arms as Cherie barreled into a corner and cowered, wheezing heavily. The masked man walked in and kicked the door shut.

"I don't go nothin' to do with this, man," she yelled.

The man pointed the gun at her. "Shut up!"

"Hey! I ain't seen you and I ain't gonna say shit. Jes' let me go, okay?

"I said shut the fuck up!"

Cherie held her hands up and quieted down. He pointed his gun back at Ben. Ben backed up slowly, looking around for something to defend himself with, then cocked his head. A look of recognition crossed his face.

"Fuck man," he said and chuckled. "You scared me. I thought we were good, Red. What's up? Did I—"

Red cut the conversation short with a bullet between Ben's eyes. He collapsed back onto the chair he had been sitting in and both he and the chair tipped over, bringing along a floor lamp that crashed loudly next to Cherie. Ben's blood and part of his skull peppered the wall behind her. She started shaking and sobbing in between great gulps of air. Red pointed the Glock casually back at her. She could prove a loose end, but she couldn't identify him so he figured there was no need to waste another round. He hoped he wasn't making a mistake.

"You. What's your name?"

"Che... Cherie. Please don't hurt me."

"I'm not going to. Are you a smart gal?"

"What?"

"Listen to me carefully. You're going to leave now and there will be no trace of you here. I'll take care of that. Guaranteed. You don't know me, and you never saw me. You got that?"

"Yes, for sure." She scrambled to her feet and started for the door but hesitated. "He, uh... I mean we were—"

Red sighed. "Jesus, girl. Really? How much?"

"Four."

Red opened his wallet, reached under his mask to wet his thumb with a disgusted glare at the girl, pulled out two hundred-dollar bills. He held it out to her then pulled it back. "Here's two. Do you want to argue about it?"

"No, sir," she mumbled.

"See, you are smart." He handed her the bills. "Now get out of here."

Cherie took one last look at Ben's body sprawled on the floor, then back at Red. Without another word, she tucked the bills into her cleavage and left. Red surveyed the room and decided that the girl did nothing to leave any signs of her presence. He walked over to the small desk that the satchel rested on, grabbed it, and pulled it open to check the contents. One of the banded stacks had been ripped open, but that was all so he closed it up and slung it over his shoulder. He noted the room looked suitably trashy enough to suggest that Ben had stayed there a few days, so the messier the better. An overturned pill bottle caught his eye. He picked it up to find it contained a few grams of white powder. He pocketed it.

He lifted a shabby curtain and peeked out of a smeared window towards a mostly empty parking lot. Satisfied he was not going to be seen, he placed the 'Do Not Disturb' tag on the outside doorknob and left the room.

Walking down the block to his car, Red sensed he had pulled the plug on this fiasco and felt assured he'd escaped any connection to the previous day's mess. He popped open the trunk to the Tesla and tossed the satchel in next to the rolled-up painting. For good measure, he crammed the painting in the bag, too. Time to go get that ribeye.

8:00 p.m.

The Hollywood Hills behind the Reynolds estate were alive with new springtime growth. It was also alive with creatures both small and large that Eve detected with her superior hearing and sense of smell. The names of the various animals she encountered in the thickly forested preserve were of no concern to her. Every animal she encountered on the scrubby trails – haphazardly decorated by nature with native sagebrush and chapparal – simply moved to the side to tamely let her pass and in turn she gave them little consideration. An encounter with a mother bobcat and her two kittens perched in an overhanging Cottonwood was interesting to her. Something about the beast was vaguely familiar and she sensed a distant kinship – but gave it no more importance than that. She had a mission. She was now certain the other was actually family, calling out to her.

She headed east. The calls were emanating in that direction. Her journey would take her through the San Gabriel foothills and onto the San Gorgonio Mountain range and beyond to the lower desert and Coachella valley. Drainage and flood control underpasses allowed her some autonomy of movement that avoided the concrete trails congested by automobiles and diesel belching trucks. Darkness was a welcome companion but when needed, she would cover herself with her mantle of invisibility.

Within the hour she had skirted the Mulholland Overlook, galloped across Runyon Canyon, slid by Griffith Park, and found herself overlooking the LA Zoo. The zoo was closed to the public at this time of night and the only alien sounds were of the scattered maintenance and cleaning crews. She rested momentarily atop a hillside ridge overlooking the grounds and closed her eyes to focus on the sounds emanating from the cages. The animal sounds provided a symphony of unknown and unheard languages to Eve's ears.

Deciding a slight diversion from her trip was warranted, she crept onto the grounds. Concealed and careful to avoid human interaction, Eve stayed close to the guardrails and safety screens that were in place to keep small – and large – hands and feet from becoming a snack in the daytime. Eve quickly found what she sought – the lion's den. Even before revealing herself from her cloak, the two large African lions lounging upon rocks were alerted to her presence. They both instantly stood as a shimmering veil appeared and Eve presented herself.

At once, a quiet descended upon the zoo. Dead silence. No squawking from the waterfowl, no chittering from the racoons, no vocalizing from the birds. Nothing.

At a picnic table under a brightly colored umbrella, a maintenance man, lunching on a foil-wrapped burrito stopped mid-bite and looked at his companion twisting the top off his thermos. Both men's eyes filled with concern and darted in opposite directions.

At the lion's enclosure, a small nod – a brief acknowledgement – escaped from the larger fully maned male – not in supplication at the presence of Eve – but in awe. An understanding passed between the two cousin species.

Eve sensed a profound sadness in the two. A sadness coupled to the longing for freedom, family, and a desire to return to their roots – to have command once again over their kingdom.

Eve shared their sadness. She thundered out at this sadness. Her wail reverberated across the grounds. Slowly, the male lion returned the roar, followed by his companion. The other animals joined in, and Eve's elegiac shout was returned tenfold from the warren of cages and enclosures. Chimpanzees pounded their fists on the caked dirt of their cages and screamed, elephants trumpeted, birds took flight and screeched, tigers snarled. The inhabitants of the zoo united in a cry of solidarity. They too felt the loneliness, the longing, the need to be free. The understanding that passed among the creatures temporarily salved their spirits and gave them a small hope that one day they would be free.

Eve could do little more than sympathize, but maybe once united with her kind, the other would offer hope for all species. She could only move on.

The two maintenance workers had already moved into their nearby truck to finish their lunch behind locked the doors.

8:30 a.m. Saturday

Charles was awakened by the soft beeping of a heart monitor and the muted bustle of shuffling feet, quiet conversations, and half heard announcements. He slowly opened his eyes and focused on the worn pin-hole acoustical tiles of a ceiling. A nasty brown stain had spread on one and the adjacent air conditioning vent had accumulated grungy gray dust balls on the louvers. *That needs cleaning*, he thought. *Must be UCLA.* He glanced to his left then to his right – a searing headache instantly reminded him of... *of what?* He vaguely recalled events through a fog – sitting at home, being struck, then falling, then mumbling, blood, hearing gunshots, then... nothing. He closed his eyes and took inventory of his body. His heavily bandaged head hurt like hell, his shoulder was stiff – it must have been dislocated or badly bruised somehow – but at least it felt operable, and the rest of his body felt normal. *As normal as a ninety-year-old,* he joked to himself. Then it all came back.

"Dana!" he croaked out.

His throat was dry beyond imagination, and he practically choked on that one single word. Charles knew it was prudent to take things a little slower. He felt around his body for whatever device was available to communicate with the hospital staff or used to control the mini television mounted overhead. Nothing. He tried to sit up but was slammed back as the room spun madly around. He knew he was weak, so he'd better just take it one step at a time. He glanced at his heart monitor and caught his breath – cripes, he needed to slow things down. He took deep cleansing breaths through his nostrils and slowly let it our through his mouth, a technique he had learned after his heart attack six years ago. He watched the heart monitor descend to an acceptable BPM. Better. Much better. He closed his eyes and immediately fell back into a deep sleep.

He dreamt. He found himself sitting at his old drafting table, drawing. Sketches and finished paintings surrounded him – his sketches and paintings. He remembered giving them all to Dana for safekeeping prior to his Marine tour overseas. His hand suddenly stopped. *What am I doing?* he thought. He hadn't touched a charcoal pencil or watercolor brush in over forty years since he returned from Southeast Asia. His hands moved as if a greater power had control. He sketched a cocoon. Sucked into the drawing, he was then wrapped tightly in the cocoon which he adorned with a silvery weave. He was unable to move. He was both in the cocoon and the creator outside. Inside, he felt all around with white gloved hands but could find no opening to leave. He stared at his hands. He hadn't worn white gloves since his Marine days. Was he back in service? Dana appeared next to him also in a cocoon. Outside once again, he witnessed one of the two cocoons shake and wiggle, then rip open on its bottom as blood poured out in bright red warm splashes that washed at his bare feet. He sunk into the floor as one sinks into sand with the ocean waves lapping the shore. Dana's cocoon opened also to reveal her head. She looked lovingly in Charles' eyes.

"We were warm, weren't we?" she asked. "But we knew it couldn't last."

Charles opened his mouth to reply but nothing came out. Dana stepped out of her cocoon and disappeared in a silvery cloud. He reached out to where she was – nothing. He swiveled around as he sensed an intense burst of oppressive heat from behind – a gigantic bonfire was raging out of control. The sight was horrific. All the known Van Gogh paintings in the world were being consumed by the rising flames. Watching with glee as the smoke rose, a dark shadowy form was alternately shimmering solidly then transparently to the side. Charles looked at it. The form turned to him.

"We didn't get the missing one, but we will," the form spoke directly into Charles' mind.

Charles awoke. His dream still fresh. He shut his eyes immediately. He knew he wanted to recall it as dreams have a habit of fading fast. The words spoken yet not spoken haunted him. He felt repulsed by the memory yet unable to shake it off. *Get up*, he commanded himself. *Shake it off*. Easier said than done. Still weakened, he could only lie there and let the dream circle around his head as an uneasy feeling in the pit of his stomach grew. He took a deep cleansing breath. Charles had learned long ago to confront these mind assaulting issues head on even if it meant wracking one's brain endlessly. He would embrace the unembraceable. Do battle with it and then let it go. It would pass.

Charles surveyed his surroundings. *Where the fuck am I?*

The door to his room burst open and in walked a fireplug of a nurse with a cart of meds. She appeared Hispanic or Asian, young – perhaps early twenties – and upon seeing Charles' eyes open, a large smile broke out on her cherubic face as she started to check on his monitors.

"Well, good morning!" she greeted happily. "How do you feel? I'm your day nurse, Reyna, and I have been waiting for you to wake up, sleepy head! I know you need your rest but it's such a beautiful day!"

Charles tried to speak but only managed a whispered, "Water?"

Reyna replied, "Of course! First let me get that bed up. You just let me do the heavy lifting. Ha, ha, lifting? It's just a button really, see? You can do it yourself. And this is what you press when you need someone. Here hold it. I'll get your water."

Reyna handed Charles the remote control and poured him a glass of water into a bright red plastic cup out of an equally bright yellow plastic pitcher. Sitting up, Charles was able to take the proffered cup and sip the water. It was cool and refreshing even though it tasted a bit medicinal to him, but it soothed his parched throat and was a welcome first deposit into an otherwise empty stomach. The whirlwind known as Reyna fiddled with the active heart monitor and made scribbling notes onto her iPad. The hallway outside of the room was getting noisier so Charles assumed the day was just dawning.

"How long I have been here?" Charles managed to croak out, weakly.

Reyna consulted a whiteboard on the wall behind Charles bed. "Just two days," she replied.

Two days! He couldn't remember what day it was. "And today is?"

"Saturday. You were admitted yesterday morning."

Friday? His mind raced to put together a timeline of events. Everything was disjointed and scrambled.

"Is my wife here?" he asked.

Reyna hesitated. "I'm not sure. I can check for you, though!"

"Please do. I need to see her."

Reyna made a final adjustment to one of the tubes feeding his arm. "Okay. You just get your rest. I'll let the doctor know you're awake and I'm sure he'll get your wife."

Charles managed a quick, "Thank you."

He needed to make sure Dana was all right. He supposed that the intruders had Dana bring them down to the gallery, and that Eve… what? What would she have done? Charles knew what she was capable of and shuddered to think of what she would do. He fleetingly thought what an irresponsible thing it may have been to bring her here. He laid back and took inventory once more. Head hurt like hell, shoulder hurt like hell, and he was sure he even looked like hell. *Still, good to go*, he thought. Minutes later in stepped a young kindly-looking gentleman with a clipboard in hand and the obligatory stethoscope around his neck. Charles observed he was a Sikh as his trim beard was netted and his black turban meticulously wrapped. A fitting bow tie finished the ensemble but the small hoop earring on his left ear was a jarring contradiction to his faith, just apparently not amongst the younger generation.

"Mr. Charles? I am Dr. Fareed Singh. How are you feeling? You had quite a blow to your head and a dislocated shoulder. I understand you struggled mightily the night of your accident."

"It wasn't."

"I am sorry?"

"It wasn't an accident."

"Ah, yes. I understand. Still, you are fortunate that there was only minor swelling of the brain – which has successfully receded I will add. We are going to do all we can to insure a rapid recovery. I am going to sit you up, here."

Dr. Singh used the remote control to raise the head of the bed slowly and adjust the pillow slightly for Charles' comfort.

"Is my wife here?" Charles asked.

Dr. Singh took a pen out of his shirt pocket and held it vertically in front of Charles' face.

"Follow the pen with your eyes only. No head movement, please."

Charles complied but continued to press Singh during the exam.

"I asked about my wife, doctor. Is there a problem?"

At that moment the door to Charles room clanked open as an orderly pushing a cart entered.

"Oops! Wrong room. Sorry," the embarrassed orderly squeaked.

As he backed out, Charles noted a uniformed police officer close the door. Charles pushed the pen away from his face.

"Why is there a policeman at my door?" he demanded.

The doctor turned around and glared at the door. Singh meticulously replaced the pen into his pocket. Knowing only what was deemed need-to-know, he recalled being advised to choose his words carefully.

"Mr. Charles. As I understand it, there was criminal activity at your home Thursday evening. You were viciously assaulted, and the police have reason to believe your life may still somehow be threatened. It is a standard precaution. I am sure the officer in charge of the investigation can answer all your questions, especially regarding the whereabouts of your wife. A call was placed to the Beverly Hills Police Department upon your waking. I expect you will be visited by them very soon."

The news was not what Charles was hoping to hear. He tried to recall the moments prior to his being struck in the head but was drawing a blank. His heart quickened with thoughts of the worst case. What did he mean *whereabouts*? He feared Dana was dead. Eve was dead. *What could be worse?* he thought. *No, stop!* he commanded himself. He decided to let it go and wait for the truth to come out. Only then would he deal with it – good or bad. Charles' eyes darted back to the door.

Dr. Singh waited for a reply. "If there's anything I can do please let me know."

Charles resigned himself to waiting. "I will. Thank you, doctor."

"A note of caution, Mr. Reynolds. You will most likely experience mild to severe headaches for some time. Upon release I will advise you of a regimen you must adhere to as well as follow up visits. And some additional prescriptions. Understood?"

Charles was lost in thought. The headaches he could deal with, but now was not the time to be hindered. Only partly following the doctor's conversation, he decided to avoid any further exchange and quickly replied.

"Yes. I do. I will, I mean."

Singh looked hesitantly at Charles, who nodded. "Good. Good. I will see you tomorrow and then we can discuss your possible discharge in a few days. In the meantime, you continue to rest and enjoy our hospitality." Singh smiled, winked, then turned and left the room.

CHAPTER 7

10:00 a.m.

Detective John Fox arrived at his cubicle at ten a.m. sharp. He checked his voice mail while sipping on a vending machine coffee. The brew was strong and bitter, and it suited him just fine. He had two messages and jotted down notes while they played. This first was from Cedars Sinai Hospital – the day nursing supervisor informed him that Charles Reynolds was awake and asking after his wife. A Dr. Singh was the attending physician and would be available all morning to confer if needed. That was good news. Friday felt like a bust so maybe now he could get some questions answered. The second was no big deal. A former partner of Fox, Billy Ashworth – a homicide detective in Hollywood – told him that the HPD were short on manpower and had requested a body from the Beverly station. A not unusual courtesy. A rookie detective named Shannon was volunteered, and Ashworth wanted to know if Fox thought he was a good cop. Ashworth told Fox he was called out in the early morning after the discovery of a gunshot fatality in downtown Hollywood. He'd been stretched thin all week and was grateful for the offer but not if the kid was a liability. Fox immediately called Ashworth back and told him that Shannon was an upcoming star and he'd be just fine. Fox had tagged him the day before to do some research on the Reynolds case, so he'd appreciate letting the kid juggle both. The kid was sharp, and it would be good experience, Fox added. Ashworth agreed to it and said he'd keep Fox in the loop. After that call he got a message to come see Chief Hellman.

Fox walked the hallway to the Chief's office. Just a little over twenty-four hours had passed since their breakfast meeting the day before and Fox had nothing concrete to report yet. News of Charles Reynolds being awake and alert would be worth sharing and at least offer a start. He arrived at Hellman's office and stood in the doorway.

"You wanted to see me?"

The chief motioned to his own ear – he was on a call – then motioned for Fox to enter and sit. Fox obliged. He sat still as Hellman nodded and gave a head shake in disgust for some reason. The chief was no shrinking violet and wore his emotions on his sleeve. He exuded *impatience*.

"Okay, okay. Yeah, I got it. Yes. Goodbye." He smacked his phone to end the call.

He shook his head and grimaced, picked up his AA sobriety coin and fingered it.

"Fuckin' mayor. You hear about the homicides last night? Three in the south and one on Cahuenga? That makes twenty-two this year to date. Last year it was thirteen. City Hall is screaming for answers and a crackdown. I know you've been putting in overtime and that's a problem what with the new budgetary constraints, but I just wanted to assure you I've got your back. You got anything yet on that Van Gogh mess?"

"Nothing yet, boss. I had a message that the guy in the hospital, Reynolds, is finally awake – I'm on my way over there now."

"Good, good. Let me know what you find out. This case is top priority."

"They all are for me, Chief."

"I know. Just give this one an extra shot," he pleaded as he looked over at a now empty side table where previously his mini bar rested.

"God knows I could use one about now."

Fox smiled and nodded in agreement. Chief had been sober for over a year now and Fox knew the cravings never stopped. Heading out the door, he caught a glimpse of Lieutenant Davis at the front desk. He nodded and lifted his hand up to his ear in the familiar 'call me' position. Davis nodded back. *He's a good egg,* thought Fox.

11:00 a.m.

Fox arrived at the nurse's station at Cedars and inquired about Reynolds. Dr. Singh was at the desk and perked his ears up at the mention of his patient. He walked over and introduced himself.

"Can I have a minute of your time?" he asked. Fox nodded and the two went into a small private lounge.

"I don't know how much you know about his injury," Dr. Singh began, "but I wanted to inform you that it may be difficult for him to respond to some of your questions."

"Why is that?" Fox asked. He suddenly thought this was not going to be the slam dunk interrogation he expected.

"He sustained a severe concussion with sizeable tissue tears. Upon presentation, we assumed an epidural hematoma but there were no signs of internal bleeding between the dura matter and the skull bone. In short, he was lucky. I tell you this because he may have some confusion while answering your questions. He will certainly recall some of the events leading up to his injury, but I do not expect a completely lucid conversation. There will be some short-term memory loss. I have informed him of this."

"Will it improve?"

"Over time, yes. Time and patience are all that is really required." Singh paused.

"Doc, I'm short on both now, but I'll do my best. At this moment, he's our only witness to what happened."

Dr. Singh took a deep breath and nodded, then turned to leave but did an immediate about-face.

"He is asking about his wife. Do you have any news?"

"Not yet, doc. Not yet."

"Well, good luck." He then rushed off, leaving Fox to ponder if he was going to have any luck at all now.

#

Minutes later, Fox knocked lightly on Charles door, opened it, and looked in. Charles was sitting up and cocked his head at the guest.

"Excuse me," Fox said. "Charles Reynolds?"

"Yes. Hello?"

Fox stepped in with his hand held out. "Pardon the interruption Mr. Reynolds, I am Detective John Fox. Beverly Hills PD. May I have a word, please?"

Charles shook his hand. He decided to be cautions with his answers. "Yes, sir. A pleasure to meet you. Tell me, is my wife here?"

"No, not yet. I've directed the nurse's station to let me know as soon as they hear from her. I do have some questions you can help *me* with though. Are you okay with that?"

Charles hesitated. "Yes, sure. I did expect Dana..." he trailed off.

Fox forged ahead. "Mr. Reynolds—"

"Call me Charles," he said.

"Charles. What can you tell me about Thursday night?"

"Thursday night?" Charles shook his head slowly. He looked off into the distance, as if lost, then answered. "A night much like every night, I guess. It was five o'clock, no, closer to six. Dana and I were enjoying a cocktail and the doorbell rang. And um, I answered it and when I got to the door, I remember asking Dana about that TV show, that one with that doctor who works underground. Have you ever heard of it?"

"No, I have not, sir."

"Well, it's quite good, but anyway the door. Well, when I opened it, a young gentleman was there with a firearm pointed at me and he had another, another yeah, oh! Two assistants, yes it was two, and I was told to go back in the house and sit with Dana and at that point I um, remember some glass breaking and I was hit I don't remember much after that except... Oh, I was crawling. Yeah."

"I know this is hard, sir, but..." Charles appeared straining to recall events.

"Yes, I remember crawling, Detective. I'm sorry, I just, I can't remember much more after that. You're going to have to fill in the blanks, I'm afraid. Is my wife OK?" Charles asked.

"Sir, when police arrived at your house after you had placed a 911 call – and yes, you did place that call – you were found on the floor with your injury. Officers conducted a thorough search of the house and it was in your basement where you keep your paintings, they discovered two corpses. A male and a female. It appeared they had been mauled by some sort of an animal."

Charles leaned back into his bed. "Was one of them...?" He hesitated to finish the query. Fox immediately held his hand up.

"No! We do know it was not your wife, sir. The coroner quickly put the age of the female victim at early twenties. No identification yet, but we know it was not your wife." Fox paused and put his hand on Charles' arm.

"Sir, we do not know where your wife is yet. We're doing our best to look for her."

Charles started to speak but stopped. The detective's mention of an animal sent a shock through him, but he felt this was not the time to reveal information about Eve. He'd press for whatever they knew of Dana. He reached with trembling hands to get his glass of water. Fox assisted him and lifted the straw to his lips. Charles took a hesitant sip. The ex-Marine steeled himself.

"There were three. I remember two men and one girl. They were there for the Van Gogh."

"The Van Gogh is gone, sir."

"I suspected as much. Was the male corpse young or old?"

"The coroner put his age at mid-forties to fifty."

"The second male was early twenties. Do you think he kidnapped my wife? He must also have the Van Gogh. Has there been a ransom demand?"

Fox was listening intently to Charles' questions. He knew he was vacillating from confused to coherent.

"None that we know of, no. But we have not been able to unlock either you or your wife's phone. We are hoping you can now with your help."

"0 8 2 6 0 8 is the code. Hers is the same. No secrets between us."

"I'll get that to the lab, sir."

"Yes. You can check all the messages. Please let me know what you find."

Charles then closed his eyes. Fox could only watch as Charles took deep breaths and exhaled slowly. After a bit, Charles appeared to have fallen asleep, but he opened one eye and looked at the detective.

"Still here?" he asked.

"Yes, sir."

"About this… animal. Any signs of it?"

"None that we found. Did you keep any exotics on the property?"

Charles closed his eyes once more, and once more, Fox sat and waited. Charles feigned sleep to cut the session short knowing the detective was likely to press the topic that Charles now scolded himself for bringing up. There was so much he could not yet disclose but he knew it was only a matter of time before the issue of Eve was pursued. Dana was his priority. Her, and getting out of this place to get to her.

Before even a minute passed, Charles started snoring softly. Fox rose and went to the door. He turned for one more glance, then left. He would be back.

In the hall, he used his cell phone to call the precinct station. He connected with the I.T. department, gave them the access codes for the Reynold's phones, and asked for a report ASAP. He was most interested in the wife's calls the previous forty-eight hours. Something didn't sit right with Fox about the missing wife.

11:30 a.m.

It was eight thirty p.m. in Madrid when Red Heard finally reached his buyer, Senor Vincente De Leon, with the good news that he had procured the desired Van Gogh. The call did not go as well as expected. News travels fast in the internet world and De Leon had heard about the mess surrounding the theft and the body count, which was something he did not now want to be part of. De Leon was no longer interested in consummating a deal that was tainted with such controversy. Red discovered that De Leon was a man of rapid negotiation who closed the door on any further discussion. With that one call from a cell phone, Red became the new owner of the Van Gogh and resigned himself to search for a new buyer. It was not lost on Red that the painting was now a liability. This was supposed to be a slam dunk – a quick buck, but now? Fortunately, his cost for the work of art was zero but as it was a market he was unfamiliar with, he needed to do a little homework. But first, a snort of the meth he picked up at Ben's motel room.

12:00 Noon

Eve had traversed the foothills above Glendale, Monrovia, and San Dimas under the cover of darkness and had spent part of the morning hidden in an abandoned outbuilding in Cucamonga Canyon. She had encountered several different animal species on the trip and was received by them in a similar fashion to her experience at the zoo. The humans she had chanced upon were judiciously avoided except for the occasional observation of their interactions with their animals. She found dogs most interesting. Of the few she watched, she noted a bond between them and their masters. A bond not unlike the one she felt with Charles and Dana. She noted one large dog that rested by a crackling fire while her masters sat and talked. The dog seemed to understand and follow the conversation. Eve knew that the animal did not comprehend the words of the conversation but listened to the tone. She did the same thing when she was with Charles and Dana. She missed them profoundly already but knew that separation was necessitated in response to the call. The call felt stronger the more eastward she traveled.

She drank from the many streams of cool water that were fed from the snowpack that rushed down from the range of mountain tops that stretched from the coast to the desert. She did not require any additional sustenance at present. Her body was lean and fit and under constant regeneration of any lost cells or fatty deposits. Eating was the last thing on her mind as she continued her trek.

The call was changing. What started as a simple discovery of her kind and an invitation, had developed into a learning experience. She was given small glimpses of places she did not recognize or understand yet but that gradually crystalized as her expedition progressed. She was entertained by images of massive greenery; canopies of nature that occasionally revealed the open blue sky. A warm, humid climate served as a perfect nurturing environment for the plants and vegetation surrounding numerous walking paths that led to massive structures with spires reaching heights unimaginable. She did not yet see what was housed in these structures, but the feeling was of security and not unlike what she felt with Charles and Dana. Many creatures like her – some smaller and some larger – and many different species all living within this different world. She was introduced to this world's masters – human-like – dressed in bright colors whose words she did not understand but whose *tone* soothed and comforted her. She knew that these human-like masters had bonded with her kind much in the same way the simple dog had bonded with its human next to the fire. She quickened her pace – this new world awaited her and there was so much to learn.

4:40 p.m.

Detective John Fox had just finished downing his late afternoon vending machine coffee. He drained his cup, observing dregs at the bottom, and studied the cup, turning it over in his hand. The cheap cups were usually printed with odds and ends, dad jokes or some inane trivia, and this one had a variety of poker hands imprinted on them. Fox was amused to draw a straight flush. He usually drew a pair of threes and that was it. Maybe today was his lucky day. It had been a bust so far.

On his desk was a spreadsheet with the complete cell phone records for Charles and Dana Reynolds earlier. As expected, the last call from Charles was the call to 911. The last call from Dana was to her sister-in-law in Laughlin, Thursday morning. Prior to that, both phone records revealed little out of the ordinary. IT had compiled a list of the often-used numbers – most were business related to Charles dealing with well-established art and collectible vendors and family members. Dana's calls were mostly connected to their children – a daughter in Michigan and a son in Germany – and extended families as well as clients of her part-time medical consulting. There were no red flags or unusual activities tied to either phone – both outgoing and incoming. These two were saints, apparently.

Fox texted these finding to Detective Shannon – the new kid on the block. Shannon was responsible for collating any information and distributing to the department heads that had any interest in the cases he worked on. Fox knew it was busy work for the rookie, but it was dues that would pay off later in his career. Shannon would get this latest out to the chief also, saving Fox a visit.

Fox also had gotten the initial coroner's report emailed to him earlier and he studied it. The two victims found at the scene were indeed one male and one female. Both died of multiple wounds inflicted by razor sharp claws or knives. The lacerations were deep enough and violent enough to snap bones and there was evidence of severe blunt force trauma to the head and shoulders. Death in both cases was quick and there was little if any defensive wounds. Whatever attacked these two did it lightning fast. The report went on to describe the damage to vital organs in detail, but Fox got the gist rapidly and again, he thought, he drew a lousy pair of threes. Identification was ongoing with nothing to report yet – neither victim had any ID in their possession although the male had a burner phone that was damaged at the scene and was sent to CSI for any possible information that could help in solving the crime. Fox's pair of threes downgraded to one big Jack shit.

He decided to pay Charles Reynolds another visit in the morning. *You don't have a bear in your basement and not know about it,* he decided.

CHAPTER 8

5:00 a.m. Sunday

Charles swung out of the hospital bed he was growing tired of. It was time to get out. He opened a plastic bag he had earlier discovered on a shelf under the side table of his bed. It held the clothes he had worn when he was taken to the hospital Friday morning. It was now Sunday morning and forty-eight hours in this place was too much for him. He recalled with a snort being shot in the leg in Vietnam in '71 and his return back on patrol two days later – a clean in an out – so this bonk on his head was just a minor scratch. His shirt and jeans had been laundered and a new pair of socks were included as well as his watch, rings, and wallet. He was pulling on his pants as a petite Philippine night nurse walked in. She raised a dark brown eyebrow.

"Excuse me? Where do you think you're going?" she asked.

"I'm leaving. Didn't you hear?" He gave his best toothy smile. "Dr. Singh gave me my hall pass."

The nurse glanced at the whiteboard behind him. She saw nothing to indicate his discharge.

"I don't think so, sir."

"No. Really!" Charles protested.

"You stay there while I double-check."

Charles sat on a bedside chair to put on his new socks. He sheepishly nodded. "Okay. I may have gotten my days mixed up, but I'll wait while you check."

"Okay. You stay there now, sir!" she ordered. She turned and left.

Charles waited thirty seconds, slipped into his shoes, and opened his room door. No policeman was on duty – good. It was probably boring duty anyway and Charles had apparently presented no threat. He walked down the hallway and entered the nearest elevator and punched the lobby button. He arrived seconds later, exited, and casually strolled out the front door unnoticed. Standing at the curb of the U-shaped driveway, he noticed several unoccupied taxis, plumes of water vapor exhaust rising into the cold morning air. He raised his hand and hailed one.

During the ride home Charles reviewed his conversation with the detective. There were a lot of unanswered questions on both sides and Charles knew the detective was going to get tougher the closer he got to the case. For now, finding Dana was imperative.

Twenty minutes later, Charles stepped out of the cab and walked up to his front door. Once inside, Charles was not frantic, but he was determined to thoroughly search the house for any signs of what possibly happened to Dana. He remembered protesting about them wanting to use Dana to take them to the Van Gogh. He headed straight for the elevator.

In the gallery he did a quick walk around. The dried blood that stained the floor closest to the entrance to the gallery did not escape his attention. He crouched down to touch the floor, then noticed the two other stains of blood further off. What happened down here must have been horrendous. He knew Eve was responsible – but as aggressor or defender? He was confident that Eve would have remain undetected following the attacks, so he quickly climbed the nearby access ladder to the mezzanine area and headed to her cage. The cage was covered with scales – some still transparent and shimmering and others rapidly losing their opaqueness. As he got closer, his heart skipped at the sight of a form lying at rest.

#

Dana awoke. She did not recognize her surroundings at first but as her eyes adjusted to the dim light she realized where she was. She was in Eve's enclosure. She slowly recognized the ceiling and the small thousands of shimmering scales encompassing her resting place – *her nest*, she thought – she closed her eyes and breathed deeply, taking in its' strange yet comforting aura. She did not panic but felt warm and protected. She tried to remember why she was here and the turn the events of the past – how long had she been here? – however many days over in her mind. Aware of another presence in the resting place, she quickly opened her eyes and looked down towards her feet. Charles sat, crossed legged, at the end of her bed – hands clasped together, eyes tightly shut.

Dana raised herself up onto her elbows and smiled. "Hey, good looking."

Charles opened his eyes, grinned broadly, and reached out for her. They hugged tightly. He kissed her and held her face in his hands. He looked at her lovingly. "They told me you were gone. Missing."

Dana looked perplexed. "What? Who?

"The detective."

"Not following you. I guess we have a lot to talk about."

"I guess we do. To start with – why are you here? Bed too lonely without me?"

Dana raised an eyebrow. "I'm sorry, but where have *you* been?"

Charles cocked his head in return. "We need coffee."

#

An hour later, both Charles and Dana were seated in the kitchen area as he poured the last ounces of a carafe of Hawaiian Isles Kona into their cups. Charles had related being hit in the head and struggling to reach his phone. Dana countered with her having to escort Mark and Allison to the gallery. Dana told him she briefly remembered turning on the gallery lights followed by a burning sensation in her chest, then waking up. Charles talked of waking up in the hospital and discussing his condition with Doctor Singh then being interrogated by the Detective the previous day.

"This Detective Fox told me they found two bodies in the gallery when they police arrived. They were pretty bloody and torn up."

"Oh my God. Do you think…?" Dana questioned.

"It had to be. Who would have thought she…?"

Charles finished his cup, set it down, tapped the table.

"But you were nowhere to be found. The police have been searching."

"Then Eve…somehow?"

"She must have."

"Which explains the scales. I could see them clearly today but two days ago they were probably invisible."

"But why would she have hidden me?"

"Were you hurt? Tell me about the burning sensation."

Dana closed her eyes and concentrated. After a second, she opened them wide, piercing through Charles.

"I remember… My God! I was shot."

Dana pulled down the knit top she was wearing to her breastbone and felt around the area. Her eyes opened even wider as she detected a scar. Charles reached over and touched it.

"That's impossible."

Suddenly, it hit Charles.

"Where's Eve?"

#

Minutes later, Charles returned to the kitchen nook.

"She's nowhere to be found."

Dana rose, turned, and looked out at the back of the house. Standing there, lost in thought, she spoke slowly. "Eve must have been mothering me. She must have…"

Dana touched her scar again. She turned to Charles.

"Why am I not dead? There's still so much we don't know about her. Isn't there?"

Charles slowly turned his head towards Dana. His eyes were unfocused.

"I'm sorry. What were we talking about? Do we have any coffee?"

Dana's medical training took over immediately – she knew that Charles' head injury – the concussion – was going to cause some short-term memory loss and that he would have trouble concentrating. She sat down across from him.

"Charles. We just had half a pot each. Do you remember?"

Charles stared blankly, then nodded. "Yes. Yes, I do. I'm sorry."

"That's all right. You've been through quite a lot, and we can't expect everything to be as before for some time. You need to rest today."

"We need to find Eve, though. Where could she have gone?"

"I don't know. Maybe she'll return soon."

"Yes. Maybe."

Dana reached out to hold Charles' hand to reassure him.

"It'll be fine," she added. But Dana did not believe it would be fine. She was now even more leery of the big cat, worried about her husband and the police, as well as the Van Gogh. And about a million other things.

6:00 a.m.

Detective John Fox rose early on Sunday. He threw on a vintage Hobie Surf long-sleeved tee, his shorts, and runners, and headed out the door. He enjoyed jogging on Venice beach before the panhandlers and circus acts took over. Jogging was a purely physical pursuit that allowed him time away from everything. Thirty-five years in law enforcement was a long time spent working even longer hours and doing very little. It was not all car chases and gun battles. The reporting, the research, the endless meetings, and conferences that he had worked his way up to, made him long for the simple work of a beat cop. But those days of busting drunken sailors in San Diego and Naples were long gone. The jogging was freedom without restraint. The smell of the ocean and the cool air brought in from the onshore flow was an indescribable treat he looked forward to. The news people called it the June Gloom. He loved it. At the end of the pier, he stopped and looked out over the Pacific. The salt air and faint odor of kingfish and Spanish mackerel assaulted his senses and reminded him of his youth spent off the Channel Islands – summer days surfing, and nights cooking the days catch over burning mesquite in the firepits.

John often thought of retiring. His Navy pension allotment went straight into his IRA account, his BHPD checks were more than sufficient to cover his lean monthly expenses, and he had no debt. What was stopping him, he often asked himself. He could imagine himself surfing every morning, but after that, what? It was the 'what' that kept him at it. The biggest problem was that it just wasn't fun anymore. As a young seaman military policeman, he remembers his watch commander telling his guard mount before dismissal to "have fun out there." At the time he found it an odd and disquieting suggestion. Cop work was not fun in the traditional sense. It took him years to discover that if you were good at your craft, if you cared about your results, and if you were engaged in the big picture, you *could* have fun at your job. Not the 'ha ha' fun but the 'damn, I'm good at this shit' fun. Fox faced the truth that it had been some time since he had that kind of fun. He decided it was time to head back and argue the retirement question with himself later. He ran.

His thoughts quickly went to the Reynolds case. He went over in his head what he knew – what was concrete. Who knew exactly what happened at the house? For sure, whoever had the Van Gogh knew. Also, he did not believe for a second that Charles Reynolds had no clue what could have caused the mayhem in his basement. Find the Van Gogh and you'll find the answers he told himself. This was no fun.

Arriving at his place, Fox took a quick shower and dressed to visit Reynolds in the hospital. After that he had the afternoon off to review the reports he received the day before, once again. He was sure he would find something he missed. He dressed in a pair of blue Penguin slacks with a brown Montana Bison belt, and a gray Greg Norman Golf shirt. Maybe he'd take up golf, he mused. He had the wardrobe for it – wasn't that half the battle? He downed a cup of two-hour old coffee – perfect – and headed out the door.

Halfway to Cedars his cell rang – his console screen showed 'Lab'. He had been waiting for this call. He pushed the phone icon on his steering wheel.

"This is Fox."

"John, this is Heidi Richards."

John recognized Heidi's voice instantly. Oddly, he felt the tiniest bit of dopamine release into his body. Heidi always seemed to have that effect on him. Heidi was the BHPD forensic crime lab supervisor. He was instantly attentive – Heidi never worked on a Sunday. Unless it was important.

"I received the preliminary blood test results back from the Reynolds crime scene. You asked me to call if I found anything. Well, we found a whole lot of *anythings*."

"I'm listening."

"As expected, we had blood from a male, Type B Neg from the first corpse and the female victim tested out as a Type O Positive. No big shakes there but then we found blood from another female Type AB. In checking medical records on the Reynolds fam, the wife is Type AB."

"Wait. As far as we know, the wife was not at the scene."

"I understand that," she replied.

"Then that's a problem."

"Uh huh, but hold on, good-looking."

Another jolt of dopamine. Fox had to smile at that – he and Heidi went way back, and Heidi was not shy about her attraction to him – and vice versa. Heidi freely shared that she was in a marriage to a corporate lawyer type with a million-dollar smile and a matching paycheck, but that they had an *arrangement*. An arrangement that Fox took advantage of one night at an off-site conference years earlier. Fox couldn't recall if it was the alcohol or the abstinence that drove them to seek each other out but felt no guilt. It was what it was. One night. Heidi was a sweetheart, but Fox wasn't a long-term affair kind of guy. Sneaking around was a lot of work.

"Lay it on me, darlin'."

"We found a fourth blood sample at the scene that we assumed was probably the perp that took the Van Gogh. Nope. That blood came back 'unknown'."

"Unknown? Could you determine male of female?"

"Honey, we couldn't determine if it was even human. We're not even sure it's blood."

"What?"

"You got it. No one here has seen anything like it. The DNA strands test out with super long antiparallel strand – twice as long as human – with traces of mammalian that are unknown but included synthetic cells."

"Speak English, please."

"OK, sugar. What that means is 'what it is, shouldn't be what it is'. Clear? We're not done yet though. We're retesting and setting up some simulations."

Fox's mind was racing. He recalled a thought from the day before – *You don't have a bear in your basement and not know about it.*

"Is you mind blown?" she asked. "Cos I got more."

"Oh boy."

"Oh boy, indeed. CSI Cuesta told me he picked up a strand of hair that he showed you and Lieutenant Davis."

Fox suddenly remembered and had a sinking feeling. One more unexplained addition to this puzzle.

He sighed. "The disappearing hair. Yeah. What the hell is it?"

"It's not hair. It's possibly fur and as far as we can tell, it's the damnedest fur we've ever come across. The strand of fur is comprised of micro scales. I mean micro mini micro! They react to light like we've never seen. It's there one second and then not. At least it was."

Fox was troubled to ask the next question. "Was?"

"The strands lose their ability to react over time. We're assuming that it expires over time once it's shed by its host."

"Jesus. Anything else?"

"This isn't enough?"

"You'll keep me posted?"

"Absolutely. On my honor. Keep your phone charged and on!"

"Will do. Thanks, Heidi. Love you."

"You too, big time."

Fox hit the 'end' icon on his steering wheel. He was now a block from Cedars, close to the hospital but no closer to putting together what happened at that house than before, but he did have some more ammunition to unload on Reynolds. The news about his wife's blood would not be received well but it had to be disclosed. He pulled into law enforcement parking next to an idling BHPD cruiser. An officer he didn't recognize was sitting in the driver's seat, sipping on a large 7-11 coffee cup. Fox exited and walked to the officer's side door, flashing his badge. The officer rolled his window down.

"Good morning, detective," the officer said.

#

Minutes later, a furious Fox pulled his cruiser out of the hospital parking structure and onto Beverly Boulevard, Lieutenant Davis was on speakerphone.

"How the hell could Reynolds have left the hospital without being noticed, Rocky? And why was I not notified?"

"I don't know, John. I'll find out though. This is the first time I heard about it. We don't put our brightest on hospital watch. You know that."

"No, but I do now!" he bellowed. "Reynolds is the only one who can help piece this together. We'd better hope to God that he doesn't go missing too!"

9:00 a.m.

Eve watched as a line of cars moved eastward on US 60. The concrete highway below would take traffic to Phoenix and beyond. Yet unknown to her, her destination was a small town west of Phoenix called Tonopah. She was sprinting across a tall sand dune outside of Indio, now one-hundred-twenty-five miles from her home. The desert stretched out ahead of her with little to deter her from her terminus. The journey to this point had been fairly trouble free and the warm sun on her soft fur felt comforting. The heat generated by her loping strides served as a storehouse for energy.

The visions had increased with ever more detail of her kind and her world. She learned she was not the dominant species of her world – there were many, many more – but hers was the one that the masters revered the most. She learned of her species name – N'Khal. N'Khal were initially raised as pets and companions, but the masters had discovered many millennia before the unique ability of the N'Khal to regenerate themselves inside and out and to utilize their power to heal. Sickness was all but eliminated by her kind and the N'Khal negated most illness and disability in their world. Death was an inevitably and accepted as part of life, but their world was one where disease and illness were no longer of concern. Eve knew her other was now waiting for a reunion.

#

Detective John Fox stood at the front door of the Reynold home. He was not in a good mood. The information he had gotten from Heidi begged for clarification and he hoped Reynolds could shed some light on what he knew – which wasn't much. He admitted to himself he still had little to nothing to go on. He rang the doorbell and waited. He suspected that Charles would know where Dana was and go to her, so the chance of Reynolds being home was slight. He trusted no one at this point. His mood soured. The door opened.

Charles Reynolds greeted him. "Good morning, Detective."

Charles had discussed with Dana his encounter with Detective Fox and both were in agreement that they would tell the detective everything they knew, including the existence of Eve. To keep her a secret from the authorities would be deceitful and not help them in their search for her or in the investigation of the missing Van Gogh. Getting Eve back was paramount.

Charles led Fox into the kitchen where Dana had just finished making a fresh pot of coffee – a Folger's Black Silk. Dana walked straight over an held out her hand in greeting.

"You must be Detective Fox. I'm Dana," she declared with a disarming smile.

Fox appeared momentarily stunned. "Yes. I, um… it's a pleasure."

"Coffee?"

Fox looked back and forth at his two hosts. "Yes, yes, thank you."

Charles piped in, "We'll have it out on the patio. It's such a nice day out."

Charles, Dana, and the detective sat on a sturdy outdoor whicker set with a low-lying table at their feet. Fox told them of the lab's findings regarding the two deceased robbers that were found in the basement. He then disclosed information on the presence of Dana's blood and the unknowns. He concluded with the information on the fur strands and the difficulty of identification. He then stood up to address the two.

"Mr. and Mrs. Reynolds. I need you both to be completely truthful with me now." He addressed Dana. "Mrs. Reynolds, I really need to know where you've been the past two days and how your blood got on the floor of the gallery. You certainly do not look hurt in any fashion." He turned to Charles. "Mr. Reynolds, there was clearly no evidence of your presence down there during the 'incident', but I know you must know what the hell was down there that did that damage. And more to the point, *where is it*?"

Charles looked at Dana. He raised his finger as if to stop her.

"I'll go first, sweetheart. It'll make yours easier to understand. I hope."

Charles then explained about the infant creature they had taken in and raised, and their experience with Eve the past year.

"We are still learning about her and what her abilities are," he concluded. "Which brings us to Thursday night." He turned to Dana. "You're on, dear."

Dana related escorting the two robbers down to the gallery and then being shot and waking in the cage. Healed. She showed Fox the scar. She finished by stating she had no clue as to the whereabouts of the Van Gogh.

"And now… we have no idea where Eve is either," she finished.

Charles added, "We're afraid of what she might do… out there. Or even what could be done to her."

Fox nodded in agreement and silently observed the two.

"This is quite a story," he pointed out. "May I see her cage?"

The Reynolds took Fox to see the cage and its failing covering. Fox bent down to pick up some strands with the micro scales.

"I saw this the other morning, after the 911 call. I had a bad feeling then and I have a bad feeling now."

"But you believe us, don't you?" Dana inquired.

"Yeah, I do. Dammit. I wish I didn't, but I do."

The three of them returned to the elevator for the short trip upstairs. Fox once again fingered the scratches in the stainless steel. He turned to both.

"Look, give me the day. I'll try to keep this on the QT and as vague as possible with my people. But if that thing of yours shows it's face anywhere, I can't guarantee any suitable outcome."

#

Detective John Fox called Heidi Richards the moment he got back into his car.

She answered on the first ring. "Miss me, sweet cheeks?"

Yet another leak of dopamine. "You know it."

"What's up?"

"Those blood tests we talked about earlier. The Reynolds case. Specifically, the one from the wife and the unknown. Can you route that to me directly? I've got a lead on what happened to the wife, and I want to run that unknown sample by someone else. Not that your guys aren't totally accurate in your findings, but I've got a guy. And he has a guy. You know the routine."

"Uh huh… yeah. Look, John. I can bury this for a couple of days if you want me to. That's what this is about, isn't it?

Fox sighed. "I see your radar is functional."

"You free for dinner tomorrow?"

Hell yes, thought Fox.

He paused. An idea came to him. "You know the Dal Rae in Pico?"

"It's a drive, but yeah. Great Veal Oscar."

"Uber over. I'll make it worth your time."

"Oh, I know you will," she breathed.

They agreed on meeting up in the bar at seven-thirty and either eating there or in the dining room if he could get a wrangle a table. The place was usually not that crowded on a Monday. The piano bar always got a bit raucous by ten-thirty, but Fox planned to be out of there by then.

CHAPTER 9

5:00 p.m.

Charles and Dana ate the last of their early supper – take-out from Da Pasquale Trattoria. Dana had ordered the Caprese Salad while Charles enjoyed his Zuppa Del Giorno and Chicken Parmigiana. Both had a glass of an excellent Santa Margherita Chianti Classico Riserva. Draining his glass, Charles looked off into the distance, focused on nothing. Dana studied him. She worried that Charles was struggling to say something.

"How was your meal?" she asked casually.

"Hm? Oh… good. The soup was a bit bland and the chicken was way too much, but good."

"They're servings are always too large. I'm surprised you didn't have the Caesar. You always liked that."

"Did I?"

"Yes. You did."

Dana emptied the bottle into both of their glasses. Charles sipped.

"Are you…?"

Charles cut her short. "I'm okay if that's what's on your mind. And, yes, I do like their Caesar. I know you're worried about me and what happened. I'm fine. I'm worried about Eve. That's all. I'm worried that that damn detective probably thinks we're lying about her. Maybe we should have just told him we had a damn Bengal tiger or something!"

Dana shot back, "Too late for that. He knew of the lab results."

"Labs can be wrong."

"But they weren't. And the scales?"

Charles put his glass down on the table and sat back in his chair.

"Oh, yeah. The scales. Damn!" Charles stared up at the ceiling.

A silence enveloped the two. He heaved a sigh, then settled.

"I'm sorry."

"You've got nothing to apologize for, dear."

"We've got to find her, Dana. If the police or anyone else get their hands on her, they'll put her away. They'll stick needles in her and prod and poke her and keep her locked up."

"We kept her locked up. Was that any different?"

"No, and that's not fair," he calmly chided. "We loved her and she loved us." Tears welled in his eyes. Dana sighed and reached out to him. They held hands in silence.

Charles was right, she thought. The police would be looking for a wild animal who had killed two people and was believed be capable of doing it again. There was no explaining her origin so any attempt would be met with skepticism. They couldn't just post 'Lost Cat' flyers on telephone poles. To make matters worse, there were no pictures of Eve. The couple had tried multiple times to photograph her, but all their efforts resulted in blurry smudges. They supposed her unique fur and scales reacted with the light in a way that prevented conventional picture taking.

Dana consoled him. "We'll figure it out, hon. She'll be back. She took care of me, right? This is our home. Her home. Maybe she was trying to find *you*. Maybe she still is."

The two sat silently, Dana caressed his large hand as he nodded and gazed at her face. A calm came over them.

"She must be frightened," Charles mused. "Out there alone."

Their solitude was interrupted by their land line ringing. Both reached for their hips – a long ingrained reaction to a phone ringing these days – and both looked at each other and laughed.

"I'll get it," he said. Charles rose, walked over to a built-in desk nook, and picked up the phone receiver. He greeted *hello* and listened intently. Dana saw him register some surprise. "Yes, that would be fine. Yes. See you then."

Charles hung up and raised an eyebrow at Dana. "We're going to dinner tomorrow night."

6.00 p.m.

Red Heard forced a sharp thumbtack through thick paint and canvas into the wall in his den. He stepped back to admire his work. Mr. Vincent Van Gogh's piercing green eyes stared back at him. Red reached over to pick up a bottle of Lowenbrau and took a swig, then raised it towards the painting.

"A toast to you, you ugly bastard," he slurred. "You fuckin' piece of crap."

Red did not have a good Sunday. He called every one of his fences to feel them out about possible buyers for high-end art and no one showed any interest – especially when he alluded that the 'potential' piece was stolen property. That was the death kiss. No one would touch or even be associated with a hot piece of merchandise. Without saying, everyone knew. News of a missing Van Gogh travelled quickly. International art dealers and high-end auction houses were notified quickly to be on the lookout. Red was going to have to suck it up and work diligently to off the piece discreetly. He loathed being burdened by the responsibility of doing the actual work needed to find a buyer now. He needed a plan of action. He popped the top off another bottle and guzzled it down. He had finished his free meth earlier in the day and had an Uber driver he knew delivering more later. That Spaniard screwed him royally, but he'd find a way. He always did.

10:00 a.m. Monday

Eve was nearing her destination. The visions and voices in her head had ceased for now, but like a compass needle that is commanded by earth's magnetic field to point north, she was inexplicably drawn towards several sand-colored low-lying buildings on the horizon. Tonopah was a small town with a big role in the state as it was near the Palo Verde Nuclear Generating Station, the largest power producer in the country. Given that the population of Tonopah was less than three thousand five hundred full time residents, most workers at the local businesses commuted from the greater Phoenix area. The largest employer within the city limits of Tonopah was housed in that low-lying building, Lan Pharmaceuticals Ltd.

Lan Nguyen hired his engineers and researchers from an office in downtown Phoenix, but most of his one-hundred-plus employees lived in the small community of Verrado. The town of Verrado was a man-made throwback to the '60s with tree-lined boulevards, Craftsman style houses, public parks, streams flowing among walking trails, a small town center, and a world class golf course. The town was less that ten years old but straight out of *Leave it to Beaver*, and a mere half hour traffic-free drive to the plant.

Lan was a supplier of cutting-edge medicines used in the treatment of several cancers. Lan had FDA approval for the mainstream pharma that he distributed, but much of his product was experimental in nature and since human testing was strictly prohibited in the US, Lan also maintained a larger facility in Ho Chi Minh City in Vietnam – his homeland – where the experimental product could be tested and made available on the black markets – for a hefty price of course. Lan put profits above all else, and he knew that the Asian market for certain medicines derived from a variety of endangered species was huge, and the profits from such products did not escape him. There was little if any oversight of his activities, so he directed his teams in both Vietnam and Arizona to undertake the task of creating hybrid genetic reproductions of both common and endangered species. It would be like printing money, Lan believed.

FDA inspectors regularly audited their US operations to ensure compliance. Inspectors, Distributors, and VIP Visitors had complete access to Lan's testing and production facilities – the ones that they were aware of. Unknown except for a small number of thoroughly vetted and sworn-to-secrecy researchers, Lan operated a covert laboratory in secreted rooms several stories underground at Lan Pharmaceuticals Ltd. In Tonopah. This laboratory was ground zero for his genetic research.

This laboratory held a female N'Khal.

The female N'Khal was simple known as Subject Zero. Subject Zero was brought over from Lan's Vietnam laboratory a year ago.

Lan had grown up among the rice paddies and farms in a rural village close to the Tay Ninh province near the border of Cambodia and Vietnam. Lan's father and mother were hard working peasant farmers and life was harsh as a war was still raging, but Lan knew of no other existence and accepted realities without question.

His grandfather often passed on spoken histories of his ancestors and the shared myths and stories they were taught. Grandfather regaled Lan with stories of the mysterious Cambodian N'Khal – invisible creatures who visited, befell no harm, could communicate telepathically over vast distances, and could heal the sick. However, as it is with the Easter Bunny or Santa Claus, this belief usually dissolved with the onset of adolescence. An unforgiving life in Southeast Asia was no place for tales of invisible healers. But Lan always believed and still did. The N'Khal was his invisible 'forever' friend.

Subject Zero was brought to Lan's attention a year earlier while on a trip back to his facility in Vietnam. His research team discovered SuZee (as they dubbed her) by accident near the Phnum Samkos Wildlife Sanctuary in neighboring Cambodia while searching for tree monkeys. The team had encountered a troop of monkeys and netted half a dozen in a trap. Upon inspection, it was discovered that one of the females had a small creature clinging to her. The team separated the creature and sent it immediately to Lan at the Ho Chi Minh lab. Lan was suspicious of the creature's origin but did not connect this tiny animal to tales heard long ago – until it disappeared for the first time. And until it was accidentally sliced severely during an experiment and miraculously closed its' own wound. Then Lan believed.

But SuZee was not raised as a loving pet like Eve was.

Lan was well past the dreams of little boys who aspired to raise their own personal N'Khal as a pet and share adventures exploring the world unafraid of any and all evil doers. Lan had 'adult' ideas. His experimental genetic experiments at the Tonopah facility had not gone as planned. His team was successful in creating hybrid species of animals destined to be butchered and processed for cures, but it was not without inherent dangers. Most of the creations failed, dying shortly after being born, and the few that lived proved sterile and completely feral, even murderous with others of their kind. Lan succeeded in creating modern day monsters of no obvious use. SuZee was his last resort and hopefully his best chance, but something was wrong with SuZee.

For months now, SuZee lie in her cage, rarely moving, her once magnificent fur now dulled and lifeless. Her limbs were tucked under her, unmoving. The prodding and the testing and the needles had taken a toll. Her powers to regenerate had declined. Small test animals that were injured and placed near SuZee in the past were given new life and cured, but all recent attempts to gauge her powers were fruitless. The N'Khal were a species that were ferociously devoted to their masters, but needed companionship, attention, and love. Any animal caged, mistreated, and untended for a long period of time would eventually become scared, withdrawn, and hopeless; and SuZee was now all that.

#

Eve sat just short of two-hundred yards from the building. The length of two football fields separated her from the call that had been a constant companion on her journey. Now, the voice had ceased, and visions stopped.

She attempted to communicate. *I am here, and I will remain here.*

8:00 p.m.

Charles and Dana pulled their silver Cadillac CTS into the parking lot of the Dal Rae in Pico Rivera at exactly the appointed time for the dinner invitation. It was a forty-five-minute drive, but rush hour traffic had cleared, and the 5 freeway was mercifully accident free.

Charles had spent the day walking around the back of the estate and the adjoining hills behind their property in search. There was no sign of Eve but he had resigned himself to that conclusion early in his search. His marine training from over forty-five years ago was something he rarely thought of this day but after hiking a few miles through the brush, he imagined himself back on patrol and summoned the skills he once mastered – his ears were alert, his vision expanded, and his footfall quiet. If Eve were present, she would have presented herself unless there was some reason not to. At noon he stopped to rest and quench his thirst out of his plastic water bottle. Three aspirin helped a bit to stave off an oncoming headache – they were a frequent but bearable reminder of that night four days ago. He and Dana had a lively discussion upon his return, positing the reason that Detective John Fox had extended the dinner invite. Charles argued that Fox was being civil and professional against Dana's insistence that it was probably bad news.

"Sure, bad news over a glass of cheap Chardonnay," Charles joked.

"Order a Far Niente, if it is," Dana quipped.

Charles had to laugh at her response. This was the girl he fell in love with all those years ago who just days ago suffered a near mortal gunshot and was miraculously healed with no ill effects. Charles loved her strength. *Her taste in wine was impeccable too*, he thought, *although at a tailgater at Dodger Stadium the host had better watch his supply of Miller Draft.* She could drink any of her peers under the table and still beat them all at cornhole.

Upon entering the restaurant, Charles swept the room quickly and saw Fox at a booth towards the rear of the building – accompanied by a striking woman of indeterminate age with long blond hair and seemingly flawless skin. Dana noticed them too.

"Well, well. A double date?" Dana kidded.

"Be good now," Charles replied.

"Yes, Daddy!"

The two made their way across the dining area. The air was filled with the scent of mesquite fired open-flame grilles and lively conversation. The bar was sparsely occupied – Charles and Dana discovered long ago that a seat at the bar was usually the best choice while the teetotalers sat in the waiting room for a table. Charles figured the place was about half full but doing good business for a Monday night.

Fox rose to greet them and introduced Heidi. After seating and exchanging pleasantries, Fox called the waiter over and ordered an expensive bottle of Chardonnay and Cabernet Sauvignon. Charles gave Dana an approving glance that Fox did not miss.

"Why argue over red or white when you can have both?" Fox offered.

"Works for me," Charles countered.

The conversation started light and breezy. They talked about traffic and weather, which was a given with any get together in Southern California. They moved on to the Lakers and Dodgers as the wines were being opened and tasted. Heidi joined in easily and Charles found her intelligent and charming, with a relaxed laugh and no pretensions. Charles decided to bide his time and wait for the real conversation to open. Fox did not disappoint.

"Well! If I may…" Fox started.

Here comes the real entree, Charles thought.

"Charles. Dana. I asked you two to join us because tomorrow I am going to request that the Beverly Hills Police Department close out the investigation into the deaths of the two robbers at your home and attribute it to an accident involving a rouge wild animal."

Charles and Dan appeared stunned.

"Seriously? That's possible?" Dana questioned.

"Well, you know better than most that your hills are home to coyotes, rattlesnakes, and mountain lions. We even had a bear a few years back. It's entirely believable that a cougar or some similar predator could have entered your basement by accident, found it hospitable, and had been staying in there for some time."

Charles looked at Fox and then to Heidi. "But what about the findings you reported to me concerning the unidentified blood? And fur?"

"And my blood," Dana added.

"Those reports have not been disseminated yet," Heidi interjected. "And I can make sure they stay between the four of us."

Fox glanced at Dana. "Look, this story of you getting shot and waking two days later is going to be met with a lot of skepticism and tough questions. Officially, you weren't even there! We had no idea where you were. We can't place you in the house Thursday night. You were visiting a sick aunt in Riverside – whatever. Done deal."

Fox nodded at Charles. "You. You were out of it the whole time. Pfft. Sure you asked about Dana once you woke – foggy memory – you forget she was with relatives. 'Oh, yeah, got it,' I say. Done deal. Now, I already laid out that the story of an animal attacking intruders is entirely plausible. Does anybody really know what happened down there? Of course. The guy that escaped with the painting. Do you think this guy wants to go to the police and tell them about some wacked out combination gorilla-lion attacking his accomplices during a home invasion he took part in? Including an assault? I doubt it. We close the file, you call your collectibles insurer for now, and that's it. Done deal."

"What about Eve?" Dana quizzed.

"We report a fatal animal attack to the Parks and Recreation folk, and they keep an eye out. They post a bulletin on their website. No one reads it. Case closed." He paused, then added, "You can keep looking for your Eve, but there's not much more I can do. I'd expend the energy finding your Van Gogh if I were you. I'll help there any way I can." Fox looked for Charles and Dana's response. "We good?"

Charles thought about what Fox presented. He surmised that Fox and Heidi had given this some thought and needed to trust their judgement. They were putting their asses on the line, too. Plus, Charles was not interested in becoming page one news on the New York Post. Or the National Enquirer. He glanced at Dana. Almost telepathically, she gave him a stoic nod.

"We're good," he announced.

Fox nodded in agreement just as their waiter arrived rolling a cart with their plates of food. "Ah! Here's our dinner! I am famished!"

Dinner was served. The wine bottles were quickly emptied and as their main courses were being devoured, the group grew quiet. Light talk propelled them through the meal.

While all their plates were being gathered, Fox ordered a round of Courvoisier for the table. Dana passed in favor of the last bit of the cabernet. The waiter arrived with the check and Charles courteously offered to pay or split the bill, but Fox would have none of it.

"Against regs, sir," Fox advised. "Company business and all that."

"Okay then. Like you say, 'done deal'!"

#

Fox and Heidi moved to the lounge following the Reynolds departure. Fox ordered another cognac and Heidi asked for a French Connection.

"John, dear, you know you are going to owe me big time. I was not expecting the Reynolds to join us."

Fox took a sip of his drink. "Would you have come if I told you?"

Heidi moved in a little closer to Fox. "Maybe. But don't forget, it was I who asked you out."

"Oh, I know. And I'm prepared to pay dearly."

"Yes. You are. But I am glad they agreed to our… arrangement."

"Speaking of which. Do you still…?" he asked smiling.

Heidi did not answer his question but slyly grinned and raised her hand to get the attention of the bartender. She looked Fox straight in his eyes. "Check please."

#

On the drive back home, Charles found himself talking excitedly about the dinner meeting but grew aware that Dana was strangely quiet. Usually, following an excellent meal out she would be quite vocal, talking about posting a review, comparing notes on their courses, and commenting on the ambiance of the restaurant. Tonight, she remained silent, eyes shut for most of the drive. Her hand went to her breastbone area several times and Charles wondered if she was in any pain. As Charles took the exit at Coldwater Canyon, he asked her if she was okay.

Dana opened her eyes and turned to him. "Eve is waiting. In the desert."

CHAPTER 10

10:00 a.m. Wednesday

Eve waited. Two nights passed without incident. On the first night of her vigil, she watched as a rattlesnake approached her, got within six feet, thought better of it, turned around and retreated. No one dared enter her sight the second evening. The tall saguaro cacti surrounding her, their limbs raised high, looked like humans in perpetual surrender.

Although the calls had ceased, Eve knew that it came from a N'Khal within the building she surveyed. Her thoughts went to home – her Beverly Hills home – many times throughout the previous night. She thought of Dana and the bond that the healing had established. It was a union that surpassed the simple bond of love and warmth and caring she had for her masters. It was a oneness with Dana now. If an animal was sentient and could pray, then Eve prayed to Dana. In her simple plea, she asked for nothing in return except to be of one mind. She had no confirmation that Dana would be of one, but the act of the request was satisfactory.

On day three, cloaked in her invisibility, Eve cautiously approached the largest of the buildings. A wide parking pad accessed by a dirt road seemed to be the hub of the humans traveling in and out of it. Both sides of the structure held areas of cover that the inhabitants often visited. There they ate, exhaled smoke from both legal and controlled substances, and gathered in groups noisily. The rear of the building held a massive door and a ramp dug into the land as a ravine. Several times a day, larger vehicles would access it for short periods of time. This side she approached and waited. Hours later, a rig approached, and the doors noisily rose open. Within minutes, she effortlessly slid in past the door frame of the building and climbed eighteen feet up to a platform that held a heating unit. She snuggled behind the heater and once again waited.

7:00 p.m.

The large door shut with a loud thud as the last of the humans in the storehouse area vacated and turned off the lights. Eve needed no light. Her keen eyesight was effective in any darkened environment. Hearing no additional movement beyond doors closing and the click of a few locks, Eve jumped down to the floor level and began an investigation of the buildings. A double door, unlocked, led to a long corridor with open offices and rooms on either side. Eve entered each open room, her eyes scanning quickly and her nose detecting traces of human activity – mostly benign. At the end of the first corridor, three additional hallways branched off. At the end of the shortest corridor, faint sounds of chittering and yelping from below found their way to her alerted ears. She kept searching to see who or what the sounds emanated from. At the end of hall, a stairwell led down. She followed the sounds. Several floors traversed, she reached the base of the stairwell and passed through an opened insulated fire rated door into a larger, fully illuminated room filled with cages. The cages were alive with several different species of animal. Dogs, cats, rats, rabbits, and monkeys populated the small enclosures. Upon entering, the animals grew quiet – as if they acknowledged the authority of Eve. Eve was no god, but she accepted their submission as she crept among the cages and inspected the broods.

With the room now silent, Eve turned back at the curious sound of clicking behind her as the door from the stairwell closed and locked. Immediately the lights shut off. Mere seconds later, the rooms' emergency lighting kicked in – creating an eerie shadowy tableau.

#

Lan was giddy with excitement. Three days earlier, infra-red sensors forming an invisible security perimeter around his compound picked up an animal of sufficient size to investigate. The system had the ability to recognize native fauna with accuracy. A lone coyote or peccary or even a smallish roadrunner was readily detected with accuracy and dismissed. This new creature was not. Images of the creature were captured and sent to Lan immediately. Lan was gobsmacked that an actual N'Khal had somehow been in communication with SuZee, and journeyed to its place of captivity, but he wasn't surprised. Much like the legendary Yeti, each society since time immemorial had their own take on mythical or magical creatures that roamed their forests or deserts or jungles. The myths all fell by the wayside as humanity discovered the actuality of these stories. But Lan now knew this singularity truth, and he fully embraced the idea that where there was one, there were more. Given that SuZee was rapidly deteriorating, this new visitor was indeed a gift from the gods.

Lan had no doubt that the creature would attempt to enter the facility, so he directed his secret research staff to make sure any path to SuZee was accessible. They prepared to capture the N'Khal once it entered the facility; once the creature reached the outer cages area, the heavily armored entrance door lock would be activated remotely. Then one of the researchers would enter and a heavy-duty tranquilizer dart carefully aimed at the creature would do the trick. Following that, the creature would be taken to a cage alongside SuZee.

What they did not prepare for was Eve's response.

7.30 p.m.

Eve's eyes adjusted instantly to the harsh emergency lighting. Slowly, the caged animals in unison sensed something was amiss and resumed their growling and barking and noisy assault. Eve cautiously stalked the rows, and after passing each cage the inhabitants would become silent. Eve's ears were alerted to the lock on the entrance door clicking loudly again and she immediately shimmered and became invisible. She hopped up on a tall cage housing a skittering spider monkey and observed the door. The door opened and a single human dressed in hunter's camouflage pants and matching military blouse, entered. As he stepped in, the door behind the figure closed and with a resounding click, locked again. Eve spied the barrel of a weapon not unlike that which she dealt with four nights earlier. The weapon was raised and used to scan the room. Eve watched as a large dog, a pit bull, in one of the cages on the ground angrily started ramming the door to its cage.

The human noticed it and shouted out an unintelligible command. The angry dog would not stop its assault. The figure walked over and kicked the cage angrily. The blow to the cage jolted its fastener and the door gave way. Immediately the pit bull shot out of its cage and ran towards the figure. The figure reached into a holster and produced a small handgun and shot the pit bull. The Pitbull went sprawling backward, blood from its wound gushing out in an arc that splattered other nearby captives. The room went mad with howls and screams from the resident test animals.

Visions of the night that the Van Gogh was ripped from its frame flooded Eve's mind. She immediately recognized the danger and instinctually reacted. Eve leapt off the cage she was perched on. Her invisible cloak shimmered in and out until she was fully visible. She landed a mere three feet from the figure. He started to raise his tranquilizer rifle while backing up but only had seconds to react as Eve sprang at his throat.

The rifle skittered noisily across the concrete floor and came to rest against a cage housing a white rabbit sprinkled with blood droplets. Reflected in the inquisitive rabbit's pink eyes was a pool of blood slowly inching across the floor, soon to reach the stock of the rifle.

In a room two stories above the carnage, Lan Nguyen observed the activity unfold on a video screen split into four quadrants, each with a different camera angle of the event. Eve appeared as a blur on his screen, but Lan knew what it was.

"Well, damn," he whispered.

Three men stood behind Lan looking on, aghast at the grisly scene. Lan swiveled around in his chair, jumped to his feet, and angrily addressed the trio.

"Did I not tell you that this creature was a formidable opponent – nothing at all resembling the idiotic creations we have been dealing with below?"

The tallest of the three, Aaron Butler, a pock-faced man in his thirties, with long stringy hair and a perpetual facial tic, jumped in. "Hold on, boss. We're researchers, not hunters. Kitching knew what he was doing. We all agreed once it entered the holding area, that would work to disable that thing!"

Lan pointed angrily at the video screen. "And does *that* look like it worked?"

Lan grabbed a second tranquilizer rifle lying on his desk and thrust it out at him.

"Do *you* want to try?"

Butler backed off; hands held out in surrender. "No. No! I'm just saying…"

"Do you have a plan? Good, because we need one that's a hell of a lot better than the last! Anyone?"

"I have a plan," piped one of the researchers – a thin bearded man with reading glasses perched on the tip of his long nose, the name Folsom was embroidered onto this shirt. "But we're going to need the big cage."

8:00 p.m.

Marta Hernandez was employed as an intern working at the BHPD Forensic Lab. Her primary job was the receiving, cataloging, and preparation of clothing and personal items to be processed for evidence in criminal activity cases. Marta would visually inspect the items and make notations for the actual lab technicians who would then subject them to the testing analyses required. Evidence from homicides gathered from the testing would then be used in association with human remains to aid in the cases and prosecution as needed. Marta thought the work was boring. Too many episodes of CSI on television reruns had Marta dreaming of scintillating conversations with square-jawed managers, trips to million-dollar mansions to gather evidence, and chasing dangerous suspects, not tagging dirty blood-stained clothing. Still, thanks to a recommendation by her boyfriend, she was dipping her feet into Law Enforcement; regardless of the entry level yawn she was enduring this nondescript Wednesday night shift.

The shirt she had pulled from its plastic bag this evening was a man's, blue and checked pattern, button down, short sleeved, cotton, slim fit, 'made in Thailand'. She noted all of this in the log and then added under 'condition' that it was worn, faded, missing the collar button, dotted with dog hairs, and blood stains from the left collar to the waist. The shirt was taken from a bag that was marked 'Walsh, Benjamin – victim, homicide, single gunshot, East Inn, Hollywood'. She had heard of this location before and then it hit her – this was the case that her boyfriend had helped with when he was on loan to the Hollywood Division last week. She looked at the plastic bag once again and noted the yellow sticker on it – that denoted low priority – and that meant it would simply be stored away unless it was ever needed. She thought it would be amusing if she took the shirt home and gave it to him as a memento of his first ever homicide assignment.

She hoped Officer Derick Shannon would be pleased.

8:45 p.m.

Dana had experienced a harrowing two days since her first vision from Eve. Bits and pieces of Eve's experiences in the desert were both enigmatic and illuminating, exhilarating and exhaustive. Dana would literally shut down at times, eyes closed, body held rigid, as images and sensations bombarded her mind. Then just as quickly as they came, they would leave her. These sessions lasted only a few minutes but forced Dana to stop whatever activity she was doing and sit or lie motionless. Following these she was able to relay the experience to Charles, who would attempt to record and transcribe them as best he could. For the past forty-eight hours, Dana relayed bits of the journey – as if she could see through Eve's eyes the sights Eve encountered – a muddy mix of the familiar and the unknown. Charles reviewed his notes continually. He concluded that Eve was now somewhere in the Southwestern desert – having trekked tirelessly night and day. Dana understood now that Eve was following the calling of one of her kind. Fortunately, the feline encountered scant resistance due to her ability to cloak her movements. When she finally reached her destination, she sat and waited.

This last session was not encouraging as something happened this night that truly scared Dana and immobilized her, rendering her helpless. She and Charles had been sitting together watching Clint Eastwood's *Trouble with the Curve* on Netflix. Dana was a fan of Eastwood and Charles was a sucker for any baseball movie, so they met in the middle this evening. Dana had not had a session since lunchtime and then it was only the briefest of one, Eve still in waiting. Halfway through the film, Dana suddenly sat up erect, closed her eyes, and toppled backwards on the sofa. Her breathing slowed as if unconscious, her eyelids fluttering as in a deep REM sleep. This session lasted much longer that any prior, and Charles began to panic – but just as quickly, she opened her eyes, her body relaxed, and it was over. Charles let her gather her thoughts.

She turned to Charles. "How long was I out?"

"No more than five minutes. You had me worried!"

Charles sensed that Dan was grappling for words to describe this latest episode.

"Is she still waiting?" he asked.

Dana's eyes darted around the room. "I'm… I'm so thirsty. Could you make me some tea?"

Minutes later, Charles sat next to Dana as she sipped the Sleepy Time tea he had prepared for her. Dana liked a touch of fresh lemon with a half of a teaspoon of Clover Honey added and Charles prepared it to perfection. He took his time. Charles knew not to press her – when the time was right, she would share. The two had an uncanny ability to know when to back off and allow space between each other. Charles often spent time alone in a darkened room when needed – times thankfully fewer and fewer as the years passed – and Dana was keen to recognize those moments.

"She entered the building tonight," she began. "She's curious, seeking the voice that directed her there. She was close, she felt very close, but something frightened her, no – she was not frightened – she was in control, but she reacted to something terrible and…"

Dana paused. "Oh, my God!"

Dana put her teacup down with trembling hands. Charles took the cup and saucer from her and set it aside.

Staring at nothing across the room, she continued. "She killed a man. Her life was threatened. She… she killed him." Dana, her eyes filled with tears, turned to Charles. "What is happening to her?"

Charles was at a loss. He slowly shook his head. "I don't know. I have to find her. I have to go to her."

Dana took his hand. "*We* have to go to her."

Charles looked into Dana's eyes as a single tear rolled down her cheek. There was no telling what they would encounter and Dana – a strong woman with a steel will – was too emotional and fragile at this moment. He brushed the droplet away.

"No," he said, in a steady restrained voice.

"But…"

"No buts. I do not know, we do not know, what this place is or the intentions of the people there. I cannot, and will not, risk your safety." Charles raised an eyebrow. "And clearly, you can communicate with her over the miles that separate us. And we normal folk do have cellphones."

CHAPTER 11

10:50 p.m.

Charles pulled his silver GMC Yukon out of the driveway and let it idle as Dana stood on the porch watching. She pulled her robe tighter around her neck against the chilly night air. Charles stepped out of the SUV and went to her. He hugged her tight and kissed her lightly on the lips. She grabbed the collar of his light bomber jacket and held him close.

"Promise me you'll be careful. I don't need you to engage in any heroics at your age."

"My age?"

"You know what I mean, smarty. Just come back in one piece. With Eve."

"I'll be in constant contact. You're my navigator. I'll check in every couple of hours or so. State line is just under five hours away. Once I get there I'll call. I'll probably need some landmark guidance at that point."

Dana hugged him quickly and let him go. "I'll do my best. Sometimes desert is just desert."

Back in the car, he rolled his window down. "We'll figure it out," he assured her with a wave.

He slowly wheeled out of the driveway and glanced in his rear-view mirror as Dana turned and entered the house. He drove to the property gate and stopped while the doors swung open wide. He lifted his center console and glanced down at a holstered Beretta 92FS Police Special. Available strictly to law enforcement, military, and veterans, he had purchased it two years prior for protection as riots and looting were rampant in the Los Angeles area, but thankfully it never left the holster except for cleaning and range practice. Dana was not a fan of firearms in the house, but the recent events had softened her stance. Still, Charles was not sure what she would say knowing the pistol was accompanying him now. He would tell her if needed.

While packing his suitcase, he quizzed Dana about her visions – asking about the sights she received on Eve's trip. They both agreed on her route out of the hills and her adherence to the foothills well into the Inland Empire and Lower Desert area. Charles and Dana had once owned a vacation rental in Phoenix and had made the trip eastward on the 10 freeway a number of times. He knew every county rest stop on the way – although he avoided them and preferred to stop at familiar truck stops and gas stations. If he had to pull over anywhere on his way, he was never less than twenty or thirty miles from a place he knew had hot coffee, a Mars bar, and a clean restroom.

None of those items were on his mind as he merged onto the 134 East in North Hollywood. He was focused on Eve. Dana's description of Eve's violence was minimal, but Charles knew what the gallery was like following the robbery. The Eve he knew was gentle and loving, but he had to admit that there was still so much that was cryptic about her. Her leaving to follow a *call* was even more perplexing. Were there others out there? Where, and how many? Charles was resolved to follow this trail to its end – wherever that would lead. He made a mental note to call Detective Fox in the morning and let him know what he was doing. Maybe he could help somehow if the authorities were needed, or plain advice asked for. An update on the Van Gogh would be nice, too, but that was going to have to take a backseat for now. He was sure he would have his hands full soon enough.

12:01 a.m. Thursday

Lan thought that Folsom's plan was foolproof. From the cage area where the creature currently nestled there was only one way in from above, and only one way out which led down to the laboratory area. The lab area was where the bulk of the research was conducted. A single door in and one more out – that led to the lowest level holding room. The holding room was where the live lab creations languished, awaiting their fate. That door was always locked securely and alarmed. The creation's holding cells were also electronically controlled. If any mishap were to inadvertently release the creations, they had no exit or way out and as an extra layer of protection, should the door to the holding room be breached from above, an auxiliary water supply system would flood the bottom two floors, ensuring that no one, or no *thing*, would survive. A service elevator that connected the basement floors to Lan's office aboveground was the only other escape route that one would have available, but Lan was secure in his belief that no one without knowledge – much less the dullard creations in the room – could find the discreetly hidden access button.

Eve currently sat next to a very large orange and black tabby sitting in a bed of her own – Lan had grudgingly okayed it as a company pet with unfettered access. Eve was curiously observing the tabby as the cat watched Eve's sturdy tail slowly sweep back and forth. Eve was amused at the movement of the cat's cocked head following her tail. After a bit, the tabby got bored and rolled over, stretched, yawned, and napped. Eve watched the door as the tabby snored.

Lan and his researchers viewed a split screen – one half showed a blur of light where Eve was in the cage area, and the second a shot of the lab area. Earlier, using the elevator to get to the lowest floor, the largest and heaviest of all holding area cages had been relocated from the bottommost floor to the lab and positioned adjacent to the door entering the room. The spring-loaded door was unlocked and raised allowing entry by an animal approximately Eve's size. This particular cage was constructed of TIG welded quarter inch steel bars two inches by two inches. A three-inch gap between each bar insured nothing larger that a fat squirrel could escape.

Folsom's plan was deceptively simple and promised success. Flushing Eve out of the cage area and into the laboratory would be accomplished by flooding the room with a smoke bomb, then de-activating the door lock to the lower floor. The creature would seek relief by using the stairwell, then barrel into the room and cage below at which time the spring catch would be released and the door to the cage shut.

Both Eve's and the tabby's ear perked up at the sound of the outer door *click* – and opening. Eve observed an arm reach through and toss a small object to the floor, then the door quickly close and lock again. With a sinister hiss, offensive yellow smoke rapidly billowed out of the tossed cannister and quickly filled the room with toxic fumes. Eve rose, started towards the offending object, then backed off. The room was instantly barraged with the rattling of cages and pleading of its residents. Eve intuitively crouched below the smoke level and scouted the room for an exit. None was found. The cacophony of pleading yelps and squeals soon reached fever pitch. Above the racket, both Eve and the tabby heard the click of the lock on the rear door leading down. Eve shot to the door as it opened ajar. She nudged it further and looked below. Taking a tentative step, a plaintive yowl from behind her drew her attention. She turned a saw the tabby snared – the cat had jumped between two cage and gotten her legs wedged in the wire trellis – unable to move. The smoke grew thicker and the pleas for help grew weaker. Whatever kinship Eve felt for this small animal immediately kicked in. She left the door and went to the tabby. Eve stood on hind legs and pushed the two cages apart from each other. The tabby struggled with her legs held in a seemingly inescapable cinch, but Eve studied the enclosures wires and slowly swiveled the cages, lifting one with the grasp of her tail, and securing the other into alignment to free the cat. Once released, the tabby shot towards the open door. Eve followed.

Lan watched the left screen with great curiosity as the blurred figure that was Eve freed the tabby. A grim smile spread across his face. Once out of frame, his attention went immediately to the right half. As expected, Eve leapt down the stairway and barreled into the trap. An unexpected guest also joined her, the tabby. Within seconds the door slammed shut.

Eve crouched, surveying the steel barriers. She paced back and forth, inspecting her prison. Her ears pricked as the sound of industrial axial fan exhausters roared from high up on the roof, emptying the room above of its noxious gas. All was quiet. Dead quiet.

2:45 a.m.

Charles reached Blythe without incident. His phone rang as he passed a large field of barren pygmy date palms that would not produce edible fruit for another nine months. The harsh heat and dry weather in this town that separated California and Arizona by the Colorado River was a surprisingly fertile growing area for alfalfa, cotton, and melons. He flicked on his steering wheel icon to accept her call and was surprised to see her face show up on his console screen.

"Dana?"

"Can you see me?" she asked.

"Yes, I can. Can you?"

"Um… no. Where's your phone?"

"It's in my pocket."

"Then all I can see is thirty-five cents in change, dummy."

"Oh. Hold on." Charles dug into his pocket and set the cell in a cradle.

"That better?"

"I don't know. Mr. Jefferson was at least smiling."

"Funny. What's up?"

Dana told him that she had recognized the lone Chevron station at Chiriaco Summit, thirty miles east of Indio, that they usually stopped by for an ice cream following their Phoenix trips, so it was one more confirmation that he was on the right path.

Then the line went silent.

Charles looked at his screen and saw Dana's cell phone drop onto her lap, facing up. He saw Dana's head slowly loll back. He knew that Dana was out of it – receiving something – but appeared safe.

"Hon?"

He waited. Dana got back on the line within minutes. She breathed slowly and spoke softly.

"Sorry! Eve's trapped. Surrounded by some sort of an enclosure."

"She's what?"

"Someone or something had her captured and she can't escape."

Charles felt his heart drop into the pit of his stomach and struggled to slow its beat. "Any idea of the location yet?"

"No, but it's well past Quartzsite. Maybe two hours."

Quartzsite, Arizona. - A small town of thirty-five hundred residents that swells to hundreds of thousands in the spring for their annual Gem and Mineral Show – a gathering place for rockhounds and snowbirds in RVs from all over the USA. Charles and Dana had visited on one of their trips and found some great turquoise Indian Jewelry and rare moonstone sculptures.

"I'll be going through Quartzsite in about thirty minutes. Are you okay?"

"I'm fine. I'm good. And she has a friend with her."

"A what?"

"A cat followed her into the trap. She broke her leg and Eve's taking care of her."

Charles grunted. "Huh."

"Did you eat?" she asked.

"Does a Mars bar and a Diet Coke count?"

"Hardly."

A silence settled over the line.

Dana broke the calm. "Please be careful. I know you think you're a warrior but that was a long time ago."

"I will. I'll check in by five. You get some rest."

"You know I won't. But I'll try."

"That's my girl. Love you."

"Love you, too." Charles ended the call as he drove over the Colorado River separating California from Arizona. In the late spring and summer months the river would be filled with jet skis spewing water flumes and boats serving as diving boards and bikini clad co-eds and drunken partygoers littering the shoreline. Even at this hour the docks would be home to passed-out revelers and cleanup crews but this time of year, it was dead quiet and dark as he traversed the bridge and entered the Grand Canyon State.

4:00 a.m.

Lan and his research engineers had rolled the jail cell containing Eve into the center of the room. Wary of her surroundings, Eve lay low, watching, and emitting the occasional throaty growl. The tabby cat was obviously a pet of the entire place and familiar with her captors, but she had settled into a crook of Eve's arm as Eve licked her cellmate's swollen leg. The tabby instinctively knew Eve was attending to her injury and quietly purred as the healing progressed.

Lan, Folsom, and Erwin – a squat black man with dreadlocks and wide eyes behind John Lennon glasses – watched as Eve coddled and licked the tabby. Butler was by a workbench, preparing a very large syringe charge for a tranquilizer gun.

Erwin pointed at Eve amidst her ministration. "What's that all about?"

Lan answered. "Do you recall when SuZee was inadvertently cut? How she miraculously healed herself in less than a day? She's repairing Chloe's leg."

Folsom jumped in. "It can do that? I wondered why that stupid cat didn't bolt out of there. Jeez, that thing is huge. SuZee was a runt. A sickly runt. Shoulda named her Su-Zero!"

"True," Lan added. "But this N'Khal is healthy. And dangerous."

"And worth a fortune, I'll bet."

Butler loaded the gun and walked over within four feet of the cage, keeping his distance. Eve eyed him warily.

"You sure that cage'll hold it?"

"Oh, I am quite sure," Lan confirmed.

"Okay. Here goes."

Butler crouched down on one knee and took aim at Eve's neck. Instantly Eve shimmered and disappeared. He raised the tranq gun.

"What the…?"

"Just shoot where you were aiming. It's still there," Lan commanded.

Butler aimed where he assumed he had pointed the gun earlier and pulled the trigger. The dart disappeared into the cage.

"Now what?" he asked the assembled watchers.

Lan advised. "Wait."

The four of them waited and in a few seconds Eve slowly materialized. She was face down, unconscious, and breathing softly. Chloe comfortably snored in her arms.

Lan addressed his workers. "Now, you all get some sleep and be back here…" He looked at a wall clock, "…no later than nine a.m. We'll run extensive blood analysis then and determine exactly what we have and where we go from there."

5:00 a.m.

From Quartzsite east to Phoenix, there were miles and miles of desert and very little else to attract one's attention. Dana had described a sand-colored low-lying building and aside from a few crumbling adobe huts and water pumping stations – all sand-colored of course – there was nothing yet to match that structure visible from the highway. Having driven for the past six hours, Charles needed a reason to stay awake, so he dialed Detective John Fox. Fox picked up on the third ring.

"Fox here."

"Detective Fox, this is Charles Reynolds."

"Mr. Reynolds, good morning. You caught me on a jog. Hold on a minute."

Charles could hear a few squawking seagulls in the background and a few passing voices. Fox came back on.

"Mr. Reynolds. Glad you called. I was going to call you later today to catch up and give you an update on your case.

"You have an update on the Van Gogh?"

"Well, no. Nothing new yet, but I did want to let you know that we…" He paused. "We successfully closed the homicide investigation – the coroner agreed to list the death as an animal attack – and we, well, basically we filed away the all the blood samples from the scene when the case closed. The information you shared with Heidi and I at dinner the other night will go no further."

Charles nodded to himself. "That's good. Thank Heidi for me please. But nothing on the Van Gogh?"

"We have our robbery recovery division in contact with the FBI's Art Crime Team and have secured the cooperation of all the major museums and private collection organizations worldwide. Any inquiries on the Van Gogh will be channeled here for follow up, too. Has the FBI contacted you yet?"

"No."

"Expect a call. Now, waddya got for me?"

"A lot," Charles replied and laid out what had transpired since their dinner. He disclosed Dana's unusual visions and Eve's journey progress leading to Charles quest up to now.

"This animal of yours is quite the specimen. Telepathic communication? Next, you'll be telling me she time travels."

"Oh yeah… I'm waiting for that. Or flies like Superman."

"If it gets weirder, I suggest you let me know. You'll stay safe?"

"I'm prepared."

"Protection?"

"Of course."

"Waddya got?"

Charles thought he heard Fox whisper a '*whoa*' under his breath when he told him what he was armed with.

"That Beretta's a nasty little piece of hardware. You know how to use it?" Fox asked.

"Detective, I do. I don't talk much about it, but I was with the 9th Marine Expeditionary Brigade in seventy-two. Over three-thousand PAVN killed and no US Marine causalities during the Battle of Mỹ Chánh Line. I know how to shoot, and I know how to duck."

"Nuff said, brother. You need anything from me?"

"Maybe more aspirin. Headaches are a killer. But I'll let you know."

"You do that. You keep in touch, and you find that pet of yours. Put this to bed. Make it a done deal. Please."

CHAPTER 12

Twenty minutes after hanging up from his call with Detective Fox, Charles entered the city of Tonopah. He pulled the SUV off the highway and onto 411th Avenue. The main artery in Tonopah, it ran north to desert flatlands and south, dead ending at West Salome Road, which ran parallel to the base of Saddle Mountain. He drove south. Reaching West Salome, he pulled onto a small maintenance turnout and parked. He dragged his stiff body out and stretched. The air was cool and clean and refreshing – energizing – and the rising sun had yet to reach this shadowed protected area. Charles opened his rear cargo door, grabbed a bottle of water, his LA Dodgers cap, a binocular case, and started hiking the peak.

Charles considered calling Dana but decided to let her get her rest. The whole visions thing had taken a toll on her, he could tell. Dana was no shrinking violet, but the week had been draining. He considered the shock that the gunshot wound and the healing had on her – she certainly seemed herself aside from the visions – and he was sure his experience paled to hers. He would do whatever it took to get both of them back to their normal life.

He rested on a rock outcropping a good three hundred feet above the starting point of his climb. The valley lay in front of him for miles. From this vantage, he could see the US10 interstate freeway stretching east to Goodyear, a thirty-mile straight line. Opening his binocular case, he hesitated. Memories flooded him of his days in Vietnam using these very same field glasses. The olive-green paint was worn and peeling, one of the rubber eyepieces had deteriorated badly, and the focus dial was not always cooperative, but the ground glass lenses were true and accurate even after all these years. A faded dark streak on the side of the left barrel was a stark reminder of the night he was on sniper duty as a spotter. His shooter had made two kill shots successfully and was zeroing in on a third. A crack from over six hundred yards pierced the silence and Charles felt a warm splash across his face. His teammate had taken a round in the neck and the blood spray had spilled onto him and these very binoculars. He was dead on impact. Charles dropped the binoculars to the ground and picked up the fallen Remington M-40, quickly zeroing in on the Viet Cong sniper and fired. A pink mist appeared those six-hundred yards away. Later that night he scrubbed the binoculars feverishly, ridding them of the mud and blood that saturated it. The streak would not disappear. Charles tried to remember the shooter's name but came up with a blank. It was just as well. He had removed himself from that experience long ago. These small moments were now fewer between episodes.

He brought the binoculars up to his eyes and started a slow reconnaissance. He focused on his trail here, followed it north on 411th and then laid out quadrants on both sides of the road. He recognized the travel center and the small retail establishments near them. He recognized a dairy farm, church, and school. He scanned further out and saw a structure that could easily be described as 'low-lying'. It was comprised of a two-story main building with three wings on each side, a large parking area, and a loading dock at the rear accessible through a side driveway. No signage could be detected from Charles' vantage point. He made note of it and continued his scan. He identified a small commercial industrial area that consisted of a dozen single story structures on a side road that dead-ended. He made note of that tract also. Satisfied that he had identified possible places that Eve could have accessed and been taken, he trekked back to his GMC.

Before he called Dana, he drove over to the areas he identified and snapped pictures on his cell. The tract of twelve buildings were all single structures, self-contained, and held a variety of businesses. There was a glass shop, a tile and flooring showroom, a business identified as Haddon Air Conditioning – *'We service all brands!'* – three empty buildings with a 'For Lease' sign on each, an Andy's Handyman Service, and so on. Charles drove to the larger building with the branched structures. Signage on the building that read Lan Pharmaceuticals Inc. in 3D letters adorned the front of the building as well as a standalone sign on the property line. Charles sent the pictures to Dana, knowing she would get them when she woke.

6:20 a.m.

Dana called Charles just as he reclined back in his driver's seat and started to nap. He picked up the cell and answered.

"Hey, babe. You're up early."

"I know. It's the big one, honey. That's the one I saw. She entered in back. Through the big doors."

"Well good morning to you, too, sunshine. I take it you got the pics okay."

"I got them the moment you sent them. I'm on my second cup of coffee. Did you eat breakfast?"

"Not yet. I'm sitting at a Subway watching two girls trying to figure out how to open the door."

"Buckeye has a Cracker Barrel. Go there. I googled Lan Pharma. Legit business manufacturing and supplying cancer drugs. You can get the FDA stuff here in the US and the experimental stuff in Mexico and Southeast Asia. So, what's your plan? Are you just going to walk in and ask if they have Eve? I know how your mind works."

"I haven't figured that part out yet," Charles conceded.

"I have."

"I'm not surprised. Spill it, sis."

"Do you recall that New England Journal article I sold two years ago? I was inundated with requests from the publisher to do an article on thirty-five recent FDA approvals. Lan Pharma was on that list as having interest in an interview. You could interview them in my stead; say you're vetting companies for me. I'm just so busy and all that, blah, blah. You get it."

"Not bad. It's an in, and I could easily check the place out. I was thinking they may conduct tours."

"My first thought, too, but according to their website those are only conducted monthly. Way too long to wait."

"Can you arrange the interview then?"

"I can make a call."

"Do it."

After Charles hung up, he noted the Subway girls had given up on getting their front door open and were calling someone – presumably their boss. Someone was going to be looking for a new job baking bread later that day. He started the ignition and faithfully drove to the Cracker Barrel twenty miles east towards Phoenix in Goodyear. Settling onto the counter barstool, Charles realized just how tired he was, but his stomach rudely interrupted that thought and overrode his need for sleep with a need for biscuits and gravy. Three cups of coffee and an Oldtimers Breakfast – which basically included one of everything good – later, he felt like himself and ready to go. Before getting back on the highway, he pulled into a Pilot Truck Stop across the street to gas up and while doing so, basically decided to surrender to his exhaustion. He pulled the Jimmy in next to a row of big rigs, reclined back and instantly fell asleep.

10:00 a.m.

Red Heard was furious. He sat on a folding chair amidst empty pizza boxes and discarded beer bottles and stared at the damn painting on the wall.

For the past three days he had not had one call from his people on the Van Gogh. All he got was excuses. No one wanted to touch it: it was too expensive or the market had tanked, whatever. He should have just let that creep sit on it, *save a bullet*, he mused. Maybe he'd give it to one of his bozo clients as a gift. Like that would solve his problem. Stupid! Maybe he'd try the Spaniard once more – surely, he could move it to some rich Eastern European that could hide it on a super yacht in the Maldives. He could offer a contingency sale – just take a percentage. Yeah, no need to fret. He could do it. No, fuck the Spaniard, he'd do it himself. He had a buyer in Portugal once who may be able to help him. No, he needed the Spaniard. He'd call him later. After another line of cocaine. Then he would be able to see clearer. Maybe two lines. He hadn't been to bed yet.

11:00 a.m.

Lan's team had been able to draw blood and tissue samples from Eve while she was out cold. He sat on an office chair observing her in the lab area while the researchers were processing the samples using metabolomics – attempting to understand the diverse and complex nature of the biological specimen in relation to the unique DNA that Eve possessed. The findings would allow Lan to figure out his next step with the extraordinary creature – foremost was her healing abilities – if the team could identify how that process worked, they could synthesize it and market it as a miracle cure-all. That was his wish, but he was already thinking that it would require a larger team than he could assemble here. Lan's group in Vietnam would be better equipped to do the work and be subject to less local oversight.

Lan curiously watched as the tabby, Chloe, roused from her sleep next to Eve, stood, and stretched, then narrowly slide out between the bars. She appeared to be none the worse for her earlier mishap.

Lan yelled at his researchers, "Get a blood sample from this damn cat. Now!"

Erwin looked up from his microscope, moved his readers down his nose, and looked around. "Here, kitty, kitty."

Chloe ran over and jumped up on the lab table and into his lap. Erwin petted the tabby then picked her up.

"This won't hurt, sweetie," he assured her.

Eve awoke, opened her eyes, and looked around. She saw Erwin move to a small table with the cat. She heard the cat *yelp* as a needle was inserted into her thigh. Eve raised her head and hissed loudly at the room. Everyone stopped working and looked around at her.

"Everyone, relax. It's not going to hurt you from inside there," Lan advised.

Folsom studied Eve, then looked at the others for some encouragement. Erwin's wide eyes and Butler's grimace was not reassuring. Work continued despite the unease they felt and the low guttural growls occasionally coming from the cage. When Chloe was released, she quickly hopped down and pranced back to the cage and slipped in. She sat next to Eve.

12:00 Noon

Lan sat at his desk in the upstairs office as his researchers stood quietly in front of him. Len studied several sheets of paper in his hands. Finished reading, he tossed them onto the desktop in disgust.

He addressed his staff. "Same as SuZee. Identical markings. I thought a healthier specimen would yield new results. What about the metabolic panel tests? The lipid panels. Nothing?"

"It's just like SuZee's, Mr. Nguyen," said Erwin as he settled into a chair in front of the desk. "Yes, there's a basic carbon and protein signature we've been able to chart, but beyond that it's either off the tables we use or non-existent. Or simply non-identifiable."

Lan folded his hands together and scowled at Erwin. "I don't remember giving you permission to sit."

Erwin sighed loudly and rose.

"Sorry."

Lan continued. "These creatures are living organisms, aren't they?"

Folsom broke in. "In terms of them acting and reacting to stimuli, yes. But…"

"What about the cat?" Lan interrupted. "What changes did you detect in her panels?"

"Nothing. Everything normal," Erwin offered.

Lan sat back. "What is the creature doing now?"

Butler chimed in. "Stalking the cage. Anxious."

"Suggestions?"

"I think it's time to bring SuZee in and let them meet."

Lan tapped his fingers nervously on the desk. "I agree."

12:30 p.m.

Charles woke up from a sound sleep. He ached all over. The driver's seat of the GMC may have very well offered a reclining respite, but he needed to stretch his legs and back. He adjusted the seat into driving position as his phone rang. It was Dana. This time on the cell phone screen.

"Did you eat?"

"Yes, I did, Mom."

"And rest?"

"Fitfully. But yes."

"Good. Find a comfy bed for the night. I can get you in there tomorrow."

"Nice! Who am I? Your publisher? Your agent?"

"No, sorry. You're just my plain vanilla husband. But you can be my business manager tomorrow."

"Boring."

"Just go to the office and ask for Lan Nguyen, he's the big boss."

"OK. Got it."

After he hung up, he googled Lan. Standard fare was found on his background – the typical bio. Born in Hanoi in 1968 to a hard-working peasant farmer and a seamstress mother who recognized early Lan's curiosity and craving for knowledge. They scraped and saved every dong they could and against all odds sent Lan to a private school where he excelled – thanks to an alert staff that recognized Lan's intellect. Four years spent as the Hanoi University of Science and Technology followed by an internship with a German Pharmaceutical company. A Wikipedia page elaborated more. He moved into operations and quickly established himself, ending up as a COO and then managing several companies upon his return to Vietnam. He started his own pharma company in Ho Chi Minh City, flourished there, then partnered with an expat in the United States – which ended badly – then took over the plant in Arizona, extending his reach. It was not without controversy, though. He was indicted five years earlier for numerous violations of the Animal Welfare Act, but charges were dropped when he pleaded it down to a couple of local ordinance misdemeanors. Charles' radar went up at that. That charge could have been anything from importing endangered species to animal cruelty on a large scale. Eve would be a big-ticket prize in any medical or cosmetic research facility. Visions of Eve being subjected to pharmaceuticals testing were tantamount to torture in his mind.

He called Dana back. "I don't know if I can wait until tomorrow," he confessed to her. He then elaborated on his fear for Eve. That anything could be happening in there was his argument.

"What are you asking? Do you want to just barge in there like a lunatic and demand to see Eve? That's not a good idea."

"I could get in there tonight. Find her if she's there."

"And then I get to come to Arizona to bail you out for breaking and entering. Again, not a good idea."

Charles paused. "Look, if they're expecting me tomorrow, maybe I can pop in this afternoon, tell them I have a scheduling conflict and chance that Lan would see me?"

Charles waited for her response.

"That sounds realistically sane, at least. I see no reason not to, I guess."

"I'll let you know what I find."

"But regardless, you be careful," she scolded.

Charles sighed.

"I heard that!"

Charles chuckled at that. He knew he had her complete support but hearing her approval buoyed him. He drove back to Tonopah.

CHAPTER 13

2:00 p.m.

He thought he looked presentable enough even though he hadn't had a shave or change of clothes since starting his trip. He pulled into the driveway and found a brightly painted visitor's parking spot. He glanced in his rear-view mirror, used his fingers to comb his tousled hair, and then opened his center console. He stared at the holstered Beretta, deciding if it would be a good idea to bring it in, and then closed the console without touching it. He exited the Jimmy and walked up the gold rock and gravel-lined pathway to the front entrance. The afternoon sun had warmed the concrete and rock that sent a barely perceptible heat shimmer rising. Upon entering, he quickly glanced around the lobby area – highly figured white marble floors, chrome and leather lounge chairs, one wall filled with awards and commendations, and the other three with photographs of the manufacturing processes that took place here. An Asian girl with straight black hair cut in a stylish pixie greeted him. A nameplate on the counter read, 'Cam Trang'. Out of nowhere, Charles recalled that in Vietnamese the name meant: 'A girl with a warm glow and energy.' It was a well-chosen name as she offered an inviting smile.

"Good afternoon. May I help you?" she asked.

Upon hearing her totally SoCal inflection, Charles immediately knew that this girl must be second or third generation Vietnamese expat. She would be equally at home in Ventura as Saigon.

"Yes. Hello. My name is Charles Reynolds. I actually have an appointment tomorrow with Mr. Nguyen. My wife Dana called earlier. She is an author for a medical journal, and Mr. Nguyen was interested in conducting an interview with her. I'm kind of her pre-interview scout. Unfortunately, I am not going to be able to make the appointment tomorrow. I was only in town for one day. Would there be any chance of seeing him this afternoon? I know it's an imposition, but…"

Charles tried his best to offer her a winning smile following the explanation.

Cam smiled back. "Mr. Nguyen is very busy today, but I can check."

She picked up her phone receiver and brought it to her ear, then motioned to the chairs in the lobby. "Please – have a seat."

Charles sat and watched her. She punched the keys on her desk phone. She spoke in a hushed tone – in Vietnamese. She was put on hold and glanced at Charles, smiling. After a bit, she hung up and looked at him. "Mr. Reynolds, someone will be right with you."

"Thank you," he replied. *This is going well*, he thought.

Five minutes passed when a door to the side of the reception desk opened and out strode a strikingly tall blonde Caucasian woman. She wore a very well-tailored business suit that accented her lean figure, tasteful jewelry, and four-inch-high heels. She walked straight to Charles and held out her hand as he rose.

"Mr. Charles, I am Patricia Stillwater. I am Mr. Nguyen's executive assistant. I'm sorry to disappoint you, but Mr. Nguyen has been called away on an important project and will be unable to meet with you. He asked if I could step in and show you around."

Charles thought his smile was a deal breaker with Cam, but Patricia's was a thousand watts brighter. Victoria's Secret had missed out on a winner, he thought.

"Why yes, that would be fine, thank you," Charles said, nodding in acceptance.

"Follow me then," she instructed as she turned towards an entrance to the offices.

Charles was given what was commonly referred to as the nickel tour. She brought him to the business offices, introduced him to the company comptroller and general manager, toured several of the production areas, then ushered him into a conference room and was treated to a fifteen-minute video of the plant operations. He viewed it disinterestedly. Charles thought the tour was all very pedestrian and designed mainly to appeal to investors or inspectors – nothing seemed out of the ordinary or particularly eye-catching. He concluded that Patricia was extremely business like – offering just enough information and probably sticking religiously to protocol. He knew it would be impossible to visit the real research inner sanctum areas where he believed Eve may be held.

Following the video, Patricia requested he fill out a review card presumable aimed at helping the plant better its tours. Surprisingly, she asked him to remain in the room until Cam returned to escort him out. He agreed and asked if he could use the restroom. She pointed out the location and bade him a good day. He figured his demeanor was benign enough not to warrant any concern. Exiting the conference room, he found himself in a long hallway. He recalled the route into this point so immediately headed in the opposite direction. Several turns later he found himself walking past an employee lounge, a locker room area, then past several locked doors with no signage. He turned one more corner and found himself in a dimly lit hallway that dead-ended except for a single door to the side. The door had a very impressive wall panel next to it. As Charles inspected the panel, the door suddenly opened and a white coated squat black man with dreadlocks and wide eyes behind John Lennon glasses walked out. Startled by Charles, he quickly closed the door, but not before a large Orange and Black Tabby cat ran out and down the hallway.

"Whoa. Excuse me, may I help you?" the man inquired. Charles noted a discernible trace of whisky.

"Oh, I'm sorry. I was looking for the restroom."

"Well, you're way off track buddy. Follow me."

Charles followed through several turns and found himself back in the conference room area. Five feet from the conference room was the clearly marked restrooms.

Charles feigned embarrassment. "Man, how did I miss that! Thanks, pal."

"No problem." The man sauntered off. Charles noticed a sway to his gait.

Charles entered the men's restroom. He washed his face and hands, looked at himself in the mirror. *What the fuck am I doing,* he mused. A knock roused him from his reverie.

A voice called. "Mr. Reynolds? Are you okay, sir?" Charles recognized it as the receptionist Cam. He exited as Cam stood; arms folded like a schoolteacher about to deliver a severe tongue lashing.

"I will show you out now, sir," she said, then turned quickly to lead the way. Charles had no choice but to follow and exit the building after a cordial thank you and goodbye.

Back in the parking lot, seated in the SUV, Charles called Dana. It went straight to voicemail – Dana was probably on the line with someone, although she could be dealing with one of her visions again. He hoped it was the former. He started his engine, then quickly turned it off. Across the parking lot he saw the squat black man with dreadlocks that had exited the secured room in an animated conversation with a pock-faced man with stringy hair. They appeared to be arguing – punctuated with finger pointing and a lot of head shaking. Stringy Hair grabbed Dreadlock's collar and shook him – hard. Dreadlocks pushed him away and back onto the hood of a car. Stringy Hair rolled off and held up his hands to ward off any more strikes. They exchanged more heated conversations but kept their distance as Stringy Hair slid into the car and sped off. Dreadlocks got into a late model Honda CRV and sat – presumable fuming.

Charles started up the GMC again and drove slowly next to the Honda, then rolled down his window.

"Hey. You okay, son?" Charles offered in a concerned tone.

The black man stared at Charles. "I'm not your son, but yeah. Yeah. I'm fine," he mumbled.

"Okay. Good. Um, hey. You know where I can get a drink in this one-horse town?"

4:30 p.m.

Charles followed the Honda back up 411th, north to the base of Saddle Mountain, then left on West Salome for several miles, and finally pulled into to the appropriately named Tin Top Bar and Grill. The afternoon sun glinted off the light red aluminum roof as they parked, exchanged names, and ambled in.

Over their first drink at the bar, Erwin told Charles that the Tin Top had been many things through time – buildings on this property had burned to the ground at least twice. Now it was a family restaurant and local nighttime bar. The clientele was a mix of business types from the nuclear power plant, a variety of day workers, locals, and a few motorcycle enthusiasts.

Over their second drink, Charles inquired about the run-in he witnessed back at Lan Pharma. Erwin cautiously chuckled. He said there was some disagreement over protocol and Erwin was called out on it, much to his chagrin. He brushed it off as nothing, but his quickness to dismiss the incident was telling. All was not well in pharma land.

The two of them moved to a booth and ordered dinner. Charles got the Mesquite grilled pork chops – thick, very juicy, and well prepared – and Erwin dug into a massive plate of Famous Tin Top Nachos. Charles decided to keep his wits about him by drinking Jack and Diet Coke with lots of ice, while Erwin was determined to finish the bottle of Chivas Regal the bartender poured from.

The two ate in silence – Charles noted Erwin appeared anxious to get something off his barrel chest. Erwin finally pushed his empty plate away from him, then set his glass down on the table after draining it.

He looked straight into Charles' eyes. "You know, I have a goddamn masters in pharmaceutical chemical engineering and a bachelor's degree in business and ethics. I'm the only black man working there. But don't sit unless told to do so," he spat out. He picked up the empty glass and studied the bottom of it. "You know what I did today? I drew blood from a damn cat. Effing' boss don't ask Butler to do the shit work. White privilege, I guess. Present company excepted. You seem like a good dude."

"Blood from a cat?"

"Yeah. To see if it was 'affected'." Erwin punctuated his last word with finger quotes.

Charles knew that Eve had sheltered a cat that needed healing. It had to be the cat he saw when Erwin opened the door. He decided to prod further as Erwin was obviously disgruntled and tipsy – a combination that promised results Charles would be interested in.

"Affected?" Charles asked.

Erwin paused. "You wouldn't believe the shit that goes on down below the public levels. We got a room full of animals that we subject to all kinds of crap – drugs, implants, weird tests – you name it. I don't know what the fuck I am doing there."

Erwin raised his empty glass to get their servers' attention. Waved her over. He stared again at the bottom of the glass. He turned it over and over in his hand. Charles knew he was grappling with something.

He looked up. "They're all fuckin' dead, you know," he muttered.

"Dead? Who?"

"Them animals. Smoked em', man. Just like that. All for…" Erwin paused as their server walked over and poured another Chivas at the table. The waitress glanced at Charles.

"'Nother Jack and diet, darlin'?"

Charles waved off a refill. He sensed a long night ahead.

"Gimme a wave if you do," she said with a wink, turned, and walked away. Erwin watched her strut out of earshot.

"We didn't need to do that. Kill 'em all. That's one of the things that asshat Butler and I were arguing about. He's a damn yes man and still an undergrad. Arrogant prick. But he gets all up and—" Erwin stopped. Took a drink. "What were you doing in there today anyways, Mr. Reynolds? I mean you seem like a straight up guy. What's your interest in Lan Pharmaceuticals?"

Charles decided to get to the point before the Chivas was emptied but needed to play it just right.

"Can I be totally honest with you, Erwin?"

Erwin chuckled. "Oh, I see. You been lying all night. Jus' kidding, man. Yeah – lay it on me."

"First off, my wife is retired from UCLA as chief medical research biologist. She's still active with the board of directors. You're exactly the right type of candidate they are always looking for – hell, they have open positions that start at a salary probably double what Lan pays."

"For reals?"

"For reals."

"What's the catch?"

"No catch. I can tell you aren't happy here. UCLA is world class. You could make a splash there. A call from my wife and you're on the next plane from Sky Harbor to LAX, first class, with a car waiting to take you to the interview."

Charles hoped he wasn't overselling and raising any red flags.

"Sounds like a dream job to me."

"I just… I just need your help with a problem."

Erwin frowned. He backed off into the booth. Charles knew he'd better get to it before Erwin misunderstood anything.

"I think that Lan Pharmaceuticals has something that belongs to me."

Erwin froze. He leaned forward.

"Izzat why you were there today?"

"Yes."

Erwin squinted his eyes. "And you didn't see that 'something' upstairs, right?"

Charles nodded. He could tell that Erwin was contemplating his next step.

"We captured 'something' last night. Big fucking thing. Kinda goes all wavy and hard to see sometimes. That sound familiar?"

"Very."

"And it belongs to you?"

"Yes, *she* does."

Erwin challenged Charles. "So you know about the N'Khal."

"N'Khal?"

Charles admitted he had never heard the word before now. He went on to tell Erwin the entire story about finding her as an infant, raising her, the invasion at home, and now his belief that the creature held in Lan Pharmaceutical was Eve. The 'why' Eve was at this exact location was still a mystery to him.

Erwin filled in the blank. "She's here because Lan has another like her."

A cold shiver ran up Charles' spine. Another creature like Eve? What were the odds?

"Another?"

"Yes. Like your Eve, raised from infancy. Problem is, she's dying. And I believe that son-of-a-bitch Lan is the one killing her!"

Erwin told him what he knew of the species and Lan's interest in exploiting her for black market purposes. Finished, the two sat, Charles absorbing this new information, Erwin silently considering his.

Erwin broke the silence. "Just tell me what I can do."

#

Leaving the Tin Top, Charles called Dana and updated her on his chance meeting with Erwin and the possibility of an ill N'Khal – *Yes dear, Eve's species is called N'Khal* – also needing rescue. He then laid out how he and Erwin would access the facility late tonight where he would be able to reunite with Eve, and Erwin would assist in whatever escape was needed. Erwin claimed that he knew of too many violations at the plant to be concerned with any retaliation and felt that Lan deserved to be exposed.

"This Erwin can get you two in and out alright?"

Charles knew what she was asking but he also knew the truth would alarm her – he didn't need to start anything. He hated lying to her – so he didn't – he simply worked around the details.

"Oh, yeah. Easy. There won't be any blowback."

"Uh huh..." she said in voice he recognized as her saying *you are going to hell for this if you are lying to me.*

"Don't worry. It's all good," he said then decided to change the subject. "Any more spells or blackouts today?"

"Yes, Mr. Smarty-pants."

She relayed that she had one incident earlier in the day while showering. Fortunately, she was able to anticipate them now, so she immediately rested on the shower bench. It turned out to be only a quick momentary flash. She could not recall any details except it had turned cold and dark, her cage now covered by opaque material. She sensed movement, but little else.

From that description, Charles surmised she had been moved to what Erwin described as the lowest floor of the building where SuZee was normally housed. Once released it would be little problem getting her out unless Lan or someone else interfered. He was ready for that eventuality.

The call ended on an uneasy note. He knew the plan was dangerous and he knew she knew it, too. But it was the only choice he had and Eve needed rescuing. The Beretta would not stay in the console tonight.

9:00 p.m.

Marta poured herself a glass of Hungry Hawk pinot grigio, anticipating Derick's arrival home from a long day at the station. Corking the bottle, she recalled their very first road trip out to Escondido where they stumbled upon this little out of the way vineyard owned by a husband and wife who tended the estate. Open only on weekends, they now visited often to taste the wines and listen to the music as well as enjoy the cool north San Diego County breezes.

This day, she had prepared a pork roast – six hours in the oven to be exact, the meat practically melting off the bone – Derick's favorite dish. Derick and Marta lived in an apartment complex in North Hollywood where the rent was reasonable and the neighborhood relatively secure. It took two incomes to make it anywhere in Southern California these days, but Marta was good with the budget, and they had been able to get her a reliable used Toyota for her travel daily now to the BHPD Forensic Lab. The schedule of a rookie detective was too unpredictable to expect her to hitch a ride with any regularity.

She had wrapped the shirt she had taken from the lab in leftover Christmas paper, hoping Derick wouldn't really notice or care. The problem with having a fiancée who was a police detective was that he tended to be very detail oriented. She was sure he would notice but hoped not. He walked in just as Marta was closing the oven door after checking on the vegetables she had added to the roasting pan earlier.

He greeted her. "Hi, sweetie! Wow! Something smells good."

"Uh huh. It's your favorite. We're celebrating!"

She walked over, handed him a bottle of ice-cold Corona Extra, and kissed him lightly on the lips.

"Really? What's the occasion?"

"Okay. It's not weird or anything I hope, but working your first homicide case is kind of a big deal so I thought, let's toast it, Detective."

He arched his eyebrow at her. She gave him a pouty frown.

"Is that bad?" she asked.

He smiled and chuckled. "No, it's not bad. Creepy, but not bad."

"And, what's a party without gifts?"

"Boy, you're going all out."

Marta handed him the wrapped shirt. He hefted it in his hands.

"Well, well. What could this possibly be? Is this that Tommy Bahama I was looking at?" He sat on a sofa and started to unwrap it. Half of the paper removed, he knit his brow, then removed it and held it up to inspect it, dried blood, and all.

"What? Wait… is this what I think it is?"

"I don't know. What do you think is?"

"This is that dude's shirt from that motel shooting last week. Has this been processed?"

"It was yellow tagged. It got checked in but was going straight to storage. I thought…"

"You thought what? That I'd love it?"

Derick looked at Marta sternly. Marta felt like shrinking down and disappearing. The silence between them grew uncomfortable. She watched as Derick carefully folded the shirt and put it back in the Christmas bag.

"You can't just take evidence home with you."

"I know. I just…" she trailed off. "Oh my God, I feel so stupid."

Derick was quick to react. "Look, you take this back tomorrow and we forget it happened. This could get you fired. And with me being a detective now." Derick threw the bag on the floor. "Shit!"

Marta slumped down on a nearby sofa and started to cry. Derick let out a deep sigh and sat beside her. He looked at her for a moment, then pulled her close and hugged her.

"Hey, I'm sorry. We all make mistakes. It's all good. Just get it back and it'll be cool."

Marta looked at him and wiped away her tears. "You're not mad at me then?"

"A little. But I'm madder *about* you." He kissed her cheek. "And that delicious dinner is waiting. Just promise me you'll keep these stunts to a minimum."

"I promise."

"Good. Let's eat."

CHAPTER 14

11:30 p.m.

Erwin instructed Charles earlier to park on a little used service road a mile behind the lab and wait for him. Once he found the spot and settled in, he opened his console and took out his holstered Beretta. He decided it would be better to be safe than sorry and shoved the pistol and holster into his light jacket inside pocket. It felt good. No more than five minutes later, Erwin pulled up next to him, nodded, shut off the engine and exited his car. They hiked through scrub brush and cacti in silence until they saw the security lights on the loading dock. They stopped short at a chain link fence on the property line. Erwin produced a small pair of metal snips and neatly cut a hole in the barrier. They both stepped through and walked to a door on the side of the larger loading dock rollup doors. An overhead light illuminated the door. Erwin reached up and smashed the bulb with his snips.

"Pretty handy, huh?"

"Yeah. No cameras?"

"Nah. This isn't LA. There's some inside, but not out here. I can take care of them."

"Lead on."

Erwin lifted a metal panel covering the entrance lock. He punched in a six-digit code, then immediately they heard an audible CLICK as the lock to the warehouse doorway released. They entered. Erwin went directly to a wall mounted alarm panel that was blinking and disabled it. Charles detected barely discernable exhaust fumes in the warehouse. Delivery trucks had spent time idling here, he assumed. Mixed with the fumes was something else he couldn't place, chemical perhaps, but it was not a pleasant odor. Erwin led the two of them through the large shipping and receiving area, past rows of boxes ready for consignment. The two went through another door and into the offices area that Charles recognized from his earlier visit. Two long hallways and three right turns later they found themselves at the door where Charles first encountered Erwin.

12:01 a.m. Friday

Erwin entered the codes with practiced ease and the door unlocked.

"Cameras?" Charles inquired.

"I put 'em on a loop when I entered the warehouse. Lan had that built in just in case."

"FDA?"

"Y-E-S," Erwin quipped. They entered the doorway and descended a flight of stairs with Erwin taking the lead. On the way down, he stopped short of the entrance and turned to Charles.

"I gotta warn ya. It ain't pretty."

Charles remembered what Erwin told him about animals that had been killed, but he was not prepared for what he saw as he entered the cage area.

As Charles stepped in, he was overcome by a lingering scent of smoke and animal carcasses starting to decay. Row upon row of cages of different sizes held the dead creatures. The dogs, cats, rats, primates, and more that once filled this room with their plaintive yelps, mews, and squeals were now silent – lying in repose with their twisted faces and pleading eyes. Several cages had been upended and battered by their occupants in a futile effort to escape. Erwin could only look at Charles as he scanned the room in revulsion. He finally spoke.

"What happened here? Why are all these animals dead?"

"Like I told you – he smoked 'em. It was the only way we… he… could capture your N'Khal."

"But to do this? What a waste. What were these animals used for, anyway?"

"What else? Research. Believe me, PETA never got a good look down here. We got some lab rats upstairs living the life of Riley. For show."

"Is this where you captured Eve?"

"No. We opened an escape route and she followed it to a tee."

"How kind," Charles groused.

"Sorry, man. But…"

"No. I get it. Why didn't I smell any of this on the tour today?"

"This cage room and the lab areas are all under negative pressure. You noticed the big fans on the roof? OSHA requires them in case of an emergency – they also do the trick of keeping the office area smelling nice and fresh through special air filtration AC units. Expensive, but they do the trick. That smoke would normally take days to get out but it's less than an hour with our stuff."

"Got it. So, from here…?"

"This way," Erwin instructed. He guided Charles to the rear door that led down to the lab level. Charles took one look back at the carcasses. He hoped they were the last he would see. A flight of stairs with a switchback brought them to the lab level. Charles scanned the room and was comforted to see no death here, only tables with test equipment – microscopes, beakers, funnels, test tubes, exhaust hoods, the works.

"This is the room we captured her in." Erwin did a quick scan. "Damn. They must have moved her. Probably downstairs."

"What's downstairs?"

"We call it the holding cells."

Charles was curious. "Do I dare ask? What exactly are you holding down below?"

Erwin hesitated, then sighed. Charles immediately regretted asking. Erwin walked over to what appeared to be a row of large metal storage cabinets. He opened one of the doors and lifted a canvas cover to reveal three cages. Inside each cage was a small hairless animal resembling a fat opossum with huge piercing red eyes. Simultaneously, the creatures hissed at them – revealing toothless gaping mouths. Charles stepped back.

"What the hell are those?" he asked.

Erwin threw the canvas back over the cages.

"We refer to them as *dinner*."

"Dinner for what?"

"You'll see. One more floor down. That's where they probably took your Eve."

Erwin led Charles to the door down to the bottom floor. This door had another, larger lock panel that required a code. Erwin entered the code – the LCD display on the panel blinked twice and messaged 'Access Denied'. He entered it again and the same message flashed on the screen.

"That's odd," Erwin exclaimed. He turned to Charles. "I've done this a hundred times with no problem."

"Try it again."

"No. I can't. It's protected by a failsafe device. Three wrong tries and you're out. If that's triggered, no one gets in *or* out of the building until security or Lan himself responds. There is another way down though."

Erwin turned and walked across the room to a large barn door divider on top mounted rollers. He pushed the divider aside to reveal a service elevator.

"This is how we get the big stuff between floors. This services the warehouse, too. It takes a completely different code in case of malfunction. Not everyone knows about it though."

Erwin entered the code by the elevator door, and it was accepted. He pressed the down button and waited. They could both hear the elevator on the bottom floor energizing and groaning its way slowly upward.

"It's old and takes a while," he explained.

"I can identify," Charles joked.

Both watched the door silently as the elevator finally stopped at their floor. The doors slid open to reveal a large box-shaped object covered by a duct taped tarpaulin. At the bottom of the tarp, Charles could make out steel two-by-two rails heading upwards. Erwin recognized the object.

"That's our big cage," he offered. "Help me pull it out."

The two of them rolled the cage out of the elevator towards the center of the room.

"This is the cage that your creature was held in."

"Well, let's get to her then," Charles said with a sinking heart. The two started pulling off the tape that held the tarp in place. They lifted the tarp off and found the N'Khal lying motionless on the floor of the cage. Charles took a deep breath.

"Open it," he ordered. Erwin balked.

"You open the cage. I've seen what she's capable of."

Charles walked next to the cage and peered in closely. He saw something on the forearm of the N'Khal's front leg.

"Wait," Charles declared. "What is that on her leg?"

Erwin moved closer to the cage. He hunched down and inspected a red band – it was marked 'SZ'. The N'Khal moved slightly, acknowledging his presence. He fell back, and quickly turned to Charles.

"That's not your N'Khal. That's our subject zero. This is SuZee. And it appears she's still alive. Your Eve must be below."

"Then let's go," Charles declared as he motioned towards the elevator. They both walked into the elevator and Erwin pressed a button marked B3.

As the door slowly closed, Erwin spoke. "I take it you're armed?"

Charles patted his jacket pocket. "Yeah, why?"

"You might want to get it out, just in case."

As the door closed, Charles pulled the Beretta out of its holster, chambered a round, and held it in two hands. The elevator started its descent. Halfway down the elevator lurched to a stop, jolting them both. The overhead light dimmed, then went out.

"Oh great," Erwin mumbled.

"Power outage?" Charles asked.

"Probably. We've got emergency backup gens. It takes a minute."

An amber emergency light flickered to life above a translucent plastic grid overhead.

"They just kicked in," Erwin added. The elevator squealed, jumpstarted with a grinding screech, and finally continued down. Upon reaching the bottommost floor, a series of clicks and whirrs sounded, then the doors opened to the holding room – darkened except for several rotating amber lights that bathed the area in a continuously moving shadow play. Charles though that if Hell had an entrance, it would look like this. He slowly stepped out, Erwin cautiously at his side. The elevator whirrs and clicks had been replaced with louder guttural clicks, chittering, and grunts.

"You wanna tell me what we're looking at here?"

Erwin spoke quietly. "Lan Pharmaceuticals does a black-market business in drugs and remedies that are not actually approved or recognized by any organization. The, let's call them subjects, that these drugs are derived from range from household pets to exotic or protected species."

As Erwin spoke, Charles surveyed the room – it held cages of various sizes, some small enough for a domestic cat, others large enough to house a lion – and in each cage he noticed movement. From one, a scaly arm reached out, grasping at the air in a dancing frenzy; from another, a set of searching eyes reflecting the amber lights from above returned his scan; from yet another, a pair of claws held one of the toothless creatures from above. In a flash, the hands brought the helpless animal up to a gaping mouth with multiple rows razor-sharp teeth. Dinner indeed. Charles brought his pistol down to his side as Erwin continued.

"The market for these exotic cures far outstrips the available material needed. Simple supply and demand. Lan is creating his own supply. What you see here are lab created animals that give him an endless supply of raw material." A nearby cage rattled, and the resident shook it violently. Several nearby cages responded in like. Erwin was forced to speak out louder over the racket.

"But Lan ran into problems. Claws that were ground into the powders that promised cures caused even worsening illnesses. Organs that were consumed to improve metabolisms caused deaths. Monkey brains that promised a long life and good health slowly tortured their consumers. It was failure on a grand scale. Lan was considering pulling the plug until last year when the N'Khal was brought to him."

"Because a N'Khal can actually heal."

"Exactly. To what degree, we were unsure, but the initial tests were extremely promising. But our SuZee was slowly withering away. The appearance of a healthy N'Khal like your Eve is a godsend to Lan. It's recharged him to double his efforts now."

"Not with Eve," Charles avowed. "Let's get her and get out of here."

A faraway breaker shunted to life as lights flickered overhead and the rotating amber flashers dimmed and slowly stopped. Power had been restored. The flickering subsided as each fluorescent came alive with full power. With the shadows now evaporated, Charles witnessed the extent of the failed experiments. Each cage held a creature or two not completely like its original model but with enough visible difference to separate it from its natural counterpart. They all had one thing in common – they were suffering examples of human greed and reckless disregard. A faux chimpanzee covered in scabs continuously beat its head against the bars of his cage. A wolf-like replicant that sported two snouts gnawed on its own forelegs. Bloodied and blinded hens pecked mercilessly at each other. It was a gut-wrenching display of insanity amidst their own helplessness. Charles wondered what madness Lan introduced into this room in his misguided attempt to play his own version of Dr. Frankenstein. He should have used his smoke to extinguish the suffering of these creatures in lieu of the ones above.

Charles and Erwin started scanning the labyrinth of cells in search of Eve. As they made their way across the room, the overhead lights flickered once again, and a series of audible clicks perked their ears.

"Oh shit," whispered Erwin. "The cages are being unlocked."

12:30 a.m.

Dana worried. She had been waiting for a call from Charles and it was getting late. She had not had any communication from Eve since the last episode in the shower and was concerned because for all her attempts to find her in any corner of her mind, she felt nothing now. She feared the worst and quietly scolded herself for not remaining positive. She consoled herself with the knowledge that Charles knew what he was doing and was confident in his skills and limitations. Sure, he was no longer a fearless twenty-one-year-old Marine in charge of a platoon, but he was a levelheaded and confident adult.

She could do little more than wait for news. As she sat in the dimly lit den, she thought of Eve and her species. She chided herself for not learning more about the extraordinary powers that Eve displayed recently. Her thoughts went back and forth between Charles and Eve.

She just wanted them both back and life to return to normalcy like before.

#

Charles and Erwin stood still as they listened to the last of the locks disengage. Both men had watched as each cage door swung outward an inch as each lock was released.

Charles spoke in a hushed tone. "How could that happen?"

"I'm not sure. All the cage locks are energized from the lab area control panel above us." Erwin glanced worriedly at Charles. "The power reset could have caused the system to overload and malfunction. How many rounds you got in that gun?"

"Fifteen. How many animals you got in the cages?"

Erwin did a quick mental tally. "About twenty. Give or take a few."

Charles gave Erwin a reproachful look. "You do know that twenty is more than fifteen, right?"

"Hey, you asked," he snapped back. "But…" Erwin reached into his pants pocket and cautiously brought up his keyring. "… you can manually lock the cages. You just push the door in enough to engage the bolt latch, it clicks in, and then you lock it. Quietly."

"There were a lot of 'yous' in that last sentence, you know."

"Yeah, I do. But…" Erwin froze as he saw a door to a cage behind Charles slowly open. Charles turned to look at whatever quieted Erwin. A furry claw pushed the door open wide and the face of a vampire bat appeared. It's round red eyes with pinhole pupils looked around, then zeroed in on the two interlopers. It backed into its cage. Amazingly, the bat pulled its own door shut with a click. Erwin fumbled with his keyring until he found the door key, then handed it out to Charles. He silently pantomimed him locking the door. Charles shook his head and motioned for him to do it. Erwin thrust the key towards Charles and mouthed 'do it'. Charles finally gave in, holstered his Beretta, took the key, steeled himself, then inserted it into the lock and turned it. Erwin nodded his head in approval and exhaled loudly.

"That wasn't so bad. Was it?" he said as the cage door behind him burst open and a large black wolverine shaped animal leapt onto his back, grabbing onto his dreadlocks. Charles dropped the keys and tried to grab the animal's tail. Erwin fell to the ground as the creation scrambled to detangle himself. Erwin screamed as the claws of the beast dug into his scalp. Just as quickly, the creature released his grip and scurried away. Charles managed to aim his pistol, but not fire for fear of hitting Erwin. He immediately crouched down to check on him. Erwin grimaced in pain as Charles inspected the back of his head – he felt the wound and withdrew his hand, bloodied but not overly so.

"Fuck!" Erwin shouted. "How bad is it?" he asked. Charles looked around for something to staunch the flow of blood. He had seen much worse.

"It's not terrible," he answered. "But we need to stop the bleeding. Hold on."

On a workbench several feet away rested a pile of shop towels. Between the towels and Charles, three doors appeared unlatched. He looked around for the dropped keys. He could not see them. Erwin leaned back against an empty cage, contorting his face in pain.

Charles held his Beretta in both hands, crouched down, and started towards the table. He walked past the cages – a low growl emitted from the first, but no other movement was detected. The same from the second door. Charles considered that the locks would be easy to engage if he had the damn key. The third door was partially opened and the resident inside skittered backwards from Charles's shadow, then emitted a screech as a powerful hind leg shot through the bars. Charles crouched and planted his boot on the bottom of the door and held it closed, but without a key, the barrier would only be temporary. Erwin called out.

"I'm still waiting on ya, man."

"I gotcha, buddy," Charles responded. "Gimme a sec."

Charles couldn't keep his foot on the cage and reach the shop towels, so he decided to just go for the towels. He scrambled onto his feet and hopped to the table, grabbed the towels, and turned back. The hind leg that had protruded from the cage was gone. Charles sighed in relief. Then, the cage door swung open. Charles held his breath in anticipation of what would exit. Seconds passed as no creature left the cage. Charles inched to the side of the workbench and side stepped his way to a walkway behind the cages – fortunately there were no cages facing the corridor between the wall and row he had just maneuvered. He moved through freely and came back around behind Erwin.

"I'm here, pal," he whispered.

"We got company, man," Erwin slurred. "And not the good kind."

A creature resembling a ragged coyote with a snarling mouth bearing a massive number of teeth stood motionless outside the cage Charles had minutes ago held shut. The animal took a tentative step forward and issued a wavering guttural warning. The warning was accompanied by the animal rocking back and forth, preparing to spring at Erwin. Charles took aim and fired – the bullet entered the creature between his eyes and the back of his head exploded onto the workbench that previously held the shop towels. Erwin panted.

"Oh jeez, oh jeez. Christ." He started trembling – scared.

The place went crazy with the cages being kicked and banged against, doors opening and a handful of unrecognizable creatures exiting to investigate. Charles held a towel on Erwin's neck and used another to wrap as a bandage.

"It's okay. It's okay," he repeated as he tried to calm Erwin down.

"We gotta get out of here, man."

"I'm not leaving without Eve."

"No. You don't understand. How long has it been since these cages were unlocked?"

Charles looked at his watch. "About fifteen minutes."

"Fuck! Well, we got about ten minutes before all hell breaks loose. If those locks aren't all re-locked by then, it's Armageddon."

"What? What do you mean?"

"There's a failsafe device Lan designed to kill everything down here in case of a security breach. Even he didn't want these damned creatures to get loose."

"What happens?"

Erwin pointed up to the ceiling. "See those pipes up there above on the wall?"

Charles looked at the walls and identified several large four-inch pipes with a mesh screen covering the end that terminated in the room.

"They'll—"

Water abruptly and simultaneously gushed forth from each of six pipes entering the room. In seconds they were already ankle deep in fetid brown water.

Charles stared at Erwin. "So much for ten minutes. What can we do?"

"You can still lock the cages and the flooding will stop. Supposedly. You have the keys?"

"No, but I think they're here close." Charles got on his knees and swept the flooded floor area with one hand, feeling under the cages for the keyring. He held his Beretta in the other hand in case any of the roaming creatures threatened him.

"C'mon, man," Erwin pleaded.

Charles reached under another cage and located them. He curled his index finger around the keyring.

"I got 'em!" he grunted as he pulled them towards him. The keyring abruptly pulled back. He pulled in, it pulled back. "Shit!"

He lowered his head into the rapidly rising water, opened his eyes, and was horrified to discover the lower half of a very large yellow and brown snake entangled in the ring, fighting to get loose. Charles recognized it as some sort of nightmare hybrid Python. The head of the snake turned, revealing a second head next to it, and zeroed in on the offending interloper. It attempted to strike back but the uprights that held the cages erect were in its way. The snake struggled to both get loose and attack. Charles raised his head to take a breath – he was not about to let some brainless and legless reptile beat him at this game of tug of war. The python was now in a frenzied state and close to pulling the keyring from Charles' tenuous grip. Charles knew that firing his Beretta underwater would result in a loss of velocity and trajectory but could still be deadly if he aimed correctly. He ducked underwater again, keeping the pistol above the water line and then brought it as close to the first gaping maw of the python as he dared and fired. One head of the python separated from its body almost immediately. Charles was shocked to see a sinewy claw from above snatch it and disappear. The second head lolled to the side. He hurriedly threaded the remains of the lower body from the keyring and shot back above the water line. He gasped for breath as the pounding of the deluge continued.

With the keys in one hand and the Beretta in the other, he started locking the open cages as the water continued to rise, alert for any remaining attackers. He shot four more pathetic creatures as he locked cages. All the while, he scanned the entire room for a cage large enough to hold Eve. He called her name loudly but received no response. He locked what he believed was the final cage, but the water continued to pour out of the pipes and was now at his thigh level. He slogged over to Erwin who was sitting on a work benchtop still tending his wound. He shouted above the spraying water.

"I've locked all the cages. When does the water stop?"

"It should stop now – you must have missed one. Double check!"

Charles turned and commenced to sweep each row and check each lock. At the end of the final row, almost hidden from sight, he saw part of a cage large enough to hold Eve. This one was also covered by a canvas tarp. He heard splashing water and detected movement from inside the cage. He hurriedly felt around with tarp – this one was held in place by ropes tied to the bottom of the cage – ropes that were submerged.

Charles heard Erwin shouting from the other side of the room, but it was unintelligible. He prayed it wasn't a loose creature that was missed. He took a deep breath and crouched down to untie the first knot, scolding himself as he remembered his hunting knife in the cargo area of his SUV and wished he had grabbed it. The rope was triple knotted by someone who obviously did not know how to properly tie one. It was a mess and took twice the effort as it was completely soaked. Needing to surface twice, he finally loosened the rope enough to pull part of the tarp upward – he was relieved as he saw familiar paws treading water. He went to the second knot on the side and started work on that. Again, he struggled with the amateur bindings. Once the third set was loose, he was able to lift the canvas for a better view.

His heart sank for a second but began beating in overtime – it was not Eve. It was a very large jet-black wolf-like creature with burning red eyes and a massive snout with lips pulled back that revealed a double row of razor-sharp teeth – a living, breathing nightmare. The wolf-creature thrashed desperately in the water and was obviously in need of assistance. The creature was bound to the side of the cage by a collar tied onto a short leather leash that kept its wolf head just above the water line, but it was clear it would drown in the next five minutes unless it was released, or the water ceased its flooding. Charles splashed over to a tall cabinet and began opening drawers in search of something to cut the leash with. He rifled through the top drawers first. Nothing. Then he looked in the ones below the water line. He felt something sharp and painful in his hand and pulled out a carpet knife. The wickedly hooked blade had sliced the webbing between his thumb and pointer finger. He bled freely but knew it would be more of an inconvenience than anything else – not life threatening but one more concern than was needed. He sloshed through the now waist deep water over to the cage – the creature eyeing him warily. The blade did short work of the leash, and the creature was freed to tread higher. He pulled the tarp completely off the cage and looked up as the water suddenly stopped gushing from the pipes feeding the basement. Relieved, he sighed and addressed the mutant wolf.

"Must be your lucky day, fella."

The wolf snarled silently at its savior as it remained motionless – eyes locked with Charles. He felt an odd moment of empathy as the beast turned away. Charles surmised that this creation must have been Lan's sick crowning glory in his collection of altered beasts. Even though this was not an adversary you wished to meet in person out of its cage, the poor creature was doomed to an eventual execution. Erwin's yelling finally caught Charles' ear.

"Hey! The water stopped!" he yelled.

"I know," Charles yelled back. "Gimme a minute." He went to a nearby work bench and pulled several paper towels off a roll and wrapped his hand. The wolf creature in the cage watched his every move but made no sound. Charles heard distant water pumps kicking in and saw debris on top of the murky water drifting away as the water started draining.

He joined Erwin resting atop a table in the center of the room. Erwin had a bottle of bourbon in his hand and two tin cups at the ready. The fouled and rusty water, now down to calf level with the occasional dead animal carcass floating by seemed not to bother him. Erwin poured them both two full portions. They both took a long gulp.

"Where'd you find this?" Charles asked.

"I have a secret stash on all three floors here."

"Thanks, I needed this. There was something I uncovered back there. It chilled me to the bone."

"A big something?"

Charles nodded. "Yeah. A big something that probably shouldn't be."

"Xerxes. Lan's biggest fucked-up experiment. Wolf DNA mostly, but a lot of nasty critter add-ons. Shark, reptile, you name it. There's even a tiny bit of N'Khal in there. Lan hoped he could get it to communicate with SuZee, but we never recorded anything remotely close. Lan removed its vocal cords so it could silently stalk its prey. What prey, I never knew. It could do things, I hear. Tell me it drowned."

"No. It's still alive."

"Too bad."

They both took another sip.

"She's not here, is she?" Erwin asked.

Charles swallowed and shook his head. "No. She's not. Not a trace."

"So what now?" Erwin inquired. "We made quite a mess down here and I do not feel like hanging around to explain it all."

"Oh, hell. I don't think you're going to have to. A handful of dead lab clones, actual live mutants, illegal activities probably fully documented – if I were Lan, I'd quietly close this part of the shop. I wouldn't ask where you were when you didn't show up for work either."

"Yep. I can probably forget about my paycheck next week," Erwin groused.

Charles grinned at him. "And any letter of recommendation."

The two sat in silence except for the dripping of what little water remained bleeding out of the pipes above, the sucking sound of the floor drains, and the occasional rustle of some god-knows-what creation still breathing in its cage. Charles finished his whiskey and finally spoke.

"I need one more favor."

"Shoot."

"I'm taking your SuZee back to LA with me."

#

Charles and Erwin took the creaky elevator up to the lab room where they had left SuZee. The researcher prepared a tranquilizer for the N'Khal and administered it. SuZee was about three-quarters the size of Eve and in her weakened state, less than half of her weight. She still presented a formidable task of transferring her up to the ground floor, but the two men wrestled up the two flights with the snoring beast. Charles hiked back to his SUV and drove it around to the main entrance. They loaded her into the cargo area and secured her with strong tie down straps in the back in case she woke and had other plans besides heading to LA. Just as Charles started to lower the back door, an orange and black blur hopped up into the truck and nestled herself in a crook of SuZee's front legs.

"Looks like you have another guest for the ride," Erwin said and chuckled.

"Guess I do."

Erwin took off his glasses and attempted to wipe them on the hem of his shirt.

"Our talk earlier. That offer at UCLA a real one?"

"Absolutely."

"Great. Plus I kinda want to see how this all works out for you."

Charles paused. "You sure you don't want a ride back to your car?"

"Nah. I've got some stuff to clean out and then lock up the place and set the alarms. Wouldn't want anyone breaking in there tonight!"

They bid goodbye, Charles started the SUV, shifted into drive, and exited the lot. He was on the 10 West in less than fifteen minutes and hit cruise control. Chloe hopped onto the passenger seat, startling Charles. She looked at him, issued an acknowledging *meow*, then got on her hind legs, placed her front paws on the dash, and looked out at the front windshield. Charles wondered what her old life was like at Lan Pharmaceuticals. She looked like a hell of a navigator now.

CHAPTER 15

2:30 a.m.

Detective John Fox sat up in bed and watched as Heidi Richards - wife of 'Thompson, Rush, and Richards - Attorneys at Law' Managing Vice President Roy Richards - strolled into the bathroom. Her nakedness excited him still even after she pleasuring him twice in the past three hours. After a quiet dinner at Mastro's Ocean Club at Newport Beach, the two had cozied up in a bungalow with a gorgeous view overlooking the Pacific Ocean and spent the past few hours in blissful ecstasy. It was the second time the couple had gotten together this week – the first being after their dinner date with Charles and Dana.

Heidi walked back dressed in a Duran Duran T-shirt and sat on the edge of the bed. Fox playfully arranged her hair that fell to her shoulders while Heidi lit a Benson and Hedges 100. She exhaled blue smoke that slowly drifted to an exhaust vent in the ceiling and disappeared.

"You know I'm gonna get a three-hundred-dollar cleaning bill for that cigarette you're smoking," chided Fox.

"I never said I was a cheap date, sweetheart. Besides, the joint you lit earlier was all on you! Not a good look, detective."

"It's medicinal," he said and grinned. "I have a card. I got it on the Santa Monica boardwalk. Ten bucks! Besides, I have a bad hip." Fox took the cigarette from her and took a drag.

Heidi raised an eyebrow. "I thought you didn't smoke."

"I don't. The cigarette does."

Heidi playfully punched him in the gut. Fox offered the cigarette back but she waved it off, then got quiet. Fox anticipated *The Talk*, something they had both skillfully avoided the past week. Heidi had always made it clear their time together was not to be taken seriously, just a pleasurable experience and nothing more – they were simply *the very best of friends*.

Fox never bought it. Regardless of whatever arrangement she claimed was agreed upon by her and her husband, he knew Heidi wanted more. Claims to the contrary, so did he.

Just as Fox was about to ask, she turned to him with tears welling up in her eyes. She took his hand and struggled to speak. Fox cocked his head in a gesture that expressed his concern.

Haltingly, she started. "I'm sick, John. I have pancreatic cancer."

Fox opened his mouth, but Heidi held up her hand. "Let me finish please. I've been fighting feeling run down and fatigued for a while, but I thought it was just due to my work – you know me, never enough hours in the day – and there's so many symptoms of other problems. And it's usually never diagnosed early, unfortunately. I just kept taking vitamins and blowing things off. Losing weight. Sleeping less."

This was not the conversation Fox anticipated. All he could think about was how helpless he felt now.

"What kind of treatments are you taking? Did you get a second opinion?

"Hold on, buster. I know you want to bring in the cavalry, but I'm still weighing my options. I may do nothing."

"Well, you can't just do nothing!"

"No, that's where you are wrong. I *can* just do nothing. I watched my aunt go through this exact same thing and she regretted every fucking chemo and radiation session her husband forced on her. They were torture. This is my decision and my choice. Besides, nothing is set in stone just yet."

Fox knew in his heart she was right and that parroting out some knee-jerk insight intent on solving something he never had to personally deal with was fruitless – and he felt a bit shameful.

He sighed. "I'm sorry. You're right. It's not my place to dictate to you your health choices. Just know I will support whatever decisions you make."

"Well, thank you, Mr. Wokeman," she replied sarcastically, and then looked away. "You know, I don't need your approval."

"I know."

"But I appreciate your concern." She looked back. "Can we just snuggle for a while?"

Fox slid over in bed and patted the sheet. "Absolutely. For as long as you want."

Heidi laid down in the crook of his offered arm and settled in. In minutes, she fell asleep. Fox lay there, next to her warmth; content, but fully awake. His mind raced a thousand miles a second bombarded by as many thoughts and images – unable to seize on a *something* that was on the edge of his thoughts. It would come to him eventually, it always did. Life was unpredictable.

3:30 a.m.

Charles debated calling Dana at such a late – or early, as it was – hour. Chloe had had enough of watching the road and dozed peacefully on the front seat. SuZee had not made a sound in the back except for the occasional rustle of her shifting body against her restraints.

The numerous Saguaro Cactus he passed all appeared to be waving their arms up high in greeting – reminding him of an old cartoon he remembered. In it, a flying saucer sat in a desert amidst the cacti, and the aliens pouring out of it were all tall, green, and covered with spiky thorns. One alien said to another, "Report back to base that these earthlings surrender easily." He chuckled to himself when it dawned on him, he had drawn that cartoon himself in grade school. *Still funny*, he thought.

He decided to call Dana. She answered after the first ring. "It's about time. Are you okay? What happened? Do you have Eve? Where are you?"

"Slow down. Are you okay?"

"I'm fine. I'm staring at three wine glasses in front of me and they're all mine!"

Charles laughed at that and proceeded to recount the events since they last talked. He gave her a detailed account of the visits to the basement and sub-basement rooms, the creatures he encountered, the issue with the locks and flooding, everything. Dana listened without interruption. He finished with a description of his new friend on the front seat and the drugged guest in the back.

Dana was silent. Charles hoped she wasn't out receiving a communication but a part of him hoped she was – he knew she would be upset at his commando theatrics and didn't need to hear it.

"Dana?" he asked. *Here it comes*, he thought.

"I should be furious with you but I'm not. You are not to get yourself almost killed over this – unless I'm there with you. You got that?"

She amazes me every time, he mused, then sighed in relief.

"Yep."

"So, what are we going to do with this SuZee?" she inquired.

"I thought we'd put her in Eve's cage for now. Do you have a better idea?"

"Not really."

"I will secure it though, for our safety. Just in case."

"Okay. But we're back at square one, aren't we?"

Charles weighed the question. "I guess we are. Erwin's going to be a non-entity there in a few hours but maybe he has some inside friends." Charles thought of the parking lot confrontation from the night before between Erwin and his fellow researcher. "Hopefully."

"Where are you now?"

"We're just passing Blythe."

"Did you eat?" Charles grinned at that query. Dana was the mother hen regardless of the circumstances. She would have made a great wartime nurse. "Lovekin Avenue has that a.m./p.m. we used to gas up at. Get something. There's a Red Roof Inn there also – you need to rest."

Charles was impressed with her road memory. "No way. I got cargo."

"Right. I forgot. Then get some No-Doze. You're still at least four hours away. And put a fresh bandage on that hand! Really Charles, a paper towel?"

"I know, and I will. See you soon. I love you."

"Love you, too!" Dana said and hung up. Charles put his cell in its cradle as a pounding in his head started. He would forego the No-Doze in favor of several Extra Strength Aspirins, grab a Zero Bar, clean his wound, gas up, and make a beeline home. Life was getting more complicated.

6:00 a.m.

Red finally got the call. His buyer in Spain heard from a private Portuguese collector that was showing unusual interest in the missing Van Gogh. His name was Anton Abreo, and he was flying from his estate in Maui to Los Angeles later that night and was visiting the Immersive Van Gogh Experience in LA the next day. Following that, Anton was scheduled at the Getty Center to meet with the Antiquity Director to discuss his Van Gogh collection and the possibility of purchasing a private collection piece on loan to the Getty. The schedule was tight, but the Spaniard had an associate in LA that could arrange a dinner following the meetings. Red listened to this with a wry grin on his pale face. He knew for certain the only person who knew he had the Van Gogh was the Spaniard, so the chance of a setup was practically non-existent, and a one-on-one meeting in a public place was a safe bet. It was all on the upside.

All Red had to do was wait for a call later confirming. Life had turned around.

6:30 a.m. PST

Lan sat comfortably on the sofa of his Embraer Praetor 600 as it cruised forty-five-thousand feet above the Pacific Ocean at a clip of over five-hundred miles per hour. The aircraft had already refueled in Honolulu and was due to land in Manila close to midnight PDT for a final fuel stop, then on to Ho Chi Minh City. The trip was long but was made so much more comfortable with his private sleeping room and an on-board flight crew that included a masseuse and executive chef. Lan made arrangements to be met at the airport by his staff from the factory and a secure van for his precious cargo. It was short notice but his people in Vietnam would handle everything flawlessly. Not like some of the bumbling staff in Tonopah. When Patricia Stillwater checked her messages in the next half hour, she would be instructed to gather the research staff and inform them that Lan had decided to dismantle the special projects division. They would have three weeks to 'debrief' him. The researchers would know that the 'debriefing' consisted of destroying all the animals and mutants as well as all records of the experiments, then shuttering the entire facility below grade. The NDA's they had all signed upon employment prevented them from seeking competitive jobs in the pharmaceuticals industry for the next two years lest they subject themselves to massive civil lawsuits. Lan was confident he would be free of any personal liability in the state of Arizona.

Lan would continue his work on Eve, finding out what made her tick and how he could use his findings to his benefit. Life was good.

CHAPTER 16

7:15 a.m. Friday

Lan's satellite phone rang, showing 'Patricia' on the display. Lan stabbed at the green button to accept the call.

"Ms. Stillwater. You received my messages?"

"Mr. Nguyen, we have a big problem."

Lan listened carefully as Patricia described the condition of the cages, lab, and holding areas. He instructed her to follow his orders regarding the dismantling of the lower half of the building and not to alarm the regular factory day workers. She reported who had shown up for work and who had not. An alarm bell went off hearing Erwin's name, but Lan told her not to worry and to simply send his last check to his last known address. He also asked her to send over a list of all visitors in the past three weeks as well. The events of the previous evening would not dissuade his in any way to change his plans in Vietnam.

There would be loose ends, of course, so now he had a new side plan – and Patricia was surely part of it.

8.30 a.m.

Charles arrived home and parked in front of the house. He shut his engine off and sat back to stretch his aching back. The six-hour drive was a killer on his lumbar, but nothing compared to the headache he dealt with from Rancho Mirage to Redlands. He had called Detective Fox an hour earlier and requested that he meet him at the Mulholland house. He was not going to wake Dana just to have her help move SuZee into the gallery. He was anxious to hear of any progress on the Van Gogh as well.

Prompt as ever, Fox pulled up next to him within five minutes of his arrival. Charles greeted him at his driver's door. Fox was dressed in Levi

514's and a black Tee that indicated he was ready for any task Charles requested.

"Good morning, Detective. I can't tell you how much I appreciate you coming over."

"Not a problem. What's up?"

Charles walked him over to his SUV and popped open the cargo door. Fox slid back a step at the sight of the N'Khal.

"Is that…?"

"It's not Eve."

"Do I dare ask?"

Fox gazed warily at the creature as Charles laid out the story in shorthand. He readily agreed to help him bring her into the basement gallery.

SuZee was awake but still had enough sedatives in her to freely surrender to the removal of her bindings and the transportation into the house and gallery. Chloe ran in and out of the two's legs during the process, annoying Fox – and his allergies – to no end. She was especially interested in some recently planted Zinnias in the hallway planter and relieved herself in them but gardened the soil following. Charles winced at that and smartly decided not to tell Dana.

SuZee was comfortably secured in the mechanical room with strong webbed strapping to prevent her from wandering and keep her secure. The room provided some measure of seclusion Charles assumed she would need upon awakening. Chloe investigated the entire gallery and finally plopped down with SuZee.

Charles inquired about the Van Gogh. Fox could only report that there had been very little progress so far, but reports had come in from sources that the painting was spotted in either Texas or Vermont or Scotland. None of the reports proved reliable. Charles saw Fox out, and on the way to the kitchen encountered a sleepy-eyed Dana exiting the master bedroom.

"You're home!" she acknowledged through a yawn.

"Yes, I am," Charles replied as he swept her in his arms and kissed her then bear hugged her. Dana broke away and inspected him.

"Where's the guests?"

"Already below. Detective Fox helped me. Not a big deal."

"He was here? Can I see her?"

"Yes – but gone already. And yes, again, but after breakfast. I'm starved!"

Dana zeroed in on the bandage on Charles' hand. "Let's get that cleaned up, too!" she directed.

"Yes, ma'am," he muttered. Charles dutifully went into the guest bathroom and pulled out a mini first aid kit. He opened it up and chose a suitable bandage for his injured hand. He unwound the bandage he had put on hours earlier and immersed his hands in warm soapy water. He brought out his hands immediately as it dawned on him.

The wound was half the size it had been at Blythe.

The pantry held some thick sliced Brioche bread, so Dana whipped up some eggs with milk, sugar, and vanilla, for French Toast while Charles laid out bacon on parchment paper for the oven. Fresh slices of peaches from their back yard tree topped off their repast. While they ate, he told her about the wound and how it was healing quickly. Dana nodded, smiled, and raised her hand to her breastbone.

"Looks like you're part of the club now."

Over coffee they debated their next move. Dana confessed that she still had no inkling of where Eve was as her visions had ceased for now. When she tried to meditate on her, nothing came. Charles reassured her that Eve would be found and returned – he wasn't about to stop.

Dana challenged him. "So, what is the next step? This Lan obviously has her. Can you track him down and see where she is now? Somehow negotiate with him. Or…?"

"That's the plan. And after what I've seen, I am prepared for an 'or'."

Dana sighed. Charles reached out for her hand. "Now let's go meet our new houseguests."

9:30 a.m.

Eve paced in her darkened cage. She knew she was travelling by the subtle vibrations that surrounded her. She detected conversations and noises, but they were flat, emotionless, and non-threatening. She stopped her pacing as slowly; distant visions began to crystallize in her mind. Visions that echoed the ones she had on her calling journey enroute to Arizona. The same images of tall, spired structures, magnificent sentient beings, many species of animals, and many N'Khal like her that were assembled – working, playing, living in harmony. She witnessed new things – bright bursts of light appeared in the air traveling across the blue-grey skies. Then closer, the lights solidified into immense craft that hovered over the jungles and meadows. She would run in these meadows and leap in the jungles and be transported in the craft. Eve felt at peace as she witnessed these sights. Hope swelled within her as she presumed she was being transported to this new world – hope that filled her with anticipation of goodness to come. Mixed with this hope was the belief that her masters, whom she loved deeply, would be there to welcome her and share the joy.

10.00 a.m.

Charles and Dana walked through the galley that a week earlier was the scene of death and destruction. The blood had been washed away, the air cleansed, and the damage repaired – but the memory was still fresh. Until they were reunited with Eve, life would be a limbo of activity – always searching and always wondering how and why it all happened. Charles pledged to Dana he would find Eve and he always kept his word. Their marriage was built on their commitment to each other and never had it wavered. This day was simply another step forward in what had become the new normal.

As they approached the mechanical room, Chloe stood in the doorway, licking her paw. She gave a welcoming meow and walked back in as if to escort the couple.

Dana chuckled. "That must be Chloe."

"Yep. My navigator."

"Not when I'm in the passenger seat!"

Charles smirked. "I don't know. She seems pretty tough."

Dana tsked, walked into the room and froze. SuZee sat on the floor, her formerly secure bindings now shredded and discarded. Charles took a step forward, but Dana held her hand up.

"No," she said. Charles saw Dana's eyes locked in with SuZee's. SuZee leisurely raised herself up on all fours and stood facing her, immobile. Charles felt around his waist, forgetting he was not armed. Chloe padded around his legs, purring as she rubbed her jaw against his ankles. Dana slowly knelt as SuZee approached her. Charles was about to speak as Dana turned and looked back at him.

"It's all right. She knows me."

Charles could only look on in amazement as SuZee circled Dana, brushing against her, then stopping to let Dana pet and scratch her as her fur slowly came alive with its silver and golden hues. After this unexpected greeting, the N'Khal laid down next to Dana and rested peacefully. This creature was not at all what Erwin had described. Charles surmised that the bond between Dana and Eve had been relayed somehow to SuZee. Maybe, for the first time in her captive life, SuZee had experienced family.

10:30 a.m.

Detective John Fox arrived at the station less that twenty minutes following his earlier stop at the Reynolds residence. For the next hour he sat in a task force meeting about security for the Golden Globes. Luckily, he was not scheduled for the event, but senior managers needed to be informed on any departmental extracurricular assignments that used their men.

Back at his desk, he poured himself a cup of coffee from a thermos he had brought in. Fresh Maxwell House – someone had had an argument with the coffee vending machine the day before and the twenty-year-old machine lost. The ten-cents-a-cup oldie was schedule to be replaced with a buck-and-a-half newbie. That was fine with Fox; *nothing beats home brewed*, he thought. As he sipped, he shuffled the built-up paperwork on his desk, checked his drawers for his favorite pen, perused inner-office emails, and generally wasted time. He had two voice mails he listened to – the first from the Chief asking about any movement on the Van Gogh case, and the second from Lieutenant Davis informing him that the Chief was on his ass about the Van Gogh case. He shook his head, hung up the phone, picked up the phone, then hung it up again. He checked his watch. He looked around the office to see if anyone needed him.

He could put it off no longer. He called Heidi.

Her phone went straight to voice mail. He did not leave a message. He decided he'd drop by the Forensic Unit to check on her. She would think he was being puerile, but he was concerned about her. He hated to admit it, but he felt good being around her. He got up to leave just as his phone rang. It was Chief Hellman and he requested to see him – ASAP.

#

Fox knocked on the chief's door.

"Come in and close it," he bellowed.

Fox walked in as Hellman broke into a wide grin. He motioned for Fox to sit.

"I've been on the phone all morning with the director of international investigations in Madrid. His art theft unit had been following up on a minor theft and ran into a chap that believed he had a lead on that Van Gogh. You up for some theatrics?"

11:30 a.m.

Red's cell rang. A gentleman named David Swing introduced himself as an associate of the Spaniard and would be responsible for arranging the meeting the next day with Anton Abreo to discuss the Van Gogh painting. David would be in attendance as a translator as Abreo spoke only Spanish. Red balked at the idea of a third party, but Swing assured him he understood the complete confidentiality of the occasion. He had made dinner reservations in a private room at The Magic Castle. Red was impressed but told Swing he would be calling the Spaniard to verify. Swing did not protest and in fact welcomed the confirmation. Swing said he would send a limo to pick him up at seven p.m. tomorrow, and he would call to confirm throughout the day. Red was more than impressed. It was going to be a big payday. After they hung up, Red immediately called the Spaniard.

The Spaniard's name was Dario Perez. Perez confirmed that Swing was a straight shooter who had performed several jobs in the States for him for over a decade.

"Trust me, my friend," Perez assured him. Red trusted very few of his associates. *After all, they are all criminals*, he mused.

"I trust you, Dario. But do me a favor – text me a photograph of this Swing."

"Por supuesto, señor. But of course. And please pass on my regards."

Red hung up. Seconds later, his phone notified him of a text. He opened it and studied the tanned and handsome face of Mr. David Swing – he had an easy smile that was quite infectious. Red thought Swing looked like a guy he had seen in some movie but just couldn't place him.

1:00 p.m.

Heidi returned from her lunch hour to see John Fox chatting with one of her young interns. *Always the ladies' man*, she thought. She couldn't blame him as Marta was a new face, had a sweet personality – although she could be a little too sarcastic – and a knockout figure. Heidi told herself she wasn't jealous, and Fox was a free agent anyway. But she knew deep down her attachment to him was growing. Better to think of other things, though. Fox spotted her enter the lab, begged off with Marta, and walked over.

"Hey, how ya doing?" he asked.

"I'm good. What brings you here?"

"Just in the neighborhood. Thought I'd pop in and see how you're doing."

"Detective Fox, you are rarely ever 'just in the neighborhood'. My office. Now."

Heidi led the detective into her office. She closed the door this time and confronted him.

"Look, John, if this is about last night, I'm OK. Really. You don't need to be checking up on me."

"I'm not checking up on you, I'm just—"

"—I know exactly what you're doing. Believe me, I appreciate it, but you don't owe me anything. OK?"

"I know, I know. I'm just – look, can we talk about this later? Are you free tonight?"

"No, I'm not," she stated emphatically. She then spoke conspiratorially. "My husband has a thing tonight I'm required to go to, OK? Call me tomorrow. And believe me, I'm fine! Now scoot! I'm sure you have more important things to do. I know I do!" Heidi practically pushed him out of her office and dramatically picked up a clipboard, referenced it, and walked away into an adjoining room. She sat at a small desk, scanned the information on the clipboard, turned it over and put it face down on the desk.

She cried.

CHAPTER 17

4:00 p.m.

Erwin had not heard from Lan Pharmaceuticals all day. The expected consequences from the fiasco the night before failed to materialize. He had promised Charles he would check in with him and report back, but he had nothing yet to report. His only real friend at the lab was Butler, whom he had had the falling out with at the parking lot. Upon reflection, it was a silly argument about chain of command issues and Erwin's hurt feelings. Hardly much of a reason to go off on anyone. He decided to call Butler and talk it out, and then get the 411 on what was happening at work.

6:00 p.m.

Charles was concerned. He was dog tired from the past couple days and spent most of the afternoon resting even though he was expecting a call from Erwin. By dinner time, it had yet to come. He knew there would be repercussions from what happened at the laboratory last evening, but Erwin struck him as a smart cookie. Charles trusted him and could only wait it out.

When his phone did ring, he was surprised to hear from Detective Fox telling him that there was an active lead now in the Van Gogh theft case. Fox would send over a picture of a suspect to see if the Reynolds could identify him.

Over dinner, he and Dana tried to recall everything about the evening of the robbery. The image of the one called Mark, the girl Allison, and her boyfriend Ben, were seared upon their minds. While the two were cleaning up after a quick dinner of roasted deli chicken sandwiches on hard rolls and potato salad, the picture came over. It was the face of someone named

Randall Heard. Charles and Dana had to concede to the detective that they had never seen the man although he could perhaps be the instigator of the contentious call that Mark had taken. If this Heard indeed had a lead on the Van Gogh it could be directly related to the theft or hearsay alone. The couple were disappointed – how many false leads had the BHPD received already that resulted in a goose chase? He had hoped that something would gel with this one and was reminded of the old phrase *'I hope you get your hope.'* Hardly a victory. Fox stated that he would have more concrete information in the next day or so but was tight-lipped to pass on any details. That raised the hope meter a bit.

Before retiring, both he and Dana went to the gallery to check on their new boarders. SuZee was resting comfortably. Her coat was already showing definite signs of improvement in the short time she was staying there, and Charles detected no obvious signs of aggression – but cautioned Dana to remain on guard. Dana sat quietly and stroked Suzee's fur as it dimly illuminated in a rainbow of colors, unlike Eve's. Chloe was perched up above the mezzanine, playfully swatting at the occasional moth that kamikazed the nearby light fixture. The twosome made themselves at home quickly, and Charles could only wonder what the future held for them all.

9:00 p.m.

Erwin agreed to meet Butler at the Saddle Mountain Brewery in Goodyear. The place had a nice selection of whiskeys, beers, good sandwiches, and pizza. When Erwin walked in, Butler was already throwing back a pint of their Taildragger Cream Ale at the bar. By the looks of it, Butler had already had a couple – Erwin hoped it had loosened his lips enough to get the straight story about Lan Pharma today. Erwin sat at one of the tall barstools and ordered a Chivas Manhattan.

Butler smirked at the order. "You're at a really cool micro-brewery and you order a cocktail? That right there's downright un-American!"

"That's just my pre-dinner drink. I'll cozy up to their IPA in a bit."

"Damn right ya will. Hey, doll…" Butler waved the waitress over. "Get us one of yer three-oink pizzas. Extra bacon. You good with that dude?" he asked Erwin. The waitress glowered at Butler.

"Fine with me."

"Yep," he slurred as he downed his mug. "So, what the fuck happened to you today? You heered about the mess at the lab, right? Bad day to play hooky, my friend, That did not look good."

"Yeah, I did."

"Of course you did. Look. I think I know what happened, man. You were pissed at Lan for that incident yesterday. You were pissed at me, pissed at the world. You decided to just go in there and fuck a few things up – but it got a little out of hand, huh? Not that I blame you. Lan's been a prick to me too. If it wasn't you, it would have been me, probably? Now Lan's shutting it all down. He's definitely not a happy camper."

Erwin nodded silently at his coworker's theory.

"But here's where I get a little confused. Did SuZee just run off on her own? Damn thing was weaker than shit and hangin' by a thread. Today, nowhere to be found! Wasn't that Lan's prize baby before that second one showed up? Did she just run off on her own while you were down there? Or maybe you saw an opportunity to further fuck with Lan?"

"No. I never saw her. I thought maybe Lan took her cos that other one was gone, too, so…"

"Well, and don't ask me how I know, but that other one is with Lan – probably at this very moment somewhere over the South China Sea on his way to his place in Nam. And… here comes our pizza!"

The waitress placed the steaming pizza pan on a stand between the two, set down shakers of parmesan and red peppers, then gave a business approved and patented big tip-inducing smile. "Enjoy! Another round?"

Erwin ordered the IPA. He had not eaten since a small breakfast at midday and was surprised at how hungry he was. He dutifully made sure he didn't intrude on Butler's half but he eyed the last slice greedily.

Conversation during dinner focused mainly on the upcoming spring training camps in Goodyear and how the Diamondbacks had blown yet another off season with no noticeable additions.

"Look," Butler advised. "We've had our differences, but you're a good dude. Do yourself a favor. Walk away from Lan and the lab. Lan can be very vindictive. I'm sure you're good and you've got nothing to worry about. But I don't know. I'm hanging in for the next three weeks and then I'm gone, too. A year's severance is a nice bonus."

10:45 p.m.

On his way back to his apartment, Erwin considered his conversation with Butler. The severance was interesting news. Lan taking the new N'Khal to Vietnam was predictable news. Being advised by Butler to walk was telling of a lot of things. He felt assured that now, once he disappeared, he would be forgotten. He made up his mind. Get out of Dodge. Pack up tonight and head west. A nice position at UCLA would be ideal.

Now that he had something to report, he called Charles as promised. He reported that Eve was on her way to Lan's Ho Chi Minh City facility and that Lan was shuttering the research at Tonopah. He told him he felt confident that there would be no reprisals for last night – giving the guys a year's salary proved to him that Lan would not wish to press the issue as long as he had his prized N'Khal.

Erwin felt good as he walked in his front door. That feeling lasted only for a second as he heard the crinkle of a plastic drop cloth under his feet and saw Ms. Patricia Stillwater sitting on his sofa with a pistol in one hand and a leash held loosely in her other. At the end of the leash was the creature known as Xerxes.

11:00 p.m.

Charles hung up from the call with Erwin. As heartened as he was that Erwin felt safe and was leaving it all for a new life in California, he was disheartened at the news that Eve was being shipped to Vietnam. As soon as he relayed the news to Dana, he saw the look of concern on her face.

"We can't leave her there, Charles," she stated.

"I swore I'd never return to that God-forsaken place. Ever."

"But it's not the same as it was fifty years ago, is it?"

"You don't know what you're asking me to do." Charles turned away and looked out at his backyard. He and Dana had spent many hours landscaping the back and he was proud of their work together. Dana joined him at his side and stared out at the back gardens also.

"I don't pretend to know all that you went through over there, but you went because you believed in what you were doing. Maybe the people and the war and the jungle changed you – I don't know – but you were a much different man then than you are today, Charles. The man I know today has never run from a commitment, regardless of circumstance." She turned to him. "Eve is part of our family and you made me a promise. And I know that was also a promise you made to yourself."

Charles turned to look at her. "I'm sorry. I just can't."

#

Stillwater told Erwin to sit down on the covered floor, then she began. "Erwin, I thought you were a smart guy. You didn't know about the cameras Lan had installed in the vents in the basement rooms, did you? Or the overhead one in the elevator. You did a good job of disabling the main alarms and closed-circuit television. Just not quite good enough."

"I c-can explain," he stammered.

"Oh I am sure you can. Let's start by you telling me what Mr. Charles Reynolds' interest in the N'Khals are. That visit earlier with some bullshit about vetting the company for a magazine article was crap. But our tour didn't satisfy his curiosity, apparently. What's his connection? FDA, Federal Trade Commission, IRS? Not the goddam PETA people, I hope."

Scared as he was, Erwin mustered a little chuckle at that. "That's a laugh! The dude's an art collector, lady! He and his wife stumbled on a N'Khal a year ago in Thailand. Brought her home. She was their fuckin' pet, for Chrissake. They actually kept her in their basement art room! He just wanted to find her. He could care less about what was going on down there. Believe me!"

Patricia glanced up at the ceiling, shook her head. "Jesus. He lost his little kitty and ends up going all Rambo on us. Lan is going to shit. Well, that part's good news, anyway."

"So, we're good?"

"Ah. Not really. You're quite a liability with all you know and I've unfortunately inherited you as my headache, and I so desperately need to rid myself of headaches! Too bad you took your work so seriously. It wasn't worth dying over, though."

"Patricia. Please! You don't have to do this. I'll go away. You'll never see me again."

"Well," she said, as she pumped two rounds into his torso. "That much is true."

Erwin collapsed onto the floor as Patricia let go of the leash from the silently salivating Xerxes.

"Xerxes, eat," she commanded.

CHAPTER 18

7:00 p.m. Saturday

The limo arrived at Red Heard's Hollywood Hills home at exactly the top of the hour. He received a text notifying him that the stretch Lincoln Town Car was waiting out front with a nice selection of beverages to sample. Red got in, helped himself to a glass of 2019 Darioush Chardonnay – a perfectly light aperitif to start the night. It was going to be a good – *no, a great* – night, he mused. He had already taken several hits of a cocaine laced joint – just enough to take the edge off.

Despite his roots in the southland, and his business status as a registered talent agent in Los Angeles, Red had never been to the Magic Castle. The private magician's club was a château-esque private residence built in 1909. Red marveled at the building as the limo wound its way up above the glow of the Hollywood lights. Upon exiting, Red recognized David Swift at the entrance to the building. Next to Swift was a small, dark man with slicked back hair that tumbled to his shoulders. Swift greeted Red with a firm handshake, then introduced him to Mr. Anton Abreo. Abreo managed a quick 'Hello', then broke into a Portuguese monologue. Swift translated loosely his greeting, how it was a pleasure to meet a fellow art lover, and how much he was looking forward to dinner. Red smiled and nodded.

They were received by a castle employee and led to their reserved dining. Abreo seemed excited at every hallway and niche on the way into the private room, babbling non-stop about the photos and art that adorned the walls. After being seated inside, they were served drinks and appetizers. Once he had his first drink in him, Abreo relaxed and addressed Red directly and intimately, in his native Portuguese, while Swift translated.

"He understands that you may have knowledge of the recently discovered Van Gogh that unfortunately was reported missing last week."

"Tell him I do," Red replied. "However, I do require a certain degree of confidentiality in this as the group that I believe has it can be quite… let's say, uncooperative, if specific authorities were to be party to the transaction."

Swift shared the reply, Abreo countered.

"He says he has been party to this type of business dealing before. He would not have made time in his schedule if he was not a reliable partner. He is wondering if in fact you have the painting in your possession. He is willing to offer a premium for…" – he stopped to huddle with Abreo for a second– "expedited service. If the number is right. What is the asking price?"

"Twenty million dollars."

Abreo responded. "Okay."

Red recognized that 'twenty million dollars' needed no translation. But now it struck him that he may have left money on the table. "That's for a two-week delivery. I could arrange for it quicker, if…"

Swift turned and huddled again.

"He said an additional two million is yours if he can get it by the end of the week. By Friday next."

"I can do that. But I am going to require a deposit. On the quick delivery monies, not the piece. Let's say five percent?"

It was agreed upon. Abreo would wire the money into Red's account the next day.

Dinner was served – Red had the prime filet mignon, Swing had the rack of lamb, and Abreo had the 32oz prime Tomahawk steak – usually prepared to share – and downed the whole thing. *The little guy could really pack it in,* Red mused. A quick house brandy topped off the meal. Following the meal, the three went into the close-up gallery lounge and were treated to an impromptu magic demonstration by one of the club members. *Quite a memorable night*, thought Red.

The limo pulled up in front of the entrance, Red bade farewell to his hosts and in twenty minutes he was dropped off at his house. Once in, he went straight for the Van Gogh he had hung on his wall. He removed the painting, rolled it up and slid it into a shipping tube he had purchased days before at the UPS store.

#

Detective John Fox and School Officer Enrique Cataldo watched as the limo left the parking lot of the Magic Castle, it's taillights joining the crowded traffic on Franklin Avenue.

"Well, do you think we were believable, Detective?" asked Enrique.

"I don't see why not, 'Anton'," replied Fox. "You mother would be proud."

"I haven't spoken so much Portuguese since growing up in Chino."

"Let's just hope that hundred grand gets deposited all right. It's a big gamble. But it's the chief's call in the first place. I just hope he signs off on the dinner tab for tonight."

Fox felt good about the evening – once the funds were deposited and arrangements made during the week to pick up the painting, this part of the Reynolds case would be over. If this Heard was just playing them, he'd be back at the starting gate. Given the dearth of leads, the BHPD were hanging their hats on this one big time. He'd call Charles Reynolds in the morning and let him know progress.

2:00 a.m. Sunday

Charles tossed and turned in bed even as Dana slept soundly through his restlessness. He could take it no longer. He got out of bed, put on a robe, and walked outside. He sat on a lounge chair by the pool watching the lights glint off the water and their reflection light up the underside of the waving fronds of the Queen Anne palms nearby. The news that Eve was now in Vietnam had brought up memories of his time there. He thought about long ago when he was a 21-year-old Platoon Sergeant in the Marines in charge of a squad of eighteen and nineteen-year-old men – men who were truthfully just fresh-faced boys fresh off a plane dressed as Marines. Soon enough hellfire would rain down from above, mortars would scream overhead, and muzzle flashes from their M-16's would burn their eyes and bore into their brains, and they would cease to be boys. He lost a lot of those young men and with each one a little bit of himself. He remembered looking in a mud-caked cracked mirror one morning after seven months in the jungle and seeing the face of an old man looking back. He never saw that young 21-year-old again. He swore he'd never return – the country had changed, sure – but returning meant that the memories he pushed back into the deepest parts of him would surely resurface. He had resisted them for half a century now, so let them lie. It killed him to have to tell Dana 'no'.

His thoughts jumped to Eve. What was happening to her? Would she become like SuZee was when he first found her? Would her zeal for life and love for them die? Even the question of *what* she was still needed to be answered. No one would be able to answer it now, due to his stupid selfishness and doubts.

He wasn't a praying man, but he raised his eyes towards the heavens and asked whatever God or force or spirit that was out there for an answer. He looked at the stars and waited. No lightning bolt came crashing down, no nearby bush burst into flames, and no otherworldly voice soothed him.

A shadow crossed over him and he looked over to see Dana standing at the patio door. Backlit, her hair and nightgown fluttering gently as the warm air escaped the house, she appeared as an angel.

Dana walked over and sat next to him. "Couldn't sleep, huh?" she asked.

He looked at her and suddenly remembered that young Marine that had fallen for this woman all those years ago. This same woman who had waited for a long eighteen months for his return from the war, without a single complaint. She cocked her head and smiled. "What?"

Charles knew he had his answer. It was there all along.

5:30 a.m. Sunday

Detective John Fox rose early, donned his shorts and runners, and took off for the boardwalk. He had done some additional research on Randall Heard following the meeting last night. There was no Facebook, no Twitter, no Instagram accounts. The website for his talent agency was slick and professional enough but lacked much in the way of background information on the man himself. Perusing the site, Fox noted that most of his clientele were young good-looking women, and the majority of their roles were bit parts in 'B' movies and videos. None of his clients were household names, yet. Fox wondered if the credits that they listed were actual jobs that Heard got for them. He was beginning to doubt the veracity of Heard's claim that he could actually get his hands on any Van Gogh, much less one so publicized within the art community. He presented himself as a smart man but dealing with such a hot art piece then publicizing it so soon after its disappearance marked him as an amateur. In addition, there was no hard evidence that linked him to the theft – but the lead was purportedly solid, the chief was taking responsibility, and he followed orders.

The morning was cool and the fog off the coast enveloped him and pressed against his skin and gave him a slight chill. Nearing the pier – his halfway point – the aroma of frying bacon from a food truck parked at the entrance drew him in. He stopped and ordered the double pork breakfast burrito and coffee. Predictably, the coffee was strong but drinkable. The burrito was excellent – the smoky bacon thoroughly crispy, a healthy bit of chorizo mixed in with the eggs and onion and peppers all seasoned perfectly, hand grated cheddar cheese that bit sharp, and the fresh salsa just the right 'picante'. *That was the extent of his Portuguese*, he mused. He finished only half of the burrito, wrapped it for later and resumed his morning route.

Once home, he showered, shaved, and dressed in a pair of light blue Calvin Klein slacks and a pink Greg Norman Polo. Gray Skechers Lorano boat shoes – no socks – completed the ensemble. A quick glance in the mirror before he left prompted him to pick out a watch from his collection. A sporty Tag Heuer was selected, and off he went.

He normally would be surfing on a Sunday, but the Van Gogh case needed attention, especially the deposit part. Traffic was lighter than usual, and he made good time. As he passed the Forensic Unit building, he decided he would not try to contact Heidi today. He'd give it a rest. As concerned as he was about her upcoming battle, pushing her into something she was not ready for was senseless. He and Heidi had been honest about their relationship so far, and he would hate himself for putting a wedge between them. He wanted her to live, but he wanted her to do so on her own terms. It was only right.

9:00 a.m.

It was settled. They would both go to Vietnam in search of Eve. Dana knew Charles had his reasons not to go, but the man was nothing if not unpredictable. She convinced him that once there, she would be able to guide them to her. She was already getting dim images from SuZee – many the same as Eve received – the hills and jungles, the buildings, the beings who inhabited her world. As Eve had followed her call, Dana was convinced she would hear her once in-country. Eve was still a mystery to her, though. Was she a hybrid creature, or a long-lost link to Earth's own prehistory, or something as yet unheard of? She was convinced that if the trip proved fruitful, they would have their answers.

10:00 a.m.

A call to Charles from the Goodyear, Arizona, police department came mid-morning. A detective with the GPD introduced himself and then inquired into Charles' relationship with an Erwin Tucker. Charles paused, carefully considered, then confessed he had met him briefly in connection with his visit to Lan Pharmaceuticals on business for his wife, and they had a dinner together, but there was no 'relationship'. He asked why, concerned that the lab break-in was going to come back and bite the two of them in the ass.

It was worse. Charles had been identified as being with Erwin Tucker the night before his fatally shot and mutilated body was discovered.

Charles was shocked. The bartender at the Tin Top ID'd them and now, the Goodyear PD was doing its due diligence and asking Charles as to his whereabouts all day yesterday. Charles told them about arriving at home and the fact of being with a Beverly Hills police detective in the morning of his arrival and his call with the same detective in the late afternoon. The GPD detective thanked him for his itinerary but pointed out that that still left a huge chuck of time unaccounted for following the call until the time-of-death. The detective informed him that he would verify with the BHPD his alibi as well as check phone records. He told him not to worry, that he would probably be cleared if his story proved true, but he was asked not to leave town until officially eliminated as a suspect. Charles asked how long that would be – the detective said he would let him know. After the call ended, Charles called Detective Fox.

10:30 a.m.

Charles listened to the phone connect and ring, tapping his fingers nervously at the kitchen counter.

Fox answered. "Charles, I was about to call you."

"Great. Look, I got a big problem."

"What's up?"

Charles laid out the substance of the phone call with the Goodyer Police Department. Fox listened raptly, interjecting an assuring '*uh huh*' as needed. When he finished, Fox paused.

"Are you still there?" Charles asked.

"Yes. Look, you probably have nothing to worry about – these guys are just gonna do what they need to do and believe me I know these guys, they'll do just as little as they need to do. But if you think any of this is gonna blowback on what happened at the lab then we might have a big problem. All we can do is wait."

Charles didn't like that advice. Waiting was not in the cards. "I don't know about waiting. Dana and I were just about to book the next flight out of LAX to Vietnam because that's where we think Eve is."

"I don't know – the GPD may clear you in a day or two. I think it would be prudent to wait."

"Well, I don't think we can. They're going to be calling you. Can you help clear it up?

"I'll try, pal. No guarantees."

"That's all I ask. Thank you."

"Don't hang up just yet." Fox updated Charles on the Magic Castle dinner with Heard – he shared both the progress of negotiations and his personal misgivings. "The way I figure it, we're there if this guy is legit, or no closer if the guy turns out to be a windbag."

"I opt for the former, and not the latter," Charles grumbled.

"I agree. Just stay in touch. I mean it. I'll do my best."

"I know you will." Charles hung up and tossed his cell phone on the counter. Dana bounced in with a smile.

"I booked us on JAL to Ho Chi Minh City on Tuesday," she said as she saw Charles twisted and worried face. "What's wrong?"

CHAPTER 19

Patricia called Lan and told him that Erwin was no longer a problem. When she told him about the N'Khal being nothing more than a lost pet of the Reynolds, Lan let out a hearty laugh – something Patricia had rarely experienced. They discussed the possibility of Reynolds following the creature to Lan's lab in 'Nam, but Lan assured her that his security details had already been fully briefed, and pictures circulated of Reynolds. The American showing up and demanding to see his little lost lamb was such a remote possibility that basically Lan brushed it off. Patricia wasn't so sure, so much so that she assured him she would keep an eye on the Reynolds' doings for a while. The Goodyear Police had already issued a warning against travel and she knew a straight shooter like Reynolds would follow it. Having friends in the local government was a skill Patricia had refined a long time ago.

#

Lan arrived at the Ho Chi Minh Airport without complications. His limo and requested box van were waiting for him. The creature was transferred to the Mercedes Sprinter van and sent immediately to the laboratory in the north part of town where the industrial areas were. Lan immediately went to his estate where he was greeted by his wife and family. Lan had built a reputation as a successful businessman, entrepreneur, and a generous steward to multiple causes. A lot of those causes were the pockets of local officials who had a habit of looking the other way when it came to regulations on Lan's businesses. Lan legally produced a variety of drugs marketed worldwide, and even more on the black market. With this new N'Khal, Lan had one thing in mind; her healing power and how he could harness it. If it took taking her apart limb by limb, then organ by organ, and even molecule by molecule to discover her secrets, he was willing to do it. He truly believed this healthy specimen held the key to his goals.

And Lan would do anything to achieve those goals.

12:00 Noon

The couple decided to go to Vietnam on the Tuesday flight against the Goodyear detective's request not to. Finding Eve was paramount – Charles would deal with whatever consequences would follow. SuZee improved by the hour and both Charles and Dana had no concern about her wellbeing in their absence. The N'Khal were surprisingly robust creatures who could weather a month with little food and water. Chloe's sustenance would be released by a timed feeder.

While Dana was sorting through their clothes deciding on what to pack, Charles holstered and cased his Beretta and packed additional ammunition. He feared putting Dana in unseen danger but would be prepared for any situation. He had the legal permits of ownership and would check online any regulations regarding bringing the weapon into the country.

A freight train of a headache rolled over Charles as he snapped the lock on the case. He sat on the side of the bed and pressed his hands hard against the sides of his head. Dana walked in with an armful of clothes,

"Charles, what do you—" She saw him and tossed the garment onto an ottoman, then rushed to his side. "Hon. Are you okay? What happened?"

Charles just shook his head slightly and croaked, "Head. Hurts."

Dana gently pushed him back into a lying position. "Here, sweetie. Just relax. I'll get you some aspirin."

"No. Take me down. To Suzee."

Dana was apprehensive. "Are you sure?"

"Yes."

Dana helped him up and supported him through halls that felt like they were closing in tightly – Charles faltering several times – and into the elevator, then into the underground hall and gallery. SuZee sat contentedly outside her cage area in the equipment room. Dana saw her eyes widen and her coat shimmer brighter than even an hour before.

"Okay, SuZee. I hope you're up for this. I know we're still new to you, but we need your help."

Instinctually, SuZee laid down as Dana helped Charles down on the floor. SuZee wrapped her legs around Charles as a low thrum issued from her. Dana watched as SuZee groomed Charles lightly and nuzzled him, then both fell into a deep sleep.

Dana stood there alone, feeling helpless. She was startled by a brushing against her leg, as Chloe requested some attention, She picked her up. It was as if the cat sensed she needed some assurance. She willingly took it and went upstairs.

4:00 p.m.

A good-looking, but disheveled, young man named Neil Bravo walked up to the front desk of the Los Angeles Police Department, Sunset Division, with a poster in hand. The poster was offering a reward for information leading to the arrest and conviction of the party responsible for the murder of Ben Walsh. Neil said he was a friend of Ben's and had some information about the last time he had seen him. Despite his acned complexion and mussed hair, the desk sergeant noted that Neil looked a lot like Johnny Depp.

6:00 p.m.

Dana sat in a rocker in the bedroom, slowly swaying back and forth, surrounded by open suitcases, stacks of clothing and sundry items lying on the bed, ottoman, and dressers. She stared off, lost in her thoughts. Chloe sat squarely on her lap, napping serenely. She lifted her head, her radar ears alerted to footsteps outside the bedroom. Charles walked in. He walked straight over to Dana, bent down, and kissed her cheek, then ruffled Chole's head.

"How do you feel?" Dana asked cautiously.

"Great. Hungry, too! Let's fix some dinner. I'll tell you about my dream."

#

Once in the kitchen, the couple moved with practiced precision. Dana fried up some thin pork chops while Charles chopped and sautéed some fresh vegetables. A glass each of Mondavi 2019 Sauvignon Blanc accompanied them in the preparation. Charles added a couple of thick slices of homemade sourdough bread with garlic butter to top off their quick meal. Over the light feast on the patio, Charles assured her that he felt wonderful and suffered no lingering aftereffects of his headache, indeed he felt more alive than ever, then described the dream in which SuZee walked him along crushed golden rock paths amongst richly manicured lawns that fronted massive residential structures. The dream was serene and peaceful and when Charles woke, he felt renewed and rejuvenated. Dana shared that she too had had experienced similar dreams – the N'Khal were passing on to them their generations' lives and history. Charles was convinced there was still so much to learn.

The light was fading as the two sat watching the pink sun sink from their view over the Pacific. They held hands and took a last sip of wine when Charles's cell phone rang. It was Detective Fox – he had news share – there was a break in the Van Gogh case.

"Good news, I hope?" Charles replied.

"Yeah. Are you sitting down? Dig this. This guy walks into the LA substation not two hours ago with a reward poster about the murder of his pal a week ago and claims to have information about the man who was with him last. Turns out the guy is none other than our Randall Heard. Apparently Heard was chummy with this stiff named Ben Walsh. I just texted you a pic of this Walsh."

Charles switched his phone to messages and waited for the photo to appear. In a second, Charles saw it and shared the picture with Dana as she had been listening with interest. They both gasped. "Son of a bitch," he mumbled. "That's the guy. That's the guy that I first saw at our door. So, he was murdered?"

"Yeah. He was found in a cheap motel Friday, the day after the theft. We figure Heard was the buyer for the Van Gogh. So now we can place Walsh at your home the night of the theft, and we can place him and Heard at a bar the next day. That's all good, but…"

"But what? Go arrest the guy!"

"Well, that's the problem. It's all circumstantial until we find him in actual possession of the painting or get an eyewitness to the murder. The kid that came in saw them exchange packages at a bar – but there was nothing at the motel – no money, no painting, no nothing. Just a dead guy in a run-down room. We need hard evidence. We've got to let this play out for now. If we can snag the guy for possession of the stolen property, that's one thing. But for murder-one, that's major."

"Dana and I will positively ID Walsh."

"You'll be expected to, but you were out for quite some time and Dana was missing. We can't even place her in the house, remember? The DA is going to need more than that."

"Shit."

"Yeah. Plus, this Ben Walsh left no DNA at your house, so it's he-said, you-said. The key is the painting. We get that from Heard and that puts all the pieces together."

Fox ended the call, wishing them safe travels and promising updates.

In some way, Charles felt sorry for this Ben guy – he certainly wanted him to pay for the theft and pain he had caused – but a bullet in his head over the Van Gogh was too much to fathom. He had to admit did not understand the criminal mind. With Erwin's murder, he realized he'd better not underestimate anyone's motives. He hoped this would serve him well in Vietnam.

6:00 a.m. Monday

Red awoke with a pounding headache from last night's party to an equally loud pounding on his front door. He hoped it wasn't his nosey neighbor asking why his car was parked sideways in the driveway again – cocaine has a way of making things move mysteriously. He'd figure it out someday. The knocking persisted.

"I'm coming. I'm coming. Jesus!" he yelled out. He swung his door open and saw two men in suits, one man dressed in beachwear, and three uniformed officers in tactical gear. One of the suited men addressed him.

"Mr. Randall Heard? You're gonna need Jesus – we have a search warrant."

"What... for what?"

The man in the suit handed him the warrant and walked past him into the house. Red struggled to read the print. The second man nodded as he went past, and the man in the beachwear stopped in front of him. Red looked up.

"Hey, you! You're that translator," Red blurted out. "What the hell?"

"Small world, isn't it?" Fox replied. Fox addressed the uniforms. "Spread out, guys. You know what you're looking for."

Red jumped over to his couch area and started picking up ashtrays, a small white powdered mirror, and bags of unidentifiable substances.

"We don't care about your stash, Heard. Where's the Van Gogh?"

"The what? What's that? I don't have it. This is like, entrapment, right?"

"Don't be cute. And no, it's not."

Red shuddered at the sound of something breaking. "Look, I'll be straight. I'm just a businessman. I heard from some guy that said he had a painting for sale, and I figured I'd middleman it to turn a profit. Can you blame me? Now you're telling me it was hot?"

"And who's the seller then?"

"I… forgot. A guy I never heard of."

"Right. I'm sure you also forgot that transaction at the bar – the Overtime – last week with someone we ID'd as being part of the crew that stole it. That, I got an eyewitness for."

Red watched as the uniforms and men in suits went through the place. A tall, uniformed officer approached Fox. "Nothing so far."

"Keep looking," Fox ordered. He caught sight of a grey leather satchel as described by Bravo, the Johnny Depp guy. He pointed it out to the officer.

"Bag that," he added. He addressed the group of officers. "Take every painting off the wall and every piece of luggage large enough for a big screen television."

10:00 a.m.

Fox called Charles and told him that the BHDP conducted a search at Randall Heard's residence earlier in the day. Fox's chief found a judge that issued it based on the eyewitness account reported yesterday, and the mounting circumstantial evidence. Multiple items were removed from his home but no painting matching the description of the Van Gogh was recovered. The forensic team had the items and would run tests to determine if any of it could be positively tied to the theft, or the people believed involved.

"Did you… jump the gun on the search?" Charles asked.

"I don't know. I'm convinced the dude has it. We'll know more after the forensic team reports back."

"Do you need anything from me?"

"No. I'll let you know if I do. You're good. You just go get your Eve – and please no heroics," Fox ordered.

"I hear ya, Chief," Charles concluded. As he hung up. Charles thought about the 'no heroics' remark. *I didn't promise*, he told himself.

10:30 a.m.

Marta walked into her workspace at the forensics lab and noticed a clear plastic evidence bag containing a grey leather satchel on her bench. She walked over and inspected the satchel – it was red tagged, which meant ASAP – then glanced around. At that moment Heidi walked out of her office. Marta waved to get her attention.

Heidi trotted over and beamed. "Oh, good! Big assignment for you today – you're moving up and you get to run tests on this satchel."

"Where did this come from?" she asked.

"We got it through a warrant search yesterday. We think it originally belonged to that murder victim whose clothes you processed a week or so ago. You need to see if you can match it up with them. The DA's looking forward to our findings. Get on it, gal!"

As Heidi strode off, Marta's heart sank, knowing she still had that damned bloody shirt from the murder victim at her house. She had promised Derick she would return it but had put it off for no good reason other than her own forgetfulness.

She sat at her workbench and nervously dialed Derick. He was on a late shift today and was hoping he was still in bed.

"Pick up. Pick up. C'mon babe," she pleaded. It went straight to voicemail. After the beep she hurriedly rattled off her message. "Hon, remember that shirt I gave you last week? I'm sorry but I never returned it. I just forgot. I'm stupid, okay? I need it now. Like right now. Call me. Please. I love you! Oh, I'm at work!" she trailed off. She hoped that Derick would get it and be able to run the shirt over. She felt stupid and chided herself. A stack of files was dropped on her bench with a loud *thud*. Heidi stood beside her, a scowl on her face, arms folded.

"You get that shirt back now and you process it properly along with the bag. Then you bring the findings immediately to my office. Then, and only then, will we have a little discussion about what I just heard." Heidi stormed off.

"Yes, ma'am," Marta sheepishly squeaked out.

Derick arrived at the lab an hour later. Marta figured there was no use dragging him into her screw-up, so she told him she'd come out to the car and get it. As she walked up to his Mustang, he had a dark look on his face as he handed it to her from his window.

"You do realize my DNA is on it, too. How can I explain that?" he asked.

"I'll do the explaining. Heidi heard my message to you. I'll probably get fired but it's not your fault. I'll make sure she knows. Sorry!"

Marta's heart dropped as Derick simply said, "Whatever," and drove off.

CHAPTER 20

6:00 p.m.

Marta timidly knocked on Heidi's office door. Nervous, she entered as Heidi commanded. Heidi sat at her desk with the easiness of a Captain Kirk aboard his own private Starship *Enterprise*.

"Well, what have you got?" Heidi asked, with a raised eyebrow.

Marta laid a printout and sheaf of papers on Heidi's desk, then delicately seated herself and remained quiet. Marta was embarrassed, mad at herself, worried about Derick, and generally in a foul suicidal mood – but she had found something interesting. Beyond interesting, she hoped. Heidi perused them. She shuffled the papers, took out a yellow highlighter, made marks, and vigorously consumed all that was given to her. Marta noticed Heidi's eyes growing larger.

She looked at Marta. "This is good. Actually, it's fucking great," she declared. She picked up her cell phone, reviewed her contacts list, and selected 'J. Fox'. Before she dialed, she looked at Marta sternly. "None of this is for public consumption. You got that?"

"Yes, ma'am," she said and sighed.

"Good. Now—" Heidi coughed, then coughed again, unable to stop until she took a drink from her water bottle on the desk. She took a deep breath and continued "Now go home. We'll discuss this further tomorrow."

"Yes, ma'am," Marta repeated, "and… thank you, ma'am."

Marta rose to leave, Heidi had one more command. "Get here early tomorrow, I'll need you standing by at the press conference." She paused, then added, "I'm still pissed at you, but you did good, girl."

#

Fox saw Heidi's name on his cell and his stomach stirred. He took a deep breath and answered the call.

Cautiously he greeted her. "Hey. How are you?"

He heard Heidi clear her throat. "Absolutely fabulous. I just got the forensics report from the lab on the items you picked up at Randall Heard's place."

"And...?"

"Do you recall those strange silvery hairs that changed colors and disappeared we found at the scene of the Reynolds murders? They were all over Ben Walsh's shirt."

"That's good. That confirms his presence there."

"And those hairs were also present on that satchel."

"Nice, but that can easily be explained as a transfer if Heard got it from Walsh."

"Uh huh. But – and this is big – we found canvas fibers with oil pigmentation on them inside the satchel. We roughly dated the fibers to be over one-hundred and thirty years old. We can probably match them to the remnants in the frame it was cut from."

Fox smacked his lips. "That connects Walsh with the bag that had the painting."

"Right. So the bag that Heard had, the bag he got from Walsh, had the painting in it at some point."

"Girl, I love you," Fox declared. Heidi laughed. It was music to Fox's ear. Both were quiet for a moment – Fox was suddenly unsure of how his last words were taken.

"I mean, I love it—"

"I know what you mean." She sighed. "Look, I gotta lot of things going on and... call me tomorrow, okay?"

"Sure. You know it, and... hey, great work."

Heidi said goodbye and ended the call. Fox sat and thought about the conversation. *That love remark was just off the cuff – it had no real meaning,* he thought. *Liar. And she sounded far from absolutely fabulous.*

6:00 a.m. Tuesday PST

Charles and Dana boarded the JAL 747-400 jumbo jet bound for Ho Chi Minh City and settled themselves into their first-class seats. Both of them had done their time flying in business and coach class for many years and neither felt more or less privileged than before. They made no excuse for their determined and hard-earned successes. They were greeted immediately by a smiling attendant and offered champagne, coffee, and tea. Both ordered coffees.

Upon takeoff, Dana immersed herself in a novel she had started recently, and Charles went online to discover 'today's Ho Chi Minh City' at a variety of websites. The city had changed. Radically. Modern high rises, massive shopping centers, numerous parks and attractions that were in stark opposition to the crumbling and run down French inspired architecture and dirty back alley feel of the old Saigon. Charles wondered what he expected. Did he think jeeps filled with NVA soldiers sporting AK-47's would be patrolling the streets and harassing the southerners? That was over fifty years ago. He knew that the country was still a communist nation but exuded a successful and a very urbanized profitable type of capitalist communism.

Dana conked out after just two hours into the almost sixteen-hour trip. Charles marveled at her ability to shut everything out and rest so peacefully. Charles was not a plane sleeper, but he was normally able to close his eyes and enter a zone – it wasn't sleep and couldn't qualify as rest, but it was a nether land of faux tranquility.

Several hours later, they were served a meal of rare filet mignon and a Wafu dressed green salad – expertly prepared by the in-flight chef. An excellent pinot noir complimented the service.

With over ten hours of flight time remaining, they busied themselves with checking on their hotel and car reservations, emails, and local news. Detective Fox had left a message on Charles' cell that the lab had returned with forensic evidence that could definitely tie Heard to the Van Gogh and possibly to the murder of Walsh. The district attorney was determining charges. Heard's lawyer was threatening legal action against him, the BHPD, the City, and even the Magic Castle. It was all smoke, he confided.

Ho Chi Minh City
11:00 a.m. ICT Wednesday

They landed in a wash of steady rain. Once the doors to the plane were opened, the humidity crept in like a determined phantom mist reaching out to strangle passengers and crew alike. The air-conditioned sky bridge that carried them inside the hectic terminal felt sticky and tangible. Dana noticed Charles taking deep breaths – she knew it was possible the air alone could open a floodgate of memories. She watched him closely. Once inside, the bustle of the airport seemed to calm him down – it could have been Atlanta, Denver, or London. It felt familiar. She was relieved to see him take charge and lead them to customs.

Dana was in charge of their papers and was amused to see Charles pointing out the maps of the city and posters on the wall advertising high end shopping. They may as well have been back at LAX looking at Rodeo Drive adverts.

They Uber'd to the Pullman Saigon Centre in a late model Kia in showroom condition. The trip was fraught with sharp turns, frantic lane changes, and grinding stops. Charles seemed to actually enjoy the bustle and sheer sea of people moving to and fro. Dana inquired if the driver was available for private hire – such a thing in the states was unheard of – and the driver whose name was Tin seemed surprised that she asked.

"I take you anywhere!" he shouted as he honked at a stalled pedicab. "I'll treat you A-number one!" He gave a thumbs-up and scribbled his name and number on a card and disclosed to Dana with a sly grin, "Seriously, call me anytime. I'm a graduate student at the University of Medicine and Pharmacy here in town. I start my residency in the fall. I can always use a few extra bucks – cash or bitcoin, of course." He snickered, and then addressed Charles. "So, sir. Please excuse me, but how was my old papa-san impression? Same as way back in the day?"

Charles raised an eyebrow to Dana. "What makes you think I was here back in the day?"

"Just a guess. You look like an ex-GI. It's the way you stare out the window. Looking for landmarks. Am I right?"

Charles laughed. "Is it that obvious?"

Tin giggled. "It's a gift. And… here we are."

The Kia pulled into the covered portico and they were immediately greeted by two sharply uniformed bellmen. Charles reached for this wallet, intending to tip Tin, but he waved it off.

"Just give me a call when you're ready to go about town, okay? I know the best spots. I can tour for a whole day if you like!"

Charles grinned. "You got it."

6:00 p.m. ICT

Dana and Charles checked in to the four-star hotel without a problem. Charles was amazed at how clean and upscale it all was. *This was not his dad's Nam,* he thought. They were both exhausted after the fight and immediately hit the shower, and then took a very restful and peaceful short nap. Upon waking, they both proposed a recon dinner out in the town – Dana called Tin and his Kia was at the entrance to the hotel not fifteen minutes later.

District One in Ho Chi Minh City was the heart of the restaurant, retail, and commerce section of the city as well as a smattering of industrial buildings. Tin maneuvered between the cabs, private vehicles, pedicabs, and motor scooters expertly, and brought them to their desired location – a popular shopping center within view of the massive Lan Pharmaceuticals complex. Tin pointed it out to them unwittingly – unaware of their focus on the property.

They seated themselves curbside at a very busy pho noodle shop and ordered a variety of dishes suggested by their waitress – a strikingly beautiful young woman in traditional Vietnamese dress. Charles and Dana tried some chilled Kim Son rice wine and declared it eminently drinkable.

Amidst the hustle and clamor of street life passing by them, dinner was casual and laidback, by design. Charles wanted to observe the comings and goings of personnel at Lan. The business obviously employed a much larger force than the one in Arizona. Charles saw employees of all classes enter and leave the building through its impressive lobby. Workers in hospital uniforms, men in work khakis, professionals in suit and tie, well-dressed women in business attire – a steady stream of people leaving their shifts and others arriving for theirs.

"They must employee hundreds there," Charles said. "It's way bigger than I imagined. I don't think I can pull off a casual break-in like I did in Tonopah."

"You had help there, remember?" Charles nodded. One day in, he didn't want to push but needed to ask.

"Are you getting anything from inside?"

"No, not yet. I'm sure it'll come." She paused, looked off, then leaned into Charles.

"Do you think this Lan is expecting you here?" she asked softly.

Charles furrowed his brow. "It's a possibility but I doubt it. Why?"

"Don't look back, but there's a man behind you who has been staring at the building and glancing at you for the past hour."

Charles looked back. Dana kicked him under the table.

"I told you not to look back," Dana scolded, then moved in closer once more. She couldn't resist asking, "So did you see him?"

"The white-haired guy? In the Hawaiian shirt?"

She nodded. "Uh huh."

"He's not from here, that's for sure. Looks European."

Dana leaned over and kissed Charles on the cheek, then whispered in his ear. "He's getting up to leave."

The white-haired man walked past their table without so much as a glance. A newspaper was tucked under his arm, and he stopped at the entrance of the shop to chat with their waitress. He pecked the girl on the cheek with a faux kiss and left.

"Well played, Mata Hari," kidded Charles. "The old guy is probably a sex tourist, and you caught his eye."

Dana screwed up her face at Charles, "Hey! I'm new at this, Mr. Bond."

"Well, enough of this subterfuge for the night. Let's take a walk."

Charles paid the miniscule bill, took his bride by her arm, and the two spent a few hours wandering around the district shops and streets. On their walk, there were some war memorials that Charles was drawn to that Dana thought he would have avoided – but he showed real interest in them. She was surprised also that he pointed out some of the landscape and architecture still standing from fifty years ago that he recognized.

#

That night, in bed, Charles and Dana made love with the fervor of newlyweds and intimacy of seasoned lovers. Lying in each other's arms, Charles confessed to Dana that he didn't know why *they hadn't done this before.*

"Uh, excuse me, we've done this *lots* before!" she protested.

Charles laughed. "No, not that, silly. I mean coming over here – it's not at all what I feared. In a way, it's like… it sounds stupid. The air, the sounds, the people. It's just a place where some very, very, bad things happened a long time ago that I never let go of – and now somehow, I realize that it's in my power to let it go. This city, this place, has moved on. I can move on, too."

He grew quiet as they held on to each other. Dana sat up and looked at Charles' face, studying every line and contour.

"I always knew you could. I was just waiting for when you *would*." She paused, kissed him hard, then reached under the sheets for him. "Hmm, someone thinks he's twenty-one again, eh?"

CHAPTER 21

9:30 a.m. ICT

Charles stirred from his sound sleep feeling more refreshed than he could recently remember. The morning light filtering in through the window with its dancing specks, and the scent of the woman lying next to him energized him – he could take on anything the day brought. He imagined he could hear the distant roar of a crowd: *Now batting, Charles Reynolds.* His cell phone came alive as he turned it on.

There was a missed call and three voicemails waiting for him on the iPhone. An irritated-sounding Detective John Fox called to pass on that the DA was not bringing charges against Randall Heard. Although it was rock solid, he was in possession of a satchel/gym bag that had forensic evidence of the Van Gogh painting in it, that alone was no proof that Heard actually received the stolen work of art. It was agreed that Ben Walsh doubtless had the painting in that bag but Heard's possession was circumstantial at best and therefore hardly admissible. Heard trying to broker a sale of something not in his possession was idiotic, but not a crime. *See: Brooklyn Bridge*, thought Charles. Strike One. Fox went on to tell him that there would be no murder charges either as his being seen in a bar by some small-time drug dealer the day of Walsh's murder was flimsy proof Heard was the trigger man. Strike Two. Fortunately, that was it – no Strike Three. Fox signed off with a promise he'd keep working on the case. Disappointed over the turn of events, Charles thought, *I'm not out yet.*

The second voicemail was Fox again – it came minutes after the first. This time it was good news that the Goodyear PD had a break in the case and were definitely taking Charles off the suspect list of Erwin's murder. He was free to go about his business. That was a swing and a solid rip down the left field line for a hard single. *No home runs today, but the day was just beginning.*

#

Tin showed up at the hotel before the lunch hour and took the Reynolds back to the noodle shop the day before.

"You must really like this place. I do know of one a few blocks away that's even better," he said as the couple left the sedan. Charles popped his head back in and handed Tin a crisp one-hundred-dollar bill. "This one suits us," he said. "Stay close today, okay?"

Tin eyed the bill with widening eyes and gave a thumbs up. "You number one G.I.!"

Charles gave Tin a phony grin. "And you not so funny."

Tin laughed and sped off. Charles joined Dana at a table again on the sidewalk. The waitress was another sweet young girl with long braided hair, dressed in the same traditional garb as their server the night before. She suggested the Bun Cha – a very trendy lunch item in the city – consisting of grilled chunks of fatty pork with vermicelli rice and dipping sauce. Both had the Saigon Special lager – a local beer that made a perfect accompaniment. An hour passed with nothing of terrible interest happening at the Lan building. Charles was coming to the conclusion that he may just have to walk up and demand to see Lan. Sometimes the simplest solution is the best. He pitched the idea to Dana and she rejected it immediately. She was about to rattle off a number of reasons why when Charles cut her off.

"Hold on," he interrupted. "Looks like your friend is back."

"My friend?"

"Our sex tourist," he whispered.

Dana's eyes widened. "Ohhh, what's he doing?"

Charles watched over Dana's shoulder for a moment and reported back. He assumed a deadly serious tone. "This is hard to believe, but I think he… yes, hold on, he ordered a drink. Here at a café. Incredible."

"Ha. Ha," Dana sarcastically replied. "So, he likes the food and atmosphere. I tell you; he was looking at you and the Lan building yesterday. Very suspicious."

"Well there's nothing wrong with being cautious, I suppose," Charles said as he rose from his chair. "I feel like a walk. Join me?"

Dana readily agreed. They paid their bill, tipped generously, and joined the pedestrian throng on the busy street. Dana glanced back and saw their café friend's nose deep in the local newspaper. Walking on the crowded boulevard, Charles considered how comfortable he felt – the cars roaring by, the local chatter, the humidity – it all seemed so benign, so normal. After several blocks of window shopping and stopping in a souvenir ship, Charles almost forgot the reason they were here. It felt like a holiday, not a mission. Gazing at an ivory carving of a mountainside village, Charles turned to point a detail out to Dana. They had wandered into a museum cum art gallery – an instant draw for them both. Realizing she was not at his side; he saw her across the room sitting in front of an enormous bas-relief sculpture of an ancient dynastic castle. He started towards her but stopped dead in his tracks as he saw their 'Mr. Suspicious' sitting behind her and off to the side in a corner of the gallery. He was instantly jolted back to reality and the reason they were in country. Dana was unaware of it, but Charles had armed himself for the day with a shoulder-mounted holster concealing his Beretta. Charles cautiously circled around the back of the room until he was behind his quarry. Surely, Lan would have scouts keeping track of strangers near his facility. Charles chided himself for how stupid he must have been to openly recon at the noodle shop. Now he had not only put himself in danger, he put Dana in jeopardy also. Charles watched as the man unfolded his newspaper once again and appeared to be reading it. It was time to get some answers.

    Charles walked up behind the daily reader and quietly sat next to him, Beretta poking the interloper in the ribs. The man looked over at Charles nonchalantly and gave a toothy smile.

    "Don't say a word," Charles commanded.

    The man cleared his throat, looked over in the direction of Dana, opened his mouth as if to say something but could only whisper, "Oh dear."

    Charles froze. The white-haired gentleman dropped his newspaper onto his lap and hung his head down, unmoving – in a trance like state. He looked at Dana and she *too* had her head down. Charles withdrew his firearm and ran to Dana's side. An alert museum worker was already kneeling in front of her, calling out.

    "Miss? Miss?" the middle-aged lady said, trying to rouse her.

Charles knelt and addressed the worker. "I'm her husband. It'll be all right."

Charles told her the spells were transient and would quickly pass – just let her be. The seconds ticked by and neither Dana nor Mr. Suspicious stirred. The realization slowly dawned on Charles – somehow, the man following Dana and Charles must be experiencing the same thing that Dana was. But how?

A full minute passed, and Dana roused. Charles took her hand.

"Are you okay?"

"Yes. Yes, I'm fine," she replied, focusing her eyes. "She's in there, Charles. She's waiting for us, and I sense an urgency. She's definitely not happy." Charles kept an eye on the white-haired man while Dana talked. "We need a plan. We need—" Charles abruptly cut her off and rose.

"What…?" a confused Dana asked.

Charles held a hand up and whispered, "I'll be right back."

Dana watched as Charles went over to the white-haired man and sat himself next to him again. The man was not surprised.

"My name is Charles Reynolds. Are you alright?"

The man eyed Charles with a degree of absurdity. "I'm sorry, mate. Do I know you?" he replied. The man had a commanding voice and a distinct Australian accent. Charles noticed a healed scar on the man's cheek – faded by years, no doubt, but conspicuous.

"No, you do not, sir. But I believe we may have a mutual interest in something very special. And it's inside the building across the street from the noodle shop."

Charles could see the wheels turning in the man's eyes. With oversized gestures, he deliberately folded up the newspaper he had on his lap. "Mr. Reynolds, I am sure this will come as a surprise, but I have been waiting for you."

#

Mr. Suspicious, the White-Haired Man, the Sex Tourist, had a real name. It was Taylor Scott. Taylor accompanied the Reynolds back to their hotel and the three settled in the lounge area that adjoined the bar. Charles and Dana shared a split of Cakebread Chardonnay Reserve while Taylor asked for a whiskey sour – prepared with egg white and Buffalo Trace, please. Taylor was again sporting a printed Hawaiian shirt, cargo shorts and sandals. The trio engaged in small talk about the weather, hotel accommodations, and local news – each camp reticent to open the main topic; why they were all there. After an uncomfortable pause, it began.

"Well, where do we start?" Charles asked.

"Where indeed?" Taylor responded.

"I'll start," Dana offered. "Mr. Scott, Taylor if I may, long story short – we're here because we believe Lan Pharmaceuticals has something very valuable to us."

"A N'Khal?" Taylor slyly tested.

Dana shot a glance at Charles. An upspoken signal passed between the two. Knowledge of the species must be more widespread than they believed. Charles nodded.

"Yes," she replied.

"Interesting. And how exactly do you know of this creation and what is your interest in it?"

"Hon?" Dana looked at Charles. He smiled and took over. He sensed he could trust this man. He told Taylor of the trip to Thailand the year previous, finding the creature and adopting it, their life together in Beverly Hills, and the Van Gogh incident leading up to Eve's response (*yes, we named her Eve*), her journey to Arizona, the visions that Dana received, and the subsequent capture by Lan Nguyen. Charles also went into detail on his attempt to liberate her, and the rescue of the sick N'Khal known as SuZee. Taylor remained silent during Charles story, except for the occasional *Ooh* and *Yes* and raised eyebrows.

"This is an incredible tale. And they have names!" he exclaimed. "To me they were simply numbers 'one', 'two', and 'three'!" Taylor looked at the faces of his audience. A look of astonishment crossed their faces at this reveal, but he could tell they were as anxious as children awaiting a new bedtime fairy tale – and ready for the hard truth behind the enigmatic creature they raised.

He began:

"In 1975, I was a sociocultural anthropology master's student at the Australian National university – a very well-respected college, I assure you. My father was an investment banker and my mother, God rest her soul, was a music teacher. I am quite an accomplished clarinetist, by the way. Mum always wanted me to be a professional musician and Dad wished I would follow his shoe steps into the financial world. I did, for a short while in fact, as I wisely invested a bit of my savings in the eighties and nineties into several start up corporations. All of them are software and computer related, actually. I did quite well, I assure you, thank you. But by then I realized that my degree and studies were chosen as such because of my love of cultures and their political, social, and religious beliefs. I did a brief stint in the military, then ten years out of uni I simply engaged in whatever I desired. I had yet to embark on any particular avenue that challenged me in my chosen major, so I took holiday to clear my mind and ended up traveling extensively in southeast Asia and found myself in Cambodia, settling into the northern part of the country – specifically at the ancient kingdom of Koh Ker. It was – I must apologize, have you heard of it?"

"No," Charles and Dan both said in unison. Taylor motioned to the waitress for another round. He continued.

"Terribly hot and humid, of course, and the access is horrendous – from plane to train to bus and then on foot. It's a tester! But I was taken immediately by the ruins, not unlike Angkor Wat or even the Bayon but Koh Ker is singular in their magnificent structures that have stood for over a century. Oh, the statuary, gardens, the intricacies of the bas-reliefs, all of it. And the history of the people, the art, philosophy, and beliefs." He paused with a faraway glance. "And especially the myths of the region."

The waitress brought the new round of drinks to their seated area. "Oh, thank you, luv. Now, where was I?"

"Koh Ker. Myths."

"Right! I have always been fascinated at how myths of different cultures have an overlap, a universal common thread that connects them. You Americans have your Bigfoot, we Aussies the Bunyip, and Asia their Yeti. So on and so forth, you get it. The more I researched and the more I visited the ruins, the more I was drawn to a particular myth that seemed to be a singularity. No creature in any studies I conducted were quite like the N'Khal. And even more disconcerting, outside of Southeast Asia, the N'Khal are rarely catalogued or known. Eh?"

Dana interrupted, "I found nothing in my research. Charles neither."

"May I ask your background, Dana?"

Dana told him about her background as chief medical research biologist at a major university and that now she occasionally provided reviews for medical and scientific journals.

"Fascinating!" he continued. "You are going to be quite interested in this next part. So anyway, it seems that the legend of the N'Khal was handed down through spoken words for centuries because I found little in the way of literature other that the last few hundred years and that was mainly the recounting of the spoken histories. Not a grand problem, I assure you, so I went on search for any art or depictions of the N'Khal inside the temples – and there are still quite a few – but the largest and grandest is the Prang – a pyramid of sort where history records its base was built deeply and into the crater of a meteor or comet that fell to earth. Well, this I had to investigate. Now, I am not an archaeologist, but I did minor in the craft, so I went down into the basement and bowels of Prang as far as one could go – it is perilous at best and special permission must be granted. By chance, while at the lowest level, I found several depictions on the walls of the strange beasts, our N'Khals. The images were chipped away, partial visuals, and faded, and could easily be overlooked by the untrained eye, but I knew what I saw. I saw the beginning of the myth. I was quite happy, I assure you, to see with my own eyes' confirmation of the birth of the myth. If my search had ended there, I would have been quite fulfilled."

Taylor took a sip of his sour and Charles perceived some degree of mischievousness in his eyes. A twinkle that foretold an even more captivating chapter yet to be revealed. Dana reached over and took Charles' hand and squeezed it in anticipation. The small gesture did not go unnoticed by their narrator. He smiled and clapped his hands together.

"Now! You're wondering how these magnificent creatures came alive amidst the relics of a thousand years, I wager. I will get to that, I assure you. I spent many months cataloging the art and statuary down at the lowest depths of the Prang and became very familiar with the layout, so much so that I began to increasingly detect anomalies in the construction of the extreme lower levels. Stairways were built that led nowhere, walls that contained certain rooms were longer and wider than the actual chambers it held, passageways abutted entire areas that were completely inaccessible. Eventually I discovered a passage that had been walled up – rather crudely in my experience – but so that it would have been neglected and dismissed as it was casually viewed. That passage riveted me. I petitioned the city marshals, as a thesis scholar – entirely made up – to investigate the walled area under the supervision of their historical society. Remarkably, they granted access and even offered assistance. The wall was three feet thick and was constructed of crushed granite, limestone, and mud. It took two months to successfully remove it without damaging adjacent areas. Mind you, I was extremely protective of the structure at this point. Naturally, I was the first through the passageway. The massive hall led down a dark and dank tunnel into a great chamber built around an object that was at least forty feet across and as high. It was badly damaged and with only my torchlight I was unable to determine its totality or original purpose but I knew it was my entrance to whatever lie beneath the Prang."

"Another tunnel, perhaps?" Charles offered.

"It could only be, I assumed!"

"How far below the surface were you at this point?" Dana asked.

"Easily one hundred meters. It was bloody cold and the air in that tunnel was stale, fetid, perhaps even hazardous to my health, but I was on a mission."

Taylor checked his watch, furrowed his brow. "I do apologize, my tale rambles on and I do have a call I must make. Should we take a break and perhaps meet back for dinner? Say seven?"

Reluctantly, the Reynolds agreed, parted, and reserved a table for three on their way to their room. Alone in the elevator up to their floor, Dana asked Charles his opinion of their newfound comrade.

"He seems square. Plausible story so far. He's no stranger to the N'Khals, so we need to hear him out and see if we can enlist him in our cause."

"I don't think that's going to be a problem. I am worried about his motives, of course."

"Motives?"

"Don't you think he's a little too eager to share? And this talk of numbers one, two, and three. There's a third then? What drew him here? Does he hear Eve?"

Charles sensed Dana's apprehension. She was good at reading people so there was little he could say to defend Taylor as he also held his private reservations. He did not want to prejudge the man, but exercised caution.

Dana continued. "He definitely demonstrated something at the museum. We'll have to hear him out I suppose, and then decide our next steps."

"Yes. We're here for a reason, let's not get derailed."

"Agreed."

7:00 p.m. ICT

Charles and Dana waited outside the restaurant not more than five minutes before Taylor showed up. They were quickly seated in a quiet section away from the busy bar. Once bottled water and drinks had been paced in front of them, Taylor suggested a toast.

"To my new friends. To common goals!"

The trio clinked glasses together and drank. Charles could not resist following up with the appropriate response. "What is your goal, Mr. Scott? My wife and I have been very candid about the retrieval of Eve. The true nature of your presence here has yet to be divulged."

Taylor tilted his head to the side and considered Charles's challenge. "I can understand your apprehension, sir... and ma'am. I have been too loquacious perhaps, but it is my way of making you fully understand my position with regards to N'Khals. And believe me, it is extremely and deeply personal. Bear with me and I assure you, the entire picture will crystalize before our waiter hands us a dessert menu." The soliloquy ended with a wide smile on Taylor's face.

Charles glanced at Dana, then back at Taylor. "I'm sorry, it's just that—"

"No!" Taylor interrupted. "A bit of skepticism is healthy and essential in this case, mate. I assure you."

"All right then. Give us both barrels."

"Both barrels? Ah! An American western reference! Lovely." He took a large swallow of his Whisky Sour – by Charles' count, his fourth of the day – and continued as their waiter approached the table. "Okay, pardner. But shall we order first!"

Their orders were placed, and a silence fell upon the three.

Taylor took center stage once again in the conversation. "The opening, forty feet across, one hundred meters down. Cold. Silent. The workers who had assisted to that point were reticent to enter. I went it alone. The jagged walls of this entrance gave way to smoother surfaces. It was as if I was walking on a ghost ship adrift for a thousand years. Time had not been kind to this structure. The pressures of plates and shifting of the earth had turned what this once was into a Mad Hatter's nightmare. But enough of the original construction was recognizable for me to make a determination that eluded any previous generations visits – the flat, engineered surfaces, covered with inch thick dust, the walls filled with protrusions – perhaps dials or controls – the resting areas with steel like chairs of a sort – this was no sailing vessel displaced by any natural disaster – this was a craft not designed by earthly hands. This was a visitor from another galaxy. A starship."

"Then Eve and SuZee *are* alien. But, how?" Dana blurted out.

"One would think. Wouldn't one? But standby," Taylor added with a sly wink as their waited pulled up with a cart overflowing with entrees. Taylor had ordered the Tomahawk filet – a twenty-eight-ounce beast, rare, Charles – the sea bass, and Dana – the petite filet. The young waiter offered to slice the filet for her but Dana passed. Taylor went deep and fast into his chop. He was halfway through before Charles and Dana had finished two bites. A bottle of Penfolds Bin 707 Cabernet was opened, tested, and poured for them. Taylor offered another toast – "To good Aussie wine," he said – then took up his tale.

"Naturally, there was nothing alive in the tomb. The features and hardware became more recognizable as ship's controls and amenities. I was careful in my examinations. If the Prang was built on its grave over a millennium ago, how long was it there before its discovery? Another thousand years? Three, ten? I am sure you know; carbon dating cannot be applied to inorganic material. So, my quest was to find evidence of the previous life aboard that ship."

Taylor poured and then drained the bottle of six-hundred-dollar wine.

"I visited daily for the next two months. Every misstep resulted in breakage; every inadvertent touch caused the breakdown of a mysterious object. *Until.*

"I found a row of capsules, all broken, disordered, but in each capsule was a spider work of translucent filaments that imperceptibly glowed; indeed, a night light of four watts would outshine the globes tenfold. To look away briefly and close your eyes was enough to prove the illumination and perceive something it concealed. I searched with my eyes, then reached into the globe and felt through the filaments. Each filament felt like it had tentacles or scales – not an unpleasant sensation – and I was able to pluck from the bottom a small round ball – no larger than a baby pea – still intact and not disintegrating at my touch. Could this be the proof I was in search of? I was not intending to destroy it by my rough handling, nor send this off to some lab where I had no control. Now, if you recall, I did quite well several years before my trip – well enough to immediately set up my own research facility in Phnom Penh."

"You set up a laboratory?" Charles interjected.

"Yes, I did. At considerable expense, I might add, but I was obsessed with my discovery and felt proprietary ownership. A few former school mates were recruited: a biologist, a chemist, an archeological scientist, a genomic scientist, so on… some names I even forget. All doctorates of sorts, I assure you."

"That must have been a giant undertaking," Dana surmised.

"Five years. Five years to process my pea-sized discovery. And in the end, my team had a complete antiparallel double helix strand of alien DNA which was twice the size of ours. And it was mammalian. With eighty-six unique chromosomes. Eighty-six! We humans have twenty-three. It was astounding."

By the time Taylor had finished pronouncing the word astounding, Charles and Dana had both put their utensils down on the table and sat rigid in awe, as the implication of Taylor's statement became apparent.

Dana took a deep breath. "You created life from the DNA. *Eve is a lab creation.*"

Taylor smiled and sipped his wine. "Yes. It took twenty years, but your Eve, your SuZee, and my number one are identical triplet sisters – N'Khals created in my facility in Cambodia from organic material that is dated to be… over eighty-five thousand years old."

The trio sat in silence digesting both their excellent meal and the mind-boggling revelation. The waiter stopped by and presented them with dessert menus. Charles and Dana held hands up to ward off the young man, but Taylor took his, consulted it, and ordered the triple-chocolate cake. Handing the menu back, he looked at his companions and queried, "More wine, then?"

#

They had more wine. On into the night, Charles and Dana asked Taylor question after question regarding his use of the DNA, the processes, the failures, and successes. Taylor described his lab in Phenom Penh and his staff, their work, and accomplishments – and his desire to keep his discoveries secret for now. He readily admitted that the implications of his discoveries would result in an unknown worldwide reaction – the type he could not envision. Interestingly, the Cambodian government staunchly refuted his claims of an ancient spacecraft under the Prang and declared it a protected national monument and thereby off limits to all except the high-ranking officials and Taylor's team – no Cambodian official expressed interest or had even inquired about the craft since its discovery. Myth and legends still held sway over the Cambodians in the twenty-first century.

"I have to ask, what brought you to Ho Chi Minh City then?" Charles prodded.

Taylor was quick in his reply. "Your Eve. I had been looking for her ever since an incident at my lab last year. I would like to believe that news of my research had somehow leaked to the scientific community and that people like Lan Nguyen who knew of the myths were hell bent on proving them a reality and covertly raided my lab, but that's a Hollywood story. What happened is less dramatic and quite unremarkable. Three idealistic animal activists in search of proof of animal cruelty in the city's many pharmaceutical and medical research facilities stumbled upon my place. Of course, they found no rows and rows of sad tortured subjects, but they did find the incubator for the N'Khal. They were able to cage two of them before my night watchman discovered them and chased them off – with their cages, unfortunately. I've got to admit, the little N'Khal were easy pickings but the activists had no idea what they had on their hands. Once they transformed – you know, basically melted into the background, their handlers probably opened their cages in a panic, left them unguarded, and out they went. This had to have happened in the Phnum Samkos Wildlife Sanctuary area near the lab. That's just across the border from the Chanthaburi District in Thailand – where you found Eve. Lan's team must have just stumbled upon SuZee while capturing wildlife for his lab. Last week, Number One and I felt the call from Eve. It was a shock as I thought the two sisters were lost to the jungles and elements forever. As enigmatic and special as they are, a toddler N'Khal would have made a tasty meal for any hungry primate or predator."

"I heard her call when I got close to the city also," Dana admitted.

"And you, Charles?" Taylor asked.

"Not so much. A little from SuZee – because of the healing – but I have not established anything with Eve like Dana has. So far. But you have no direct connection with Eve, so…?

"Through One. The sisters have finally reunited in their call and One guided me here."

"Your One is here? In Ho Chi Minh City?"

"Of course."

9:00 a.m. PST
Los Angeles

Detective John Fox was just finishing his third coffee of the morning – the new machine was in, and he had to admit it was actually quite good – when Lieutenant Davis sauntered up to his desk, a thin file in hand.

Davis greeted him. "Morning, John."

"Rocky. You look like the cat that ate the canary."

"I had my guys on the street last night, three days away from the Globes – we did a little cleanup duty."

"Homeless?"

Davis tossed the file on Fox's desk. "Yep. Us and the sanitation guys in hazmat all night."

"Ah, yeah. Thank God for industrial-sized sanitizer. What's this?" Fox opened the file.

"We got a call about a disturbance at the Sunset Seven Motel about two a.m. You know the place? It was near the homeless encampment we were supervising. Some guy and gal were going at it pretty good – arguing, not screwing – breaking stuff, trashing the room, the gal screaming and the guy smacking her around. We bring them both in. The john claims she wasn't who he called, the escort claims she was, and he stiffed her. Or he didn't, you know."

Fox was looked at the picture of the woman and her record. He shrugged.

"Cherie Swan. Solicitation, possession, misdemeanor assault, blah, blah. And you brought me this why?"

"The gal's sitting in the cell and yelling her head off that she wants out and she wants to see somebody about a murder she witnessed. She kept yelling and yelling, so I pull her out and sit her down. I get her a Dr. Pepper, she settles in, then tells me a story about a call at Hotel East about ten days ago. Claimed the deal was never 'consumed'; some guy in a mask 'jacked her at the door', they bust in and the guy just flat out pops her date. Single bullet dead center to the guy's noggin."

"Jeez! That's my guy Walsh."

"Right."

"But the guy was masked? That's no help."

"Yeah, but before the gun goes off, she heard Walsh call the guy Red."

Fox's ears perked up. "Where's this Cherie now?"

"Home, I'm assuming. We released her on her own – no bail LA – remember? Promised to appear and all that. She's got a couple of kids and swore she'd witness if we dropped the disturbing the peace charges."

"This is good. We can place him with Walsh at the Overtime earlier the day of the murder and now have a witness to Walsh identifying him by name in the hotel room. Still circumstantial, but it's another link in the chain. I'll get this to the D.A. and see what he says. And see if she'll come in and talk to me. Maybe something else she witnessed can help."

Lieutenant Davis left as Fox continued to look over the lean file. He reached for his coffee, looked at the empty cup, then over at the gleaming new coffee machine calling to him in the corner.

"Aw, hell," he swore as he got up and walked over to the new addition.

11:30 p.m. ICT

Charles and Dana sat in the backseat of Tin's KIA with Taylor in front as they barreled down a darkened tree lined road. The overhanging foliage of the King and Canary Island Palms reached high over the roadway as if to snatch up the invader and toss it from its sanctuary. They passed houses and huts and tents where flames from firepits leapt up toward the moonlit sky and their tenders drank beer and sang. Tin pulled onto a dirt road that dead ended in front of a stilted wooden framed house with a thatched roof. A Land Rover was parked to the side under a covered tent.

Taylor turned to address the couple. "I have a Tung friend who lives here and lets me use the place when I'm in town. He's not here now though, he's on tour if. He's a traditional folk musician and in much demand. C'mon in!"

Charles and Dana got out and started towards the house.

Tin rolled down his window and yelled, "Hey, boss! You want me to stay?"

"I'm not sure how long we'll be," Charles responded.

"No problem. I've got homework with me," Tin said as he held up a textbook and a sheaf of papers.

"That works," Charles said, as he gave Tim a thumbs up.

#

The inside of the house was sparsely furnished with low level furniture resting on wooden plank floors. The kitchen took up most of the middle of the room, one corner held a sleeping mat with walls that were filled with various stringed instruments hanging by hooks, and a small ancestor worship area was set off to the opposite side. Charles and Dana's attention was drawn immediately to the altar of the worship area – specifically a shimming, silver and gold color changing shape resting on the floor. It was Number One.

Taylor motioned for the two to sit on a bench across from her. As they sat, Taylor hunched down in front of the beast and gently patted her awake and spoke to her.

"Hey, darling, we have company. Come greet our guests."

Number One raised her head and focused on the two guests. A low hum vibrated from deep within her – Dana recognized this as a contented purr – as she raised herself and rubbed her lithe body against Taylor's torso. One then padded softly, cautiously, to Dana. Such a lady! She laid her head on Dana's knees as Dana reached out to pet the N'Khal. Her hum grew louder as her tail swept slowly behind her.

"She likes me," Dana exclaimed, looking at Taylor.

"Because she knows you," added Taylor with a smile.

Charles motioned to Taylor's cheek scar. "Did… she…?"

"Actually, yes. I suffered an auto mishap a few months ago. Three broken ribs, a collarbone fracture, collapsed lung, and this. Don't let the scar fool ya, mate. I almost lost my face. My Sheila there took care of me." Taylor paused. "Crikey, I think I've given her a real name!"

Dana ruffled the beasts' ears, nodded approval. "I think it fits."

"It's settled then. Sheila it is. How about a nightcap, all?"

More nodding all around. Taylor produced a bottle of Remy Martin XO Cognac. Taylor saw a look pass between the two Americans.

"Yes. It's good stuff, I know. But tonight's special."

He poured a serving for each in a paper cup, but the bartending was interrupted by the honking of a car horn outside. Taylor gazed out the window of the bungalow.

"Excuse me a minute, all," he said, and with a clap of his hands, Sheila followed him out the front door.

"I wonder what that's all about?" Dana mused.

Charles just shrugged his shoulders and helped himself to the poured drinks. Minutes later, Taylor walked back in. Sheila was noticeably absent. He noticed the quizzical look on the couple's faces.

"That was one of my associates. He's taking my N'Khal back to Cambodia tonight. One less thing to worry about tomorrow. Now, where were we? Oh, I see you've started without me. Good on ya." Taylor picked up his Cognac and raised his cup up into air. "A toast, then?"

Charles and Dana did the same. "What are we toasting and what's tomorrow?" Charles asked.

"Here's to that young man who drove us here."

Charles furrowed his brow. "Why?"

"Because he's helping us get your Eve back – tomorrow!"

CHAPTER 22

12:00 Midnight

Lan reviewed security camera footage of the street across from his facility. He could not believe that Reynolds had made the trip to Vietnam, much less accompanied by his wife. He surely underestimated the will of the man and his desire to reclaim the creature. And now it appeared that a second set of eyes had been monitoring the place for the past few days also – a man Lan had never seen before and that no one on his staff could identify. What was his game, mused Lan, that he was also nosing around? Press, most likely, or worse – someone from Asia's version of the damn FDA – the National Medical Products Administration. He ordered his security team to continue their surveillance – he was to be notified whenever they showed up again.

The creature had grown increasingly tense and skittish since arrival. Lan kept her caged and in a solitary steel-walled room. If she somehow escaped the cage, the room would continue to contain her. Feeding was performed once a day by a two-man crew in combat gear. A variety of tests were performed while she was under sedation. Lan had seen what the creature was capable of first-hand and wished no rerun of the spectacle. At this time tomorrow, Lan would have the results of tests and could then determine the fate of this animal.

The little boy that Lan was all those years ago that daydreamed of having a N'Khal as his best companion would have been devastated at what his older self was about to do – but that optimistic child was buried so deep down in Lan's heart that the protestations of the boy would never be heard. Lan snapped off his computer screen and watched the LED lights dim to nothing. The creature was housed in a fortress with no way out. Anyone attempting to rescue it would suffer a similar fate.

9:00 a.m. ICT

Tin wheeled the blue and black bespoke Range Rover owned by Taylor Scott into the parking lot of Lan Pharmaceuticals. An eight-hundred horsepower V8 engine, double-walled reinforced body with bulletproof glass, and dual wheels in the rear made the SUV/APV feel like an F-35 fighter jet dominating the city street. Tin had never handled such a massive boat and clearly enjoyed it.

Taylor, Charles, and Dana exited and walked towards the entrance of the building. Charles was carrying his Beretta in a shoulder holster flat against his body, concealed by a light beige windbreaker. Dana sported a casual skirt and blouse, and Taylor was in his Hawaiian shirt and cargo shorts, jack boots, and carrying a large computer bag. The conversation on the Rover centered on their plan to rescue Eve as peacefully as possible – Taylor assured the team that Lan was a shrewd businessman first and foremost and would negotiate the release to his advantage, and between the Reynolds' and Taylor, an agreement could be reached amicably. Charles was not convinced and reminded him of the Arizona incident and was not expecting this meet and greet to be anything more than a bust. Upon their entry to the building, they were immediately confronted by two very professional looking men in black business suits.

The tallest of the group addressed them in English, "Good morning, gentlemen. Ma'am. May I ask you your business today?"

Charles answered, "We would like to see Mr. Nguyen, please."

"Is Mr. Nguyen expecting you?" the tall man questioned the three.

"No, but we do have personal business to discuss."

The tall man conferred with his associate, turned, and walked away, talking into his sleeve. Charles assumed he had a concealed walkie-talkie. The trio waited patiently while the tall man talked, looked back several times and finally rejoined the group.

"Mr. Nguyen is unavailable. His secretary asks that you make an appointment at the front desk, stating your business, and you will be contacted within forty-eight hours."

Taylor looked at Charles and Dana. "I think we can do that. Lead the way, sir."

Charles was surprised that Taylor was so accommodating at the request but did not hesitate to let him take the lead. This was his show – today at least. If a rational argument that resulted in Eve's release could be arrived at, Charles wouldn't have to adopt an Indiana Jones act – something he thought of and rejected outright. The Aussie had proven himself capable of sizing up a situation, *So lead on, my friend*, he thought.

The reception area was situated back at the center of the lobby room they had entered and consisted of a large, long counter with half a dozen administrative personnel busy at their computer screens or walking papers and correspondence to other desks. High ceilings and a gigantic mural on the back wall reminded visitors this was indeed Vietnam. A lazy pastoral scene of farmland and grasses, workers in rice paddies, farms, and animals, graced the wall in vibrant colors. Muzak wafted softly from hidden speakers, occasionally interrupted by a low volume PA announcement by a female speaking in dulcet tones. Taylor motioned the two to relax on the sofas in the waiting area – he would handle the request.

Charles and Dana sat comfortably on the leather sofa as Taylor was greeted by the smiling face of a young receptionist, smartly dressed in a casual pantsuit, highlighted hair up in a bun, and very little makeup on her smooth face. Charles remarked to Dana that he did not recall such good-looking women during his time in country fifty years ago.

"Well, you only had eyes for me. Didn't you?" Dana chuckled.

"You got me there, gorgeous," he replied.

Charles watched as Taylor pointed them out to the woman at the counter. She looked at them several times and nodded, her previous smile replaced by an impersonal business expression. She started to reach for her phone, but Taylor gently touched her hand and shook his head imperceptibly in disapproval. The girl appeared to have seen a ghost – the color had drained from her face, and she was noticeably nervous. She lifted up a hinged section of the counter, walked through it and over to them, followed by Taylor.

"Mr. and Mrs. Reynolds, please follow me." Her eyes darted around the room as she cleared her throat. "Mr. Nguyen will see you now."

Charles, surprised at this, immediately rose, and gave Taylor an inquisitive look.

"Powers of persuasion, mate," he offered with a wink.

The receptionist proceeded through a double door that led them down a long corridor. At the end, they entered a walnut-paneled and red carpeted anteroom. Another set of nine-foot-tall doors led to their destination. As she reached for the doors, the receptionist turned around and addressed Taylor.

"You should probably wait here. I would like to announce your visit first, sir," she said.

"No! We will announce ourselves," Taylor replied. To Charles' and Dana's surprise, Taylor forcefully grabbed onto the receptionist's upper arm and opened both doors leading into the room. Taylor barged in as Lan stood by an ornate sidebar, pouring a drink. Lan looked up to see the intrusion and focused on the receptionist being held by Taylor.

He set his glass down. "What is the meaning of—?" Lan appeared to recognize the three intruders.

The receptionist burst out, "I am sorry, Mr. Nguyen."

"It's quite all right. Is she really needed here? You can let her go," he stated.

"No, she stays," Taylor replied, then spoke to her. "You, sit over there." He motioned to a chair next to the sidebar.

Charles and Dana were clearly in the dark as to what was unfolding.

Charles spoke up. "Taylor, we didn't—"

Taylor cut him off. "You want your Eve, right? Pull your socks up, mate. Relax."

Lan held his arms out in surrender. "Really, Mr... I'm sorry, we haven't been introduced. You are?"

"Taylor Scott. And these are my associates, Charles and Dana Reynolds. And please, stand right where you are. No calls, no alarms, nothing. In fact, sit." He motioned to a chair near the receptionist.

"This is ridiculous, I am not going to follow the order of someone the likes of you."

Taylor took two steps towards Lan. "The likes of me?' he chuckled. "What do you know about the likes of me? Here are the likes of me, Mr. Nguyen," Taylor said as he raised the bottom of his Hawaiian shirt and revealed a wide belt of explosives surrounding his waist. Dana inhaled sharply.

"The likes of me has enough C4 to level this room and everyone in it as well as a sizeable portion of the building. Now sit."

Lan sat.

Charles rose quickly and walked next to Taylor. He spoke in hushed tones. "Are you serious? Do you know what you're doing?"

"Sorry I left it out, but I was three years Australian Special Forces during my wandering years, mate. Yeah, I know exactly what I'm doing."

"OK, but this is your idea of negotiation?"

Taylor cocked his head and whispered. "In and out, in and out. It's all good, I assure you. Now please withdraw your little popgun from its holster to show this bloke we mean business."

Charles did as directed and casually folded his arms across his chest.

"Now listen up," Taylor started. "We're offering you the deal of the day. Apparently, you ran off with this fine couple's property, surely without their prior approval, and they would like it back. Nothing more, nothing less. Let us get to the little missus, and we'll be on our way. Easy, eh?"

Charles saw Lan's eyes moving rapidly at his unwanted guests, his body releasing tension. He recalled the look of resignation in the posture of held hostages he had seen before. The shoulders relax, the lips part ever so slightly, and the eyes adopt a thousand-yard stare. Lan was all that and more. Charles was hoping that the investment in this lab, the people he employed, the chemicals and inventory stored, plus the impact of an explosion near a highly populated district, was not worth squandering over the life of a creature he had yet to fully decode. A creature he knew was not rightfully his.

Lan slowly stood. "I will take you to her."

#

Outside his office, one of Lan's security team, deaf to the conversation in the soundproof office, came to attention as Lan escorted the group out.

"Is everything okay, sir?"

Lan waved him off with a smile "No problem, Tay. Just giving a tour to VIP investors."

As Lan led the group away from the guard down the numerous hallways and stairwells to the room, his mind raced.

The secure steel-clad room that Eve's cage rested in was made of two layers of one-inch-thick cold rolled steel, sandwiching six-inch thick concrete blocks. A small IED detonated in that room would evaporate anything in it instantly but anyone outside of it would only hear a loud 'thump' and perhaps experience the ground shaking. A C4 charge the type that Taylor was wearing would simply detonate mostly unnoticed and do no harm to the facility.

Lan was not giving up this easy, he told himself. This building, the people, the investment, were nothing compared to what he ultimately wanted. Lan calculated that once he had the group in the room, his men could quickly disarm them. Lan had called the security guard 'Tay', when in fact his name was Khahn. 'Tay' was a code word for 'need assistance'. By now, Khahn would have reported the code to his supervisor and the interior cameras were being monitored as the team prepared to respond. Lan's security detail were not hardened combat veterans, they were untested, but they were intelligent young men and he hoped they would act accordingly to defuse the situation. The way Lan figured it, the group would not even reach the steel room Eve was in and the offending trio would be dealt with. Lan was not at all concerned that his precious N'Khal would be forfeited.

#

The young receptionist's name was Song. She had been employed at Lan Pharmaceutical for less than a year. She hoped that this job would be a steppingstone to use her business management degree she recently received. So far, it had been a dreary slog of duties that any first month intern could do. Now she found herself a captive in something she did not comprehend. She had never been behind the closed doors of Lan Pharma and found herself wondering what truly went on in the rooms and offices she was passing. She followed the group tightly, with no need to be prodded further. The group went down a flight of stairs and entered a large room – the room was filled with unidentifiable lab equipment on worktables that fronted rows of cages. The sounds from the cages were cries of agony. It shook her to hear the yelps of dogs mixed with the shrieks of monkeys and the pleas of the cats. She quickly realized that this was a testing area for researchers. Her idealized fantasy of white-coated professional men and women looking through microscopes and whirling liquids in beakers was the sanitized advert version of what actually went on in a business such as this. Song felt ill just hearing the cacophony of pain. As they passed through yet another door, her stomach turned even further. More cages. This time with creatures barely recognizable, sucking in deep breaths of air and emitting ungodly sounds. Claws and hands reached out of barred cages. She quickly resolved that if she escaped this terror, she would seek new employment elsewhere. Anywhere.

#

Finally, through this room of horror, they entered yet another corridor. Taylor stopped the group before they reached the steel room.

"Hold it right here," he commanded.

Lan turned around. "We are almost there."

Taylor motioned to Charles, nodding his head upward at a wall mounted video camera.

"You see that? We know we're being watched," he said as he loosened his explosive belt pack with an audible 'click'. "Smile for the camera, Mr. Nguyen."

Taylor removed the belt pack and instructed Lan to raise his arms. Lan protested, but a wave of Charles' Beretta convinced him to comply. Taylor fitted the pack around Lan's waist, securing it with a double-clicking sound followed by an audible *beep*.

"What was that?" Dana asked.

"Trigger release. It's armed now. If he tries to remove it, it goes 'boom'. It's insurance."

"Is it really necessary?"

"Aye, it is. You may not know this, but the man is a murderer. Ten times over. I drilled a little deeper on his so-called pharmaceutical businesses. The 'medications' he sells on the black market have been responsible for scores of deaths. Patients hungry for any kind of cure seek them out and pay the price. Usually with their lives. He sells poisons as cures. Don't underestimate this man."

#

Lan's composure was melting. He was now a walking bomb. By now his men had viewed the explosive belt and were deciding how best to react. He assumed their gung-ho posture would melt also and would adopt extreme caution in bringing the incident to a successful close, and most importantly, not harm the man who signed their paychecks. After all, *money talks, does it not*?

#

Charles and company arrived at the room unhindered and the five of them entered. The receptionist immediately backed away from the cage – until she realized it was empty. Taylor stood by the door to insure it would not inadvertently close and lock the group inside, as well as look out for the cavalry. The remaining foursome stood silently – eyes on the cage. The silence was killing the young woman.

"What are we looking at?" she asked no one in particular.

Dana turned to her. "Wait," she instructed.

In the cage, a translucent shape took form, rapidly turning solid in colors of silver and gold. The young girl audibly gasped as Eve presented herself and immediately recognized her masters. She sprang to her feet and strained against the bars, trying to reach out while making purring sounds, pleas, mixed with yowls – she wanted to be near her family.

"Oh my God," whispered the young receptionist. "What is that?"

Taylor interjected, "Open the cage and get her out. Now."

Charles went to the cage, released the outside latch, and opened the door. Eve stepped out warily, then immediately rubbed against Charles' legs as Dana joined them. Eve proceeded to protectively pace around the two, excited, but cautiously eyeing Lan – the man she recognized as an enemy.

"Get in the cage," Taylor said to Lan.

"What?" Lan cried.

"Get in the fucking cage."

Lan started towards the cage, keeping his distance from a low growling Eve.

"My men will be waiting outside. You'll never get past reception."

"We'll see about that," he replied as Lan entered the cage. Taylor closed the gate and latched it. He then spoke to the Reynolds, with a head nod toward the receptionist. "You two go. Take her, too. It'll be crowded on your way out I believe, and no one will probably notice."

Charles snorted. "Really? What makes you…"

Taylor reached over to a panel on the wall adjacent to the door that had three buttons. Charles had noticed numerous similar panels on the wall in the hall and corridors. Taylor hit all three buttons with a closed fist. Under each button was a symbol – one for fire and one for gas and one for seismic. Blue strobe lights lit up and multiple alarm horns sounded. Taylor had initiated an emergency fire and gas evacuation of the facility. In mere moments, the building would be overflowing with fleeing employees.

"Well, okay then," Charles retorted.

Taylor added, "Dana, try to warn Eve she must become hidden. Now go. Have Tin drive to the house. I'll join you later."

The noise of the blaring horns and the general rumble of the jammed workers abandoning their posts would drown out any calls from Lan.

"Are you sure?" Charles yelled.

"Yes! Go now!"

Charles, Dana, and the receptionist exited the room – several panicked staff members jogged past them, unflinching. No security personnel were present as far as they could see. Charles turned to the receptionist.

"Lead us out of the building. No games or else," he ordered.

She nodded, unable to speak. Eve followed behind the group and then she was gone from sight, but Charles knew she shadowed closely. In a matter of minutes, they were jogging alongside groups mass migrating to the exit. Whatever trusted security Lan had employed was spread thin, unorganized, and apparently not in any hurry to find their leader. The tall security man that first approached Charles when they arrived was actually climbing over desks and furniture on his way out. Lan's best turned out to be paper tigers.

#

The explosive belt that Lan Nguyen was fitted with was not a complex device. Taylor assembled it so that texting a programmed code to the receiver would activate it. Taylor closed the steel door to the secure room that held the cage that held Lan and raced throughout the building in search of the emptied rooms until he found the security office. Taylor was relieved to see that it was closer than expected and was vacant – rats on a sinking ship always exited wisely. For a multi-million-dollar enterprise, Lan's surveillance system was decidedly amateur by current standards. He appraised the equipment, then shut it all down, removed the hard drives from the open bays, tapes from ancient VCRs, and disks from backup drives. He was surprised that the words 'Radio Shack' was not emblazoned on any of the hardware.

He left the room with everything he assumed he needed and hurried back to the steel room. He entered and stepped up to the cage and displayed all of the material he had gathered in with Lan.

"What's this?" Lan screamed.

"It's your home movies and my assurance," he said. Taylor threw all of the data he had collected into the cage with Lan. Lan unleashed a loud volley of cursing as Taylor closed the heavy door – shutting the protests out – and leaned his back against it. He took out a cellphone from his cargo shorts and looked at it just as a short trim man in a black suit appeared from around the corner, training an AK47 automatic rifle on the Aussie. Taylor held up the cellphone for the man to see.

"Hey, mate! You know what this is, right? You know what happens if I drop it?"

The man stared blankly at Taylor, then started shaking slightly.

"Catch!" Taylor belted out as he tossed the cell in a high arc at the man.

The man dropped the rifle at Taylor's feet, lunged back for the phone arcing towards him, and caught it in mid-air as he tumbled to the ground. The man looked at the phone, perspiration beads dripping down forehead, and gingerly pressed the OFF button. As it powered down, Taylor picked up the AK47, racked it – selected Auto, then pointed it casually towards the man.

"By the way, did I mention that you shouldn't turn the phone off either?"

The security man's eyes widened in terror.

#

Once the door to the room was closed, Lan started shaking uncontrollably. His worst fear would soon be realized. He tried to tear at the belt pack but even if he could get it off, it would do no good once detonated. He heard a scuffle outside the door and for a brief moment thought maybe the intruder was getting his just rewards.

When there were no more sounds audible from outside, Lan relaxed slightly. Then his belt detonated, and Lan saw red.

CHAPTER 23

The visible three and the invisible one made it out safely, with their fellow refugees dispersing in all directions. Once reasonably clear of the building, Charles motioned for the young receptionist to leave them. She didn't need to be told a second time. She mouthed a *Thank you*, turned, and ran. Charles and Dana rounded a corner and found Tin waiting by the Range Rover.

"Open the cargo door, Tin!"

Charles jumped in the passenger seat, Dana in the rear. Tin climbed in the cab.

"Open it, open it!" Charles pleaded.

Tin focused on Charles. "Okay, okay! But why—"

Thump – something large and heavy jumped in the rear of the SUV that shook the Rover's body. Tin's eyes widened.

"Now close it. Please."

Tin pressed the cargo door button, looking in the rear-view mirror. Nothing was visible. He reached up to adjust it. Charles reached over and covered the mirror with his hand.

"Don't look back. Just drive. Trust me."

Tin did just that. As they pulled out of the lot and onto the frontage road heading away, three police cars with sirens blaring and lights flashing raced past them followed by four fire trucks in emergency pursuit. Through all of the noise, Charles thought he heard the sound of a distant thunderclap.

#

Charles and Dana rode back to Taylor's friend's place in silence. Tin had been warned beforehand that the group were in search of something that they would rather not reveal so he wisely avoided questions, but halfway to the house, Charles decided that Tin deserved to know as he felt responsible for the outcome. Charles told him the whole story about them, Lan Nguyen,

Taylor, and Eve. Tin nodded throughout the story, cautiously glancing back at the now visible N'Khal resting her head contentedly on Dana's lap.

When they pulled up in front, Tin shut off the engine, then stared silently out the window. Charles wondered if he had misplaced his trust in this kid. It was a lot, no, a mega lot, to take in. Tin turned in his seat and addressed Charles.

"When I get home tonight, I am going to cross Lan Pharmaceuticals off my list of prospective employers."

"Good idea," Charles responded. "I think Taylor Scott may be interested in someone like you. What do you think about relocating to Phnom Penh?"

1:00 p.m. PST

Randall 'Red' Heard was slowly unraveling. His girlfriend in Dana Point wasn't answering his phone calls. The Spaniard wasn't answering his phone calls. He believed his prized house that looked out upon the vast wealth of Los Angeles was being surveyed continuously.

He peeked out of his front window almost hourly now, sure that the cargo van emblazoned with Tom's Electric on its side was a front for the police – watching him and waiting to pounce. The red Chevrolet Malibu that passed this house twice daily were plainclothes cops. He thought he heard drones in the sky – drones with cameras that sent video straight to the cop's main headquarters. He hadn't left the house since the warrant search. Uber Eats and Grub Hub made deliveries daily now. His cleaning service notified him that they were discontinuing service, citing staff shortages – but Red knew. He knew. The cops had gotten to them. All of them. They had nothing on him. So, what if he was seen with that unfortunate loser Ben Walsh the day he was murdered – just a friendly drink with an old pal. So what if he tried to broker a deal on a piece of merch that he didn't have – the guy who had it flaked on him. The cops had shit. Red's lawyer promised he'd sue the pants off the city and anyone else besmirching his good name.

Red lit his third joint of the day – he surveyed his surroundings. He hadn't put anything back in place since the search. Empty Chinese take-out cartons, discarded pizza boxes, cheeseburger wrappers, and drained thirty-two-ounce drink cups littered the place. Red didn't care. He'd call a new cleaning service tomorrow. He'd put his cabinet drawers back in place tomorrow. He'd pull out the vacuum – *he had one, right?* – tomorrow.

He pondered why this was all happening to him. He knew. That goddam painting. That piece of crap ugly motherfucking painting. He should take that damn thing and bring it back to that rich couple's house and shove it up their asses. Serve them right for all the trouble and pain it caused him. Yeah. That's a plan. Get out of these wrinkled and stained clothes, shave, and shower, then drive over there. Tomorrow. With the painting. If he could remember where it was. *Where was it again*? No matter. He'd look for it. Tomorrow.

#

Tin left the couple shortly after delivering them and their N'Khal. Dana let him pet Eve and she gave him a reassuring nip on his hand. He claimed she drew blood but when Dana looked at his hand, there was none. Charles gave Tin a large bonus for his help but Tin refused, against Charles insistence. Charles placed it in Tin's shirt pocket anyway along with a look that Tin wisely accepted. Taylor showed up an hour later, a half bottle of Four Roses Bourbon in one hand, a shopping bag in the other. Taylor immediately walked over to Eve and introduced himself with a pat on her head and a vigorous scratching of her cheeks.

Once settled in the house, drinks passed around, take-out chicken tenders and fries plated, they discussed the day and their next move.

"How did you leave Lan? Charles asked.

Taylor hesitated, and Charles immediately knew the answer, but Dana interjected.

"Yes. What happened?"

Taylor looked Dana in the eye and cocked his head slightly. Charles intuitively knew that Taylor wouldn't sugar coat what happened, but he would pick his words carefully.

"I believe he was fine when I left him. I couldn't tell you where he is now."

Dana remained silent for a moment, then spoke. "Are we going to be all right?"

"I don't think he's going to cause us any trouble if that's what you mean. The authorities may be a different matter. I was able to dispose of the surveillance data on their security room, but… you never know about any redundant backup systems. There are no extradition treaties here or in Cambodia if that's a concern. You're coming to my place in Cambodia, of course. Settle in for a day or two then it'll be off to Los Angeles," he announced.

Charles was going to answer and let Dana absorb everything, but she queried. "How does Eve get home? It's not like we can buy her a seat on JAL."

"Dana. You and Charles will be my guest on my private jet, with Eve in a conditioned cargo section. That's if you two don't mind havin' this old bloke spending a little vacation time in LA?"

"How can we say no? Of course." Charles replied.

"Then it's settled. We leave first thing in the morning."

"We still have clothes at the hotel," Dan protested.

"No. You don't. I made one more stop following the activity at Lan Pharma. I arranged for your belongings to be packed and delivered here by sunrise tomorrow. Bill's paid, too." Taylor anticipated a protest and held his hand up. "No. Like you say, 'It's all good.' No argument tonight. Okay?"

They agreed.

#

Charles did not realize how tired he was as he lay in the bed next to Dana. Dana had gotten a second wind. She propped herself up on an elbow and scrutinized Charles.

"I think our friend Taylor proved himself today, what do you think? Did he kill Lan? Would he tell us if he did?"

Charles gave her a sheepish grin and chuckled. "I think we've got Jason Bourne on our team with a side of Charles Bronson. I think the less we know the better. It certainly seems like he's got things figured out."

"I know. It does." She paused and Charles closed his eyes. She continued. "Do you think we could see the spaceship he found?"

"Uh… that's a big no."

"Really? Why?"

"You heard him – it's a tightly controlled area. I don't think anyone wants a couple of tourists barging around down there."

"You're right. I'm not sure I would really want to see it anyway."

"Oh, now you're not sure. Why not?"

Dana paused. "It frightens me when I think about it. I never thought of Eve as an *alien*."

"Technically, she's not."

"I know but she came from alien DNA."

"Dual citizenship!"

Dana smacked Charles on his shoulder. "I'm trying to be serious. I mean, really – this is world shattering kind of news. When this gets out—"

"*If* this gets out," Charles corrected.

"*When* this gets out. And it will, what's our response?"

"We send a spacecraft to wherever it came from and wait eighty-thousand years I suppose. I don't think we panic. What would it accomplish?

"I don't know. It's all too much." Dana shook her head and lay back onto her pillow. "Somewhere out there, Eve has relatives, or ancestors, and sentient beings they interact with that live and breathe as we do, with another sun than ours to heat them, and a different sky that rains down on them. When they look up at night, do they see our sun? Why did they come to us in the first place? It makes you really wonder."

Charles answered with a heavy breathing in and out. Dana pulled some covers over him and kissed him lightly on his forehead.

"Sleep tight, earthling," she bid him.

5:00 a.m. ICT

Taylor knocked lightly on the door to Charles and Dana's room at daybreak. Charles responded with a quick, "We're up."

"No problem, mate," Taylor replied. "Your suitcases are here already and I'm leaving them by the door. Brekky in one hour and then off to the Penh."

Charles heard Taylor whistling to himself and fade away. He turned to Dana.

"Brekky?"

Dana translated. "Breakfast. I just hope it's not kangaroo."

6:00 a.m. ICT

The first thing Charles did as he entered the kitchen was look for anything that resembled a kangaroo. He saw nothing. Ah, relief! He did see Taylor dishing up a traditional Aussie breakfast of fried eggs, sausage, bacon, tomatoes and mushrooms, thick toast, and baked beans. A pot of coffee was center stage of the table, and he and Dana poured themselves a big mug each.

"Tank up, everyone," Taylor instructed as he put a jar of jam on the table as a finishing touch. "We'll load up after you eat and be in Cambodia in time for a late lunch or early dinner. The border crossing is excruciating – else its half the time – but… I know a few shortcuts, I assure you. I can't wait for my Sheila to meet your Eve!"

CHAPTER 24

3:00 p.m. ICT

The Range Rover pulled onto a dirt roadway off of Route1 just outside of the Phenom Penh city limits in the early afternoon. They passed countless driveways leading to western style homes, stilted wooden structures, and small roadside stands selling fruits and ices. From the dirt road they turned onto a gravel driveway tunneling through think jungle brush that gave way to a black asphalt road, then a smooth concrete driveway that took them up to an impressive and beautifully detailed wrought iron gate mounted on massive sculptured concrete posts attached to a ten-foot-high concrete wall. Charles turned to Dana and mouthed, *Wow*.

"Who owns this?" he asked Taylor.

"I do," he responded with a grin. "Relax, we're still two miles away."

Charles again turned to Dana. This time she mouthed, *Wow*.

The long driveway through overgrowth brush gave way to open fields and meadows on both sides. Charles spotted a small lake with a boathouse and dock one his left, a fenced horse track with stables on his right. Several beautiful horses grazed lazily on the open center of the track. A small rise took them in view of Taylor's house. House was a pallid description of a magnificent French styled country home. The multi-level structure featured a traditional hip design roof, a charming stone and stucco exterior that featured multiple pane windows accented by iron balconies. Taylor escorted the couple and Eve in and immediately brought them to a dining room fit for a noble. The group was seated by the house cook and supped on a lunch of tableside prepared Caesar salad, roasted game hens, grilled asparagus with parmesan cheese, all topped off by a nice, imported Aussie wine. Eve padded around the table, seemingly content and acknowledging both the diners and staff. Charles assumed the staff and household members were all aware of Sheila, as they seemed quite unfazed by Eve's presence.

Following lunch, Taylor gave a quick tour of the eight-thousand square foot home, the Olympic sized pool, two tennis courts, and guest house. Charles and Dana and Eve were then brought to a flat lawn area adjacent to the gardens. Taylor excused himself momentarily and returned with his N'Khal, now dubbed Sheila. The creation was an identical twin of Eve. They both cautiously left the side of their masters and met in the middle of the lawn. The two stopped short of each other, stood still, and emitted a lowing and purring in harmony. They next circled each other in what Charles assumed was a formal greeting, then rested each other's heads against its double – perhaps they were communicating – and immediately broke into a full out race across the length of the immaculate two-hundred-yard lawn. At the end, they both tumbled and played with a joy neither the Reynolds nor Taylor had witnessed.

"The sisters have reunited," Taylor noted.

"Yes! We've seen her play before, but this is a whole new level," said Dana.

Taylor walked out towards the two N'Khal in play, then looked back at Dana. "They belong together!"

Charles bristled. *And that was the rub,* he thought. That was the reason for his cooperation in retrieving her. So that he could get Eve back for himself. He would have none of it. Damn the private plane ride – he was compelled to speak up.

He got Dana's attention and whispered, "If this guy thinks we're giving her up after all we've been through, he's sadly mistaken."

Charles rose to confront Taylor, but the Aussie shouted from a distance as he walked back. "I hope it won't be a burden having Sheila join you two for a while! I don't mean to be presumptuous!"

Charles looked back at Dana. She gave him a shrug and an admonishing smirk. Charles returned her scolding with a sheepish grin. He returned to his seat. He felt like a shmuck. After putting his life on the line for them, Charles felt ashamed that his mind went where it did.

"Well, what do you say? Do we?" he asked his wife as Taylor rejoined them.

She said yes.

It was settled, then. Taylor would bring Sheila on the trip to LA to complete the reunion of sisters and stay for a visit in Beverly Hills.

#

Preparations for the return trip to LAX were made for the next day. The afternoon was spent touring Taylor's Laboratory in the city. Dana was especially interested in the research facility given her profession. Charles was relieved that there were no lab rats or any other animal testing being conducted. Taylor assured them that the lab was a pure research facility dedicated to genome mapping of DNA for the thousands of species that had yet to be cataloged. That and their successful rebuilding of the N'Khal. Charles questioned how pure the DNA was that was retrieved from the ship and how true to the original were the copies of the creatures. Taylor admitted that there were indeed missing sections early on that needed to be augmented with feline DNA, as that appeared to be the closest match earth could offer, but as more research was completed, those sections were assembled properly. In the end, there was no more than a five percent earth feline supplement. Taylor explained how he visited Koh Ker twice yearly and re-entered the spacecraft in search of the final prize – additional organic matter of the original crew. The craft so far held fast to its secrets. Vague allusions to the masters of the ship still existed in millennium-old tablets but no definitive answer was arrived at. It was posited that the visions the N'Khal transmitted to their masters were perhaps remnants imbedded in their DNA at best, and no real conclusion could be drawn. *He would remain committed until he achieved his goal,* thought Charles. His respect grew.

6:00 a.m. ICT

The next morning, Charles, Dana, and Taylor climbed aboard his Gulfstream V ultra-long range heavy jet for the nineteen-hour flight to LAX. Eve and Sheila were mildly tranquilized and seemed entirely content to snuggle up to each other, grooming one another, and generally in compliant moods. Once arrived, the human passengers would be greeted with a stretch limo for the final hour drive to Beverly Hills – followed by the N'Khal siblings in a privately converted armored truck courtesy of a few strings pulled by Detective John Fox. On the phone with him at forty-thousand feet, Fox relayed that he was eager to catch up with the couple and see how their trip went.

"I've got a lot to tell. We are definitely looking for any news you have, John," Charles replied.

"Yeah. I wish I could tell you we have Heard in custody on both the Van Gogh theft and the Walsh murder, but we don't. I do have... a personal matter I'd like to pick your brain on though."

Charles hesitated at first but decided not to press. "Okay. Whatever you need. Let me get settled in and we'll meet up somewhere."

"Thanks. I'll give a call in the next day or so."

Charles hung up and pondered what Fox could possibly want to discuss. He had been open about everything he and Dana had been through – but Fox said it was a personal matter. It must not have anything to do with the cases. He decided to let it ride and roll with whatever Fox presented.

8:00 a.m.

Detective John Fox had called the forensics lab twice in as many days only to be told that Heidi was out of the office. Yesterday, he finally called her cell and there was no answer.

He was rightfully concerned as she had confided in him her physical problem – the cancer. He wanted to be there for her, but she made no bones about them being separate entities with no strings attached. He had to finally admit to himself that he felt differently. Their time together recently had to mean something, didn't it? He wanted to help her through this, and he had decided to ask Charles Reynolds for help, but he did not want to overstep his bounds with Heidi. He would ask Charles if it was possible for Heidi and his Eve to meet and see if any healing could be performed. People went to Sri Lanka or Mexico City for miracle cures, why not to the Reynolds thingy? It was a long shot that Heidi would approve it as treatment, but her stubborn I-can-do-it-all personae be damned. He would at least set the stage and see if the players would arrive. In time, he hoped. A lot of stars needed to align if this was to happen. The Reynolds needed to get back safely with their creature; Heidi needed to understand that he was only there to help; she needed to agree; and then it all needed to actually work. Fox was a born skeptic, which worked to his advantage as a detective, but the last part of his plan was the hardest to accept – and the only part that really mattered.

#

Heidi glanced at her phone – she had received over a dozen calls in the past few days and returned none of them. She asked for and received a week off of work due to what she said was 'family business'. It wasn't a lie – she and her corporate lawyer husband, Roy, had travelled to Sacramento to file and receive a one-day divorce. Heidi and Roy admitted after the first year that the marriage was a mistake. It was good for his business, but his travelling and philandering were not what Heidi volunteered for. So, they settled on an arrangement. They would both be free to pursue whatever physical pleasures they desired in exchange for a good front and a comfortable living. Roy reveled in the agreement and took complete, loosely confidential, advantage of it. Heidi often thought about Roy's dalliances. She wasn't obsessed or shrewish about them in any way. She didn't ask and he didn't tell. *That was fine with me*, she thought. *If he knew of my activities, he would be shocked.* Why? Because she didn't have any – except for one night long in the past with Detective John Fox. And now, with the recent turn of events, her mind was flooded with thoughts of Fox and her together. She was happy when she was with him – so much happier than at any time in her life. She realized she wanted to spend however much time she had remaining with him. Together.

10:00 a.m.

The Gulfstream landed at LAX and taxied to a private runway strip. Charles thought he could get used to this kind of service. Taylor was quite excited on the ride to their Beverly Hills home. He pointed out the Staples Center Arena and the landmarks in downtown LA like a kid seeing Disneyland for the first time. He marveled at the Hollywood Hills sign. He asked if he needed permission to hike up to it. Charles couldn't remember when he last witnessed someone so excited about the sights he everyday saw.

Charles knew their residence was in no way comparable to the Taylor spread in Cambodia, but their guest was gracious enough to acknowledge his appreciation of the simple French style architecture and surrounding areas. The N'Khal arrived shortly after they did, and before they could even step inside the house, both Eve and Sheila took off around the back to stretch their limbs, led by Eve – anxious to acquaint the newcomer to the property.

Taylor was shown to the guest room which he declared was 'aces', with the invite to join the Reynolds out on the back patio in an hour for cocktails.

At the appointed time, the three sat in the warm afternoon sun, sipping vodka gimlets, and sharing a cheese tray.

"It's a right nice place you have here, Charles. Very comfy," Taylor offered.

"Thanks. It's a little shy of five acres – mostly wooded but accessible. Dana and I did most of the landscaping back here. She's the green thumb and I'm just all thumbs with anything plants."

"Don't let him fool you!" Dana added. "He's responsible for that grove of palms and bamboo over there. It's a great wind barrier. He's just too modest."

"Well, it's a great looking spread. I see our gals are enjoying it."

The two creations were still romping and tumbling, then perked their ears at a new sound. They both jogged over to a tall brick wall behind the house. Chloe had made an appearance and was meowing at them. The N'Khal sat at the base of the wall and watched as Chloe bounced down and greeted first Eve, then made her way to the new arrival Sheila. Instant friendship was achieved, and more games were played.

Charles rose. "I guess it's time to meet the final piece of the puzzle. Let's go see SuZee."

Everyone headed into the house, including the twins and Chloe, and jammed into the elevator. Taylor noted the scratches on the doors. He nodded towards them.

"That from that night?" Taylor asked no one in particular.

"Yes. Neither of us actually witnessed how it came about, but we've no doubt it was not a friendly encounter," Dana volunteered as the elevator settled gently.

"Glad we're on their side," Charles noted.

Once inside the gallery, they went to the equipment room where SuZee was resting. Eve and Sheila held back as Charles went to retrieve her. Charles noted that she had gained weight in their absence, her eyes were clearer, she was alert, and responsive. He greeted her and led her out. As Sheila and Eve had done previously, they looked at each other, then approached and performed their familial dance of greeting, nuzzled as a threesome, then all took off to explore the room. Chloe did her best to keep up with the group but pooped out after a bit, preferring to lounge and watch. Charles watched as they reveled in their reunion. "Makes me wonder how they would react to a male N'Khal approach."

"Well, mate," Taylor answered. "That would be interesting. Near as we can tell, the entire species is female."

"They're asexual?" Dana inquired.

"Bob's your uncle! The chromosome counts are off the chart, so… but we haven't figured out exactly how just yet."

Charles gave out a low whistle. "Can these three reproduce?"

"I see no reason why not. Cloned sheep can – of course that's with normal sexual reproduction. But who knows? There's still a lot of mystery I'm hoping to uncover."

Charles was mildly interested in the monumental tasks Taylor had assigned himself, but after the past couple of weeks he had no desire to tackle any more mystery. If Taylor could find a piece of DNA from the stewards of the craft, he had no doubt that he could replicate the true masters of the N'Khal.

It had been an adventure, that's for sure. He had successfully recovered the more precious of the two missing pieces of the household, he was back home in the place he felt most comfortable, Dana was doing very well and he appreciated her doubly, the residuals of his assault were a dim memory now, and he felt he had conquered a huge mountain climb that had been his white whale.

Aside from recovering his Van Gogh, Charles submitted to himself that life was good and he couldn't imagine it getting any better.

CHAPTER 25

2:00 p.m.

Randall 'Red' Heard couldn't imagine life getting any worse. As he was fighting to tear open a bag of white powder in the bathroom, clad in only his stained underwear, his lawyer called. The ringing scared him. He spilled the powder. He tried to scoop it up but it was impossible. *He could vacuum it,* he thought. He screamed a *What* into the phone. His lawyer informed him the courts had rejected his lawsuits as without merit. Fuck! What a damn waste that man was. Waste, waste, waste! He paused his tantrum. He couldn't waste this powder. He could vacuum it up! Yes.

He couldn't find his vacuum cleaner. He looked in the hall closet, in his bedroom, in his laundry room, the garage, everywhere. He even looked in the tall storage cabinet hidden in the maintenance outbuilding at the back of the property. Surely, he didn't put the vacuum there, but…Maybe. Someone. Did? No luck. He did find a tall box he didn't recognize. Was the vacuum in there? No. He remembered. It was a box he had hidden away. But why? It was a tall steel box with a combination lock. *What was the damn combination*? He couldn't remember. He grabbed a hammer and quickly destroyed the lock. He showed the lock who the boss was! He was! He opened the tall box, and it all came back to him. It was a tube. A tube containing something. He fumbled with the lid on the tube, pulled it off. Something was rolled up inside the tube. He removed it. It was a painting. He unrolled it and flung it on the ground as if bitten by a viper. It was the painting that haunted his nightmare. That damn, ugly, homeless, bum that watched him now – followed him, sitting in a van that read 'Vince's Electric'.

He shook his head and realized what he needed to do. It was so simple. He laughed at his revelation. So easy! Get rid of it. Throw it away. No, he reasoned – it would be found if he just trashed it. Some unlucky soul would be condemned by its torment. No one should be subject to the damning glare of that man in the painting. Be done with it. Bury it deep in a grave.

2:40 p.m.

Detective John Fox rose from his desk and slipped into his John Varvatos lambskin leather jacket. He was set to meet Charles Reynolds shortly to update the family on the case and then ask for the favor. He had yet to talk to Heidi – that was going to be the tricky part. His desk intercom phone buzzed – it was Melody Frahm at the front desk. He picked it up.

"Detective? There's someone here to see you. A Cherie Swan? Are you expecting her?"

Fox had to think for a second. Right, the 'visitor' from the Walsh murder. "No, I am not." He checked his watch. "… but send her in."

Fox stood by his desk as a Frahm, a smartly uniformed officer, escorted a black lady dressed in pajama bottoms and an off-the-shoulder too-tight muscle tee.

"Miss Swan?" Fox asked, pointing to a chair by his desk. "Have a seat."

Cherie sat and immediately started. "You the detective I need to talk to? I hope so. First off, I didn't do nothin' at that hotel room that them cops say I might have did. I was visiting. That's all."

"Visiting who, exactly?"

"That dead guy. Dan, or Ben. You know."

"Ben Walsh."

"Yeah, Ben Walls. That's him. Anyway, like I told that lieutenant the other day, I knock on the door, then some man comes outta nowhere and pushes a gun in my back. Walls opens the door and I get pushed in. Two seconds later the guy pops my date. Dude called him 'Red'. That's important, huh?"

"That is very important." Fox paused. "Do you recall anything else that can help us identify the killer? Anything. Don't talk. Think."

Fox could see Cherie concentrating, hoping she could add something that would help identify Heard. Any little bit. Cherie opened her purse and took out a worn red plastic wallet with traces of glitter on it. She reached in and produced two one hundred dollar bills. She tossed them on the desk. Fox looked at them but did not touch.

"What is that, exactly?" he asked.

"He had a big old wallet full of cash and he pulls out this measly two hunert dollars. For my time and for me to shut my mouth probably. I don't want it. It's blood money. Besides, there's a reward, right?" Cherie raised her eyebrow slyly at Fox.

"Oh, there is a very substantial reward."

"Good. Cause there is probably some of that D and A on them."

Fox glared at the money, thinking this Cherie may be smarter than she presented herself. Of course, there was DNA on the bill, but how many of her client's DNA was stuffed in that same wallet? He nudged her.

"What makes you think so?"

"Because I remember him looking at me all greedy like. He lifted his mask up just a little bit and licked his fingers wet to pull those two bills off of his load. You know how you do that. Those bills probably got his spit on them. You can check that out, huh?" Cherie flashed a smile and folded her arms in a pose of supreme accomplishment.

"Yes, we can, young lady." Fox smiled back. "Yes, we can."

If there was a solid reason to call Heidi now, Fox had it. He bagged the bills and gave Cherie a receipt, then personally escorted her out. Cherie made sure everyone in the precinct office knew she was in line for the reward monies, and Fox assured her that she was.

He returned to his desk and first called Charles Reynolds to tell him that he would be leaving soon to stop by, then called the forensics lab and alerted them he had a hot item of evidence in the Walsh murder investigation that he was personally bringing over, and would Heidi happen to be there? The lab assistant who answered was Marta, who informed Fox that Heidi was on family leave but that she would personally expedite the evidence and that she was familiar with the case. Fox was surprised by the family leave comment – surely, she had not taken ill that fast? If she was bedridden or even in the hospital, she would take his call, right? Her supervisors would know. The chief would know.

Fox knocked on the door frame to the chief's office in clear site of the man. Hellman was in and, as usual, on the phone. Hellman waved him in and proffered a chair.

He hung up and cleared his throat. "What's up, John?"

Again, Fox had a real reason to visit as well as snooping around about Heidi.

"I might have DNA evidence placing Randall Heard at the scene of the Walsh murder. Indisputable, no less. Maybe."

Hellman scowled. "So, it's a yes, no, maybe. Spill."

Fox relayed the conversation with Cherie Swan and the possibility of the bills being Heard's. He showed the chief the bagged bills.

"If it is, that's solid. We can make a call to the D.A. and have Heard here and charged by noon tomorrow. That's good news if it pans out. See that it does."

"I will. I'm bringing it over to the lab now – I already called to expedite it. I understand the Lab Supe is out on leave?"

"News to me. Why?"

"Oh, no reason. She was heading up the lab on the evidence so…"

"I can check with HR if you want me to."

"No, no heed to. Just curious."

The Chief gave Fox a judgmental look.

"Go nail Heard. Get back to me with a win."

Fox snagged the bag of bills and stood. "Will do, sir."

6:00 p.m.

Marta Hernandez was working the weekend afternoon shift when Detective John Fox walked in, glanced around, and went straight to her desk. She knew that the detective was working on the case that she had gotten reprimanded for. She hoped she hadn't brought any trouble to Derick. She stiffened slightly.

"Marta, right?"

"Yes, we talked earlier. What can I do for you, Detective?" she nervously replied.

"Can you operate the rapid DNA machine?"

"Yes, of course,"

Fox handed her the plastic pouch containing the hundred-dollar bills. She saw the name Heard on the flap – she hesitated. This was the case.

"We have this guy's DNA already. From the search warrant items earlier this week. Was there a problem?"

"No – everything's fine. This is new evidence we just received and if it's a match to Randall Heard's, we've got him. Heidi praised your work on this."

Marta let out sight sigh – inwardly relieved.

Fox noted it. "Are you okay?"

"I'm fine," she said and grinned. "How soon do you need it?"

"How soon can you get it?"

"The rapid DNA can match what we already have on this Heard in about three hours. Will that work?"

"That's perfect."

"Great. I can start actually in the next half hour." Marta picked up the bag and started to walk away. Fox interrupted her walk.

"One more request. Is everything okay with your boss?"

"Heidi? I'm assuming so. Why? Do you know something I don't?"

"No. No. Just used to seeing her around."

#

Fox drove to his home in Venice. He had wanted to press the young girl about Heidi but thought that Marta likely was unaware of her boss's illness and didn't want to open something needlessly in the department. He felt like he had no choice and resolved he would simply stop by Heidi's regardless of her wishes the next morning. He gave Marta his card with instructions to call him as soon as she could verify the DNA on the bills. If it was a match, he could arrange for an arrest warrant and take him down tomorrow. Fox felt that at this hour tomorrow, he would have Heard in custody and charged with Murder One.

9:00 p.m.

The Reynolds enjoyed a night of peace and quiet. Their houseguest, Taylor, had rented a car – a Lamborghini from a local company called Royal Exotic Car Rentals – and was spending the evening cruising the Sunset Strip and Hollywood Boulevard to see if he could see any star's limos on their way to the Golden Globe ceremony at the Beverly Hilton and parts beyond. A lot of the streets would be closed for the night but Taylor was excited to witness the glitz and glamour near the heart of the action he so often heard of. Of course, the pizzazz was also accompanied by the homeless encampments and the flotsam and jetsam of the city but the Aussie was undeterred in his desire to take it all in. Charles set him up in the guest room for his stay and did not expect him back for hours – if at all – the guy proved a venerable perpetual motion machine.

Charles and Dana shared a bottle of 2019 Justin Isosceles Cabernet – toasting their success in Vietnam and looking forward to things returning back to normal. Charles had expected Fox to stop by, but he called just an hour earlier and begged off – asking if he could postpone until tomorrow. Charles agreed – there was still a hesitation in Fox's request that bothered him. Fox did disclose that he now had – hopefully – solid DNA evidence of Randall Heard's presence at the murder of Ben Walsh – and was sure Heard would spill the truth about the Van Gogh after he was arrested. The two agreed to a breakfast together at the Reynolds. With the three sisters safely tucked away in the basement gallery, the night was theirs.

11:30 p.m.

Patricia Stillwater, the former executive assistant to Lan Nguyen in Arizona, sat at a stoplight at the intersection of Ventura Boulevard and Coldwater Canyon Drive, approximately fifteen minutes from the Reynolds property. She commanded a 2022 Chevrolet Express van that had been outfitted with a 6.6-liter V8 engine, heavy duty shocks, and a completely reinforced steel caged cargo area. Xerxes rested in the back, silent by design, but alert to Patricia's soothing voice. The creation was also compliant by design, thanks to a computer chip imbedded in its brain. Lan's brilliant programming allowed a limited range of commands to be transmitted that Xerxes had been trained to obey. The fearsome creature proved quite capable in the lab.

In their last communique, Lan had requested that Patricia recover SuZee after dealing with Erwin. She was notified just today of Lan's unfortunate demise in Vietnam, but the recovery of SuZee was still her mission. She would accomplish it in Lan's name. If the Reynolds and their unidentified partner – whom she believed were responsible – were to suffer any harm, it wouldn't break her heart. She would find it karmic, in fact. With SuZee back, she would continue Lan's quest to find and synthesize a black-market health and healing potion and achieve his goals by proxy. She would continue his work in Asia of course; she had plans to shutter the entire plant in Tonopah, not just the basements, and remove all traces of research. Patricia had complete power of attorney over Lan's property and holdings – unbeknownst to his family – but she would treat them fairly and set them up – just not in charge of Lan Pharmaceuticals as that was her role – she was now completely in charge. This last task would be a pleasure.

A twenty-four-hour liquor store was on the corner of the intersection. She decided to stop in and get a pint of Seagram's 7 whiskey to steel her normally calm nerves.

12:00 a.m. Monday

Charles and Dana Reynolds were asleep in their bedroom as soft rock music drifted throughout a brilliantly concealed intercom system. The house alarm system was disarmed in expectation of Taylors' return sometime later that evening. Life had returned to normal for the most part. *Home sweet home,* dreamt Charles.

In the basement gallery, Sheila and SuZee slept peacefully in the overhead cage that served as Eve's home as Eve sat – unmoving – staring intently at the kiosk that held the Van Gogh painting. She was happy to be home with her family but missed the man on the wall. *I will find you,* resolved Eve.

Taylor Scott drove the Lambo south on Pacific Coast Highway, radio blaring as his favorite group, Midnight Oil, sang his favorite song 'Beds Are Burning'. He had an amazing night out in LA and was ready to exit on San Vicente Blvd and return to Beverly Hills. *I love LA,* thought Taylor.

John Fox had just hung up with Marta Hernandez. The Rapid DNA machine had matched Randall Heard to the bills Cherie Swan had received from him following the murder of Ben Walsh. With an LAPD arrest warrant, he would have Heard in jail and perhaps recover the Van Gogh. *I miss Heidi*, reflected Fox.

Randall 'Red' Heard chucked the last bit of shoveled dirt onto the grave that held the box that held the tube that held the Van Gogh now a safe four feet deep discretely hidden on his property. He laughed. It now belonged to the worms. He felt good. No, he felt great! Tomorrow he would leave for Cabo San Lucas on an extended vacation where he learned his lover from Dana Point and her husband were vacationing. Once there, he would offer a fishing trip to the couple and take them both out on the boat. He planned only a one-way ticket for the husband. *Screw this place*, thought Red.

12:25 a.m.

Patricia Stillwater deftly maneuvered the Chevy Express off of Mulholland Drive and maneuvered down a slight embankment and onto a service road two miles from the back of the Reynolds five acres. She stopped the van after a half mile of snaking turns through heavy overgrown Mexican Palms and violet Jacaranda trees that safely concealed her from passing traffic. She rolled down the driver's side window and let the cool evening air into the cabin of the van. The air was redolent with the scent of oranges from a small backyard grove nearby. The groves in Southern California had all but disappeared except for the die-hard gardeners in the hills and the commercial groves in the Inland Empire. She twisted the cap off of her Seagram's and brought it to her lips and drank. The golden-hued fluid pleasingly burned her throat on its way down. *It's going to be a good night*, she told herself.

Her plan was simple and doable. From Erwin she knew where the Reynolds kept their darling little pet. She had consulted the original construction plans for the Reynold's home online – city building permits were a snap to get these days. It may be Beverly Hills but the commercial firewalls that protected the municipal sites were simple enough to bypass from her private IT source. She and Xerxes would enter the house through a rear window or door – whichever proved easiest. To avoid detection and the sound of the elevator, she would access the basement using a back stairwell that had been constructed for the lower level in case of power outages. The stairwell was located adjacent to the elevator through a standard entry door that opened into a walk-in linen closet. Once in the closet, a hinged door at the rear opened to the stairs. Once she was down, she could access the gallery, locate SuZee, and reverse course. SuZee was half the size of Xerxes, and the massive hybrid wolf would effortlessly carry her by her neck with ease. Up and out and they would be gone.

Patricia finished the whiskey and tossed the empty bottle out the window. She glanced at her companion in the rear-view mirror.

"Xerxes, ready," she commanded.

The beast sat up, hunched slightly because of the low cage roof, awaiting more instruction. Patricia exited the van and walked to the back door, opened it, and the beast jumped out. She clipped on a leash, grabbed a toolkit from the cargo area, closed the door, and set off on foot through the brush towards the Reynolds back acreage. The two silently trudged through the overgrowth slowly, she wordlessly, he alertly, with an overcast sky offering scant illumination to guide them. A coyote howled in the distance over a rabbit kill that was then joined by a choir of responses from its family on the hunt. Xerxes halted to listen for more, but Patricia tugged on his tether and the trek resumed. Twenty minutes later they were at the property line delineated by a flimsy wooden rail fence badly in need of repair. Patricia only had to lift a top cross beam and they were on their targeted land. The house was still several acres away down a hill with more native terrain before they would reach the football sized backyard. They pressed on.

1:30 a.m.

Charles lay in bed, awake for just a few minutes. A creak or a door closing must have interrupted his slumber. He felt good. He marveled at this new peace. His nightmares of being back in the jungles of Vietnam had ceased. Whereas a car backfire or a distant fireworks explosion would previously send a shiver up his spine, those sounds no longer bothered him. Loud sounds were just that – loud sounds. He had Dana and the trip to thanks for that – and somehow SuZee had played her part. His mind was clearer than it had been for some time and this new feeling of gratitude comforted him. He closed his eyes and started to drift off but was alerted by a barely perceived sound in the hall. He debated delaying a nighttime exploration but thought better of it and quickly rose from bed, threw on his robe and after a glance at Dana – insuring her soundly asleep – left the room.

The hall from the master bedroom led toward the center of the house past the elevator. Stepping past it, Charles noticed the linen closet door ajar. He reached for the doorknob when the guestroom door across the hall opened – Taylor had returned.

"Allo' mate! I hope I didn't wake you?" he whispered to Charles.

"No. No, it's okay. I was just lying in bed and heard a sound. Not a problem. Glad you made it home all right."

"Easy as pie! Say, could I interest you in a nightcap? The two of us? A *final final* I call it?"

Charles grinned. "I'm up – so I can't say no. Being a good host and all."

"So be it!" the Aussie added.

The two went into the bar/media room and Charles poured them both a generous brandy. Taylor regaled Charles with his evening drive and his star-struck sightings, claiming to have seen Mel Gibson at a stoplight holding a sign.

"It turned out to be just a homeless guy, so I told him he had a nice beard and gave him a fiver," Taylor added.

Charles topped off their snifters and the conversation resumed.

Earlier, Patricia had entered the house easily enough through the sliding glass door – a child's lock at best – and found the stairway to the basement without a problem. She and Xerxes walked the long hallway silently to the gallery door. It was secured so Patricia pulled out a lock pick gun from her bag and quickly disabled it. She and Xerxes entered. She produced a small LED flashlight and searched the wall for a light switch. She located it, flipped it on and the gallery lit up.

Patricia didn't have to spend a lot of time looking for SuZee – it appeared she was lying on the floor in front of a large three-sided kiosk that had a frame affixed to it but no picture was displayed. *Curious*, Patricia thought. It was not a matter that demanded a great deal of contemplation though, as her prize was there and no more searching was required. In and out, she thought. Xerxes ruffled against Patricia's leg, anxious to do whatever bidding she commanded. Patricia cleared her throat loudly to get the N'Khal's attention and addressed her.

"Hello, SuZee."

It was Eve, not SuZee as Patricia assumed, that stirred from a sleep, raised herself up and turned to face the new visitors.

"Remember me? It's time to go home, girl."

In the overhead cage, Sheila and SuZee were alerted by Eve, and both watched the scene below unfold. In unison they quickly vacated their comfortable nest and each started to steal quietly on opposing tracks through the mezzanine of steel that held the gallery lighting and load bearing columns in place.

Patricia once again reached into her bag and produced a tranquilizing gun. Eve recognized the mechanism and crouched down readying a defense from its poisonous bite. A deep guttural sound emanated from Eve, followed by two joining echoes from above.

Patricia quickly scanned the ceiling structures, confused. She waved her gun back and forth, unsure what was now stalking her. She finally saw the two identical N'Khal.

"Oh, you have friends, I see. Well, so do I. And he's quite accomplished in his work."

Xerxes strained at the leash with such strength that he raised his forearms off the floor in anticipation of battle. Patricia could barely hold on. A soundless snarl revealed his potent sharp weapons for the girls to see.

Sheila and SuZee sensed the terrible danger and dropped to the floor on either side of Eve. Patricia waved the tranq gun wildly, unsure of her next move. Eve took a step forward and issued an ear-shattering roar. Patricia fired but Eve evaded the dart with lightning speed.

Patricia had no choice. She released the leash.

"Xeres, kill," she ordered.

Upon command, the mutant wolf leapt forward to attack Eve. Xerxes clearly had the size and power advantage, but Eve's long limbs easily kept his sharks' teeth at bay. The battle was joined by Sheila and SuZee almost immediately and it was crystal clear that their slashing claws, whip like tails, and iron-vice jaws were superior weapons against him. Within seconds, the wolf was fighting for his life. Patricia was dumbfounded at this turn of events. She had expected a quick knockout of the N'Khal and a rapid escape. Instead, she witnessed her number-one weapon rendered impotent, scrambling to escape. The N'Khal continued their relentless assault, each in lockstep with the other to nullify this threat. Bloodied, bruised, and clearly outnumbered, Xerxes withdrew from the fight, galloped back to Patricia, and wilted prone on the floor at her feet. The N'Khal sisters sensed no more danger from the foreign creature and reassembled in front of the Van Gogh kiosk, tending their minor wounds. The N'Khal would fight to protect, but not to kill unless there was no alternative.

2:10 a.m.

Dana awoke in a panic to the sound of breaking glass. Was she having a nightmare? Reliving the terrible event of the past? She immediately reached for Charles, but he was not there. She hurriedly put on her robe and left the bedroom. As she cautiously entered the hall, she was relieved to hear Charles' voice talking to Taylor – telling him not to worry, the glass was one of a dozen, and he would go find a broom.

Dana's heart slowed down. *Men!* Can't live with them and well, so on and so on. She considered joining the two late night revelers but noticed the linen closet door ajar. What were those two doing? She started to close the door but noticed the back wall also ajar. The last time she had even tried to use that stairway was the week they moved in years ago. Maybe one of the 'kids' had been messing about – N'Khals proved curious creatures for sure. Dana turned to leave the closet but just as quickly did an about face and walked down the stairwell.

The door to the gallery opened once again and Dana entered and immediately halted. Patricia swiveled around at the sound, tranq gun raised and trained on Dana. The three sisters sensed the danger and rose immediately, slowly stepping forward. Dana took in the scene and held a hand up as if to order them to stay. Dana would not play the victim ever again if she could help it. She saw the bloodied mutant wolf on the floor, bleeding and nursing its wounds. Charles had told her about the creature he had saved from drowning – this must be it. The woman she did not recognize.

"I don't know who you are but I'd put that down if I were you," she said forcefully.

Patricia stood her ground, unflinching.

"Oh, you must be that madman's assistant," Dana continued. "You must be as crazy as he was to think you could come here." Dana saw Patricia's eyes darting back and forth, weighing her chances of a clean escape.

Patricia kept the gun pointed at Dana. "You're his wife, then? The guy that broke into our facility with that loser Erwin."

"If you mean the *guy* that rescued our N'Khal and freed the one that Lan abused with the help of the only researcher I hear had any integrity, then yes.

Patricia scoffed. "Integrity. Pfff. He begged for his life like—"

She was cut off by a droning from behind her. All three N'Khals were fading and reappearing – in and out as each moved a step closer to her. Dana caught a subtle shaking of the tranq gun as Patricia's resolve started to melt. No more death here, Dana decided. This was designed to be a place of peace and tranquility and the recent events had marred that dream. She would have it back regardless of the cost.

"Think hard, lady. One pull of that trigger is all you're going to get, and the odds are not in your favor. And by the looks of it, your helper there on the floor isn't much interested in your welfare at the moment."

Patricia looked at Xerxes, compliant and still, its eyes averting her.

"I …" She couldn't finish her thought.

"It's over. Drop the gun."

Resigned, Patricia muttered a swear word and pitched the tranq gun on the floor. Dana picked it up. She motioned for Patricia to move out of the gallery.

"Let's go," she commanded.

Patricia reached for Xerxes' leash but Dana stopped her.

"Leave it."

#

Charles went to the utility closet in need of a broom to sweep up the glass that Taylor had broken. He was sidetracked by the odd sound of voices coming from a lower combustion vent in the wall. The vent was part of a fresh air exchange system connected to both the outside and into the gallery. He recognized Dana's voice and an additional one. Sensing something not right, he rushed into the bedroom and retrieved the Beretta from his top dresser drawer, insured it was loaded, then ran into the hall and towards the elevator.

He exited the elevator and ran to the gallery door. Halfway there, he saw Patricia Stillwater exit the gallery. Charles immediately raised and aimed his Beretta at her.

"Easy, hotshot," Patricia said.

As she stepped forward, Dana appeared in the lighted hallway, tranquilizer gun at Patricia's back.

Dana smiled. "I hope you cleaned the mess up there. I took care of downstairs already."

Charles lowered his gun. "I'll call 911."

The door next to the elevator opened and out walked Taylor, brandy in hand.

"Well, I'm late obviously but always up for a get-along!"

"Are you good with ropes?" asked Dana.

"Junior yachting champ, three years in a row!"

From the gallery door, a dark shape slipped out and stepped into the light. Xerxes was up, limping, but mobile. Charles had met the beast before and knew that even though the beast was wounded, it was still capable of enormous damage. Dana slowly scooted around Patricia, tranq gun now on the beast, and stood next to Charles, who had raised his Berretta once again.

"Do. Not. Say. A. Word," she ordered Patricia.

Patricia smiled. "I don't have to," she replied. "I'm sure this clever creation senses my danger now and will make an appropriate response. Oh, she remembers her last command quite clearly."

Charles still had his gun trained on Patricia. "Tell it to stop. Or halt, whatever."

Patricia looked at Xerxes, studying it. Xerxes returned her stare. "I will if you let me go."

Dana looked at Charles. "She's responsible for your friend Erwin's death. She admitted as much to me. We can't."

Taylor piped up. "Whoopee, a Mexican standoff!"

"Is he always this annoying?" Patricia asked.

Charles and Dana stood their ground, Patricia smirked, and Taylor raised his glass and took a sip.

Silence.

Charles studied the creature who was now staring at him. The creature appeared to be deciding his actions – Charles hoped he could get a solidly aimed shot off if the animal lunged but was unsure of the effectiveness on the muscular hybrid. The tranq gun that Dana held would probably overdose Patricia – the last thing he wanted.

Without warning Xerxes took a step towards Charles. Then another.

Patricia affected a malicious grin but the grin quickly faded as Xerxes tucked its tail between its legs, went into a submissive crouch, and inched forward towards Charles. Charles slowly crouched down as the beast moved closer. When Xerxes was a foot away, it lay down and rolled over, exposing its belly. The creature was smart – Charles assumed the animal must have recalled its near drowning. *He remembers,* thought Charles. Erwin said that the creation was made up from other DNA including a tiny amount of N'Khal. Perhaps that portion accounted for Xerxes supplication.

"It likes ya, mate," Taylor softly said.

Charles set his gun down and reached out with an open palm. Xerxes tentatively sniffed, then nibbled at his fingers.

Patricia was furious. "Xerxes! Kill. Kill that sonofabitch!" she screamed.

Xerxes looked back at Patricia as Dana stepped toward her, reared back, and cuffed her hard across the face with a closed fist.

"Nobody calls my husband a sonofabitch!" she shouted.

Patricia went down on one knee in pain. Xerxes gave a silent snarl of approval and returned its attention to Charles.

Taylor clapped loudly. "Bravo!"

Charles decided not to call 911. They would hand Patricia Stillwater over to Detective John Fox in a few hours and spare the Beverly Hills Police Department's finest of having to spend half a day writing reports of whatever weirdness they encountered at the Reynolds residence once again. Dana approved.

CHAPTER 26

7:05 a.m.

Detective John Fox arrived at the Reynolds at seven a.m. prompt. He was greeted at the door by Charles and led in. Upon his entrance, he saw an attractive young lady with blond hair and a large bruise on her cheek, bound tightly in ropes, sitting on the floor of the entryway, handcuffed to a very large man with a shock of white hair, dressed in cargo shorts and a loud Hawaiian shirt. The gentleman sat on a lawn chair and drank from an extremely large mug of steaming coffee. The man raised his mug in acknowledgement.

"G'day, mate!" he greeted.

Fox exhaled sharply and mumbled, "Oh boy."

\#

Over freshly baked croissants – handmade by Charles – smothered with Irish butter and topped with excellent Bonne Mamam Strawberry preserves, Fox listened as Charles and Dana recounted the events of the early morning. He finished off his second croissant, dabbed his mouth with his napkin, and took a drink of coffee. He set his cup on the table and took a deep breath.

"You know this could have ended very badly for both of you had you not had the assistance of your man-made alien DNA lab-created creatures living in your basement that protected you from a mutant wolf creature."

The couple nodded quietly. "And I swear to God Almighty I cannot believe I actually said all of that with a straight face," Fox said.

"We can't either," Dana countered with a sly grin.

"As for Ms. Stillwater, I'll call the Goodyear police shortly and have them send a unit to *quietly* pick her up at the station. They will probably require a statement from you, Dana. I assume that's not a problem?"

"Not a problem."

"And an arrest warrant for first-degree murder is being signed," he checked his watch, "as we speak, for Randall Heard. Hopefully we will have him in custody in the next hour. From there, it's a longshot, but maybe he'll actually admit to knowing the whereabouts of the Van Gogh."

"That would be nice," Charles interjected.

"Yes, it would."

Fox looked down and grew silent as he played with the handle of his coffee cup. He looked up at the couple.

"I have a favor to ask."

8:15 a.m.

Heidi Richards left her doctor's office in Chino Hills following her early morning appointment. It was a long drive from Pasadena but Doc Hedderman had been her family physician for years and she trusted him over any fancy young Oncologist she had been advised to see. He reminded her of Disney's Geppetto. His kind eyes, still bright and lively at eighty-five, his gentle but stern voice, and his warm bedside manner made her feel like she could overcome anything. She had an hour's drive back home at this time of day and used it to reflect on what the doc had told her. She was not at all surprised at the news that there was very little that could be done at this point to stop the metastasizing of her cancer. Pancreatic cancer was difficult to detect early, and in her case, had spread quickly.

She felt bad putting off John Fox's phone calls and texts. Today she would remedy that.

8:30 a.m.

Detective John Fox brought Patricia Stillwater to the BHPD and placed her in custody until she could be remanded to the Goodyear PD. They seemed quite excited to hear about her activities in California and immediately dispatched a cruiser to LA where Patricia would have to cool her jets now for the next six hours. Fox was driving out to join the warrant serving party at Randall Heard's place when his cell buzzed – and was surprised to see Heidi's name come up.

He pulled his cruiser over to take the call.

"Heidi! Hi," he answered.

"Hi, John. I'm sorry I haven't returned your calls. I've been out of town.

There was a pause – Fox heard her take a deep breath and sigh. He didn't know what to expect next. "John. Roy and I are divorced. We both knew it was just a marriage of convenience, but I had had it. And with what's going on now…"

"Yes?"

"With what's going on now, I need… I need you more than ever," she said, her voice cracking.

Fox was both heartbroken and hopeful. He heard something in her voice that he had not heard before. She sounded overwhelmed. At the same time, he wanted to share his news, but he didn't want to do it over the phone.

"Can we meet later?" he asked. Heidi agreed and suggested a late lunch at the Ombra in Glendale. If all went well, he'd be done with Heard and available for a lazy rendezvous. Besides a superb selection of wines and craft cocktails, the place had a fantastic made-from-scratch Italian menu, and Fox knew it was one of Heidi's weaknesses.

9:40 a.m.

Fox pulled up in front of Randall 'Red' Heard's home well before any black and whites had arrived. There were no cars in the driveway. *Was he even home?* Fox mused. It would be a gigantic shame if all of the work and effort that had been put in to get to this point was for naught. The Chief was still under the gun from the mayor despite the great BHPD cooperation he received for the Globes and he needed another win. Fox got out of his cruiser and started to walk up the steep driveway as a blue Nissan Murano with an UBER sticker on it pulled up and went past him and over a ridge – taillights sinking below his line of sight. Fox walked cautiously up on the side of the drive until the Nissan came into view. A heavy-set young Latino driver sporting an out-of-place bowtie was loading suitcases into the rear hatch of the car as Red was on his cell talking animatedly. Fox withdrew a service revolver from his shoulder rig and marched up towards the car, pistol in both hands, aimed at Heard. The damn cruisers should have been here by now, but it is what it is. Please don't make this harder than it is, he thought. Red saw Fox and immediately went to the driver and grabbed him in a headlock, dragging him back towards the front of the vehicle. The driver wrestled but was held firmly in place covering Red. Fox marched towards Red and his hostage. With his free hand, Red pulled out a .22 pistol from the small of his back and held it against the Latino's temple.

"Get back, man!" he screamed.

"Randall Heard. You know me. Detective John Fox, Beverly Hills PD. You have an arrest warrant issued in your name for the murder of Ben Walsh."

"Yeah, I know you – the phony translator. Thought you could trap me, huh? Your little charade failed, dude! You move any closer and I'll break this guy's fuckin' neck. Then I'll shoot you. I swear I will."

"There's no need for that. Let him go and we'll talk. You don't want this."

"You don't know what I want. You have no idea the hell I've been through! I just want to get the fuck out of here for one thing. This place is driving me crazy. You all are driving me crazy. And I'm not crazy! I got rid of crazy! I did!"

"Hey, relax. I know you're not crazy. But if you don't let him go, you'll never have the opportunity to tell your side of the story."

Heard whispered in the hostage's ear. "Tell him I'm not crazy. Tell him it's all good, okay? Tell him!"

"He's... not crazy," the Latino barely choked out.

"Say it again!" demanded Red.

"He's all good."

"It's the painting you know, Detective."

Fox shook his head, not understanding. "What about the painting?"

"It's cursed," he said and laughed. "It mocked me! It's sucked the life out of me. It's... I'm a failure! That's my fate!"

Fox watched as Red whispered something into the young Latino's ear while two black and white police cruisers came up over the steep driveway and screeched to a stop. The officers inside flung open their doors and pulled their service weapons out and aimed them at Red. Fox turned to address them.

"I got this under control, Officer," he said as a shot rang out.

He turned back and saw Red collapse onto the ground and the young Latino break away. Fox lowered his weapon and holstered it. He stood there transfixed as the two officers approached the body. The first officer kicked the gun away from the fallen man, the other checked for a pulse. There was none. Fox roused himself, then walked slowly to the back of the Nissan and unloaded the suitcases. He was surprised to find them incredibly light. So much so that he placed one down on the ground and opened it. It was empty. *Why?* he wondered. He turned to see the driver sitting by the side of the driveway so he walked over and sat next to him. The driver looked at Fox.

"I don't think he was crazy, but he must have been very sad and lonely," he said.

"Why do you say that?"

"The last thing he whispered to me was, 'There's nothing left. Please forgive me, but what else can I do?'"

The young Latino grimaced and shrugged his shoulders, then added, "Do you have a smoke?"

Fox shook his head. "No, I do not. But today I wish I did."

11:30 a.m.

The drive to Glendale to meet Heidi was fraught with calls from the Chief and the shift supervisors of the responding officers. He ignored them all. He argued with himself over his handling of the incident. Fox couldn't figure out if Heard was ill, depressed, or just insane. He certainly did not expect Heard to end his life. The man must have been under pressures Fox couldn't imagine. He was clearly guilty of murder and warranted to be held responsible for it, and he probably knew the whereabouts of the stolen Van Gogh, but justice in either case could not now be served. It was not a satisfying ending for the BHPD, the Reynolds, or for Fox.

He pulled up in front of the Ombra and immediately saw Heidi's car. She would normally be waiting for him to escort her inside to get seated, but she was not in the vehicle. He walked in the restaurant and went straight to the bar. Sure enough, she was sitting at the bar, a clean Vodka Martini in hand. She glanced over to see Fox enter, waved him over. He thought she looked exhausted. Tell-tale signs of sleepless nights etched new lines across the corners of her eyes. She was free of any makeup that would have concealed her now sallow complexion. Her blond hair was normally silky smooth but now appeared brittle and dry. He sat next to her and gave her a peck on the cheek.

"Hey, you okay?" he asked.

She gave him a counterfeit smile. "I feel as good as I look. What does that tell you?"

"The truth? A sick you would still outshine a well Miss USA any day!"

Heidi took a sip of her drink. "This helps, although it's supposedly not good for me, so say the doctors."

"Ah, doctors. They're all quacks."

The bartender placed a whiskey sour in a coupe on the bar in front of Fox.

"I ordered for you. Added egg white of course."

"Of course." Fox raised his glass in a toast.

"What are we toasting?" Heidi asked.

"My murder suspect confirmed his guilt today."

"That's good, isn't it?"

"It was a messy confession."

Fox knew Heidi would understand his description.

"Oh. That's… a bummer."

They both quieted and sipped their drinks. Fox swiveled his stool to confront her head on. No time like the present, he decided.

"How much time do you have?" Fox asked.

Heidi tilted her head and shook it slightly. "You mean… today? I wouldn't be very good company, I'm afraid."

"No. I mean how much time have the doctors given you?"

"I…" She shrugged.

"Listen. Don't speak, please, until I'm finished. I'm crazy about you. I want to spend every waking hour with you. I don't want you to go off somewhere and deal with this cancer without me. I love you. I know it's irrational and fantastical, but I think the thing that saved Dana Reynolds can save you too. I don't know how it does it or what, but I believe it can cure you. If we don't try this, we'll never know. What do you say?"

Heidi moved back slightly in her chair. She drained her Martini and waved to the bartender for a refill.

"Well?" Fox asked.

She studied his face with narrowing eyes. "Did you say you loved me?"

He hesitated. "Yes. Yes, I did. And I do."

Heidi leaned forward, reached out and held his face in her hands. The two shared a lingering kiss.

"I love you, too. And no matter what happens, or how long we have, I also want to spend it with you. And Hell yes, we'll give it a try," she added.

4:00 p.m.

Charles stood at the entry to the gallery where hours earlier the three sisters had become one in their fight to protect Dana. Eve sat in the middle of the room while Sheila and SuZee chased each other above the mezzanine. He was in awe of the bond the three had formed so quickly. What must their home world have been like? This species that was below their masters yet above all other living creatures that could perform miracles of healing and commune over miles. This was a truly enigmatic and special sentient species. What terrible sin did Earth commit that deprived this world of such a special gift? Sadly, Charles knew that if the N'Khal were revealed to the world, every unscrupulous individual or corporate entity like Lan's on every continent would emerge to violate and abuse their uniqueness for their own benefit. What must their world have been like to be given such an inheritance?

Charles walked towards the sitting Eve. She held vigil, waiting in front the kiosk that held the Van Gogh. Like the storied faithful canine companion who sits at the foot of its master's grave, she was waiting for the Man on the Wall to come back home and complete her family here. Charles sat next to her and rubbed her back, a soft purring emanated. It was musical in a way he had never heard – palpable yet comforting. Eve leaned against him. Charles knew that the love she felt for the Reynolds was not diminished by the missing portrait, but felt it was a tacit disappointment.

Taylor spoke to the Reynolds at length of his desire to return soon to Cambodia and made clear his desire to bring all three N'Khal home. Charles grappled with the offer but recognized from the start that he and Dana were only temporary caretakers of Eve. She belonged with her sisters away from the spying eyes of civilization. She deserved to be with her family. Taylor was even planning on bringing Xerxes to his lab to remove the chip and let him live out his life. Surprisingly, the mutant wolf approached Taylor that morning and would not leave his side. "Maybe it was the Aussie accent," joked Dana.

Maybe it was the permanent scent of alcohol, Charles thought.

10:00 a.m. Tuesday

Detective John Fox and Heidi arrived at the Reynold's home the next day. Charles noticed the difference a few weeks had made in the sick woman's appearance. John had informed him of the disease's progress and although Heidi walked in unassisted, it was clear she was assuming a brave exterior. Small things usually unnoticed were present. A halting stride in an otherwise fluid walk, a few seconds of unfocused discussion, a grimace in pain that sprang out of nowhere – things that added up to someone undergoing a terrible trial.

Charles' recalled that the Reynolds had been touched by the disease years earlier. His sister had perished of this malevolent hateful sickness ten years prior. She had a particularly bad case of laryngeal neck cancer and had undergone a jaw replacement, chemo, radiation, everything. And everything failed. Not bearing to see her suffer alone in some cold nameless institution, he and Dana moved her in for whatever hospice was left. The night before she passed, Charles sat with her as she struggled to breathe. The cancer had simply grown out of control and was tenaciously closing in on her windpipe.

"You look tired, bubba," she whispered with labored breath. "You get some sleep. I'll be fine."

"You sure, sis? I can stay," he assured her.

"No. You've had a long day. I need my sleep too."

Charles reluctantly gave her a dose of morphine that seemed to help her rest. Before retiring he sat down on the living room sofa and prayed to the God that he had given up on years before that all the pain would just stop. Hers of course, but his too. She was dying incrementally in front of his eyes and there was nothing more he could do.

The next morning, he went to check on her and discovered her half on and half off the soiled bed. She was cold and the room silent. The oxygen generator had shut down sometime during the night, but it was of little consequence. She had suffocated to death, and it was over. Oh, how he wished for a magical moment then. But in her memory, he would endeavor to help his friends now.

Dana greeted the two as old acquaintances and sat them in the living room as if they were there for nothing more than a casual visit. Charles marveled at how easy Dana could engage guests and make them comfortable, a skill Charles still found awkward.

"I understand you live in Pasadena. Is that right, Heidi?" Dana asked.

"Yes, near the border of San Marino."

"Oh, such a lovely area all the old homes and cottages. Near the Huntington?"

"I'm only three blocks above the grounds,"

"Charles advises the curators there sometimes,"

Charles shrugged. "It's not a lot. Special pieces mostly."

Heidi nodded and started to speak, but cleared her throat, and the coughing started. Violent and constant. Heidi reached for a tissue Dana offered for her mouth, and as she settled down and took the tissue away, the blood was noticeable.

"I'm sorry," she apologized, as her eyes filled with tears. "It's just…"

Dana comforted her. "No please. Let's not pretend this is a Sunday brunch party – you're here for a reason, so we should get to it." She looked at Charles.

"How does it work?" Heidi asked.

"Let's go to the guest room," Dana suggested.

The four of them went into the guest room and Dana helped Heid lie down on the king-sized bed. The drapes were drawn, but sufficient light filtered through so the room was dimly lit without glaring. A lamp on the dresser next to the bed cast a soft, comforting glow.

Dana sat next to Heidi and held her hand. Charles addressed her.

"We've kept Eve a secret here in our home for over a year now. We didn't know what she was or what she was capable of until Dana was wounded. Eve took it upon herself and recognized that she needed help. I have no idea if she will be able to do the same with your cancer. But John believes she can, and so do I. Just remain calm and let the her lie next to you. Then the rest is up to her."

"You're the boss," Heidi said.

"Ready?" Charles asked. Heidi nodded. "Don't be afraid. She's quite gentle."

Dana opened the door and Taylor walked in with the N'Khal by his side. She greeted Dana and Charles with a soft rumble then saw Heidi. She strode to the side of the bed and put her paws on the top of the mattress, looked at Heidi, and then caught some scent beyond human perception. She quickly hopped up on the bed and proceeded to lie next to Heidi and started a low thrumming as her brilliant coat started to shimmer and change colors. In a matter of a few minutes, Heidi and the N'Khal were almost transparent – a blur of a barely visible, translucent form. Fox approached Charles.

"Now what?" he inquired.

"Now we wait."

They left the room and pulled the door to – just enough to hear sounds if needed. Taylor approached Charles.

"Can I have a word, mate?"

Charles glanced around and walked him across the hall. "Sure, what's up?"

"That was Sheila I brought into the bedroom."

"Sheila? Why? Where's Eve?"

11:00 a.m.

Charles and Taylor entered the gallery to find Eve still holding vigil in front of the main kiosk that held no canvas.

"She wouldn't budge. Don't worry, Sheila will take care of that young lady I'm certain. But her? What's the attraction?"

Charles explained that after the Van Gogh was installed, he and Dana spent numerous evenings at the gallery with Eve and always ended up at this spot. The Van Gogh was a special addition to the collection and Eve must have sensed their appreciation and attention to the rarity. Eve must have developed an extraordinary attachment.

"Who knows what goes on in that mind? We're still just scratching the surface," he added.

"Do you think the painting is still here in California?"

"I can't say for sure, but if Randall Heard had it, it may be."

Taylor rubbed his chin and gave Charles a roguish glance. "I have an idea."

12:10 p.m.

Heidi dreamt. She was in a verdant jungle, walking amongst rows of green golden-tinged plants and silver trees. N'Khal and other species shared the walkway as did men and women of all colors and indeterminate ages – all long-limbed with brilliant swirls of shimmering clothing clinging to their sinewy bodies. She somehow knew the name of the race was the N'Ghap. They were both the planet's masters and servants – all caretakers. They enjoyed a freedom from tyranny, hate, war, greed, and all forms of evil that the planet had endured millions of years previously – but amazingly, the race had evolved and escaped the behaviors that destroy worlds. The N'Ghap now bore the fruits of universal knowledge, fellowship, servitude, and true love.

Heidi saw a sky filled with birds flying in formation and roosting on tall towers and spires. Laughter erupted from nowhere and everywhere. She reached out to touch a delicate flower and as her finger approached it, it took flight – its petals now wings, its stem, its legs.

Heidi drifted away from the vision of that perfect world to one of brilliant light streaking out of her body. Each streak produced a pain that bit sharply but healed instantly – the beauty of pain released. She never knew such a thing could exist but she surrendered to it.

She then fell back, retreating from the bolts of light, as a warm darkness overtook her.

#

Taylor left Charles in the gallery with Eve and returned with a small disc and length of chain. He threaded the chain through a clip on the disc and asked Charles to place it on Eve's neck. He hopped over to the kiosk and with his pocketknife sliced a tiny sliver of canvas that still remained in the frame that had held the Van Gogh. He returned to Charles and offered it to him.

"Hold on to this," he said.

Charles took it.

Taylor continued. "I put Sheila through a battery of tests and tasks in Cambodia. The N'Khal are super sensitive. Eve heard the call from SuZee over hundreds of miles, right? It could be thousands. I'm not sure, but their sense of smell is equally keen. That's a GPS tracking device you've placed on her neck. We're going to see how much bloodhound she has in her. Let her get the scent of the canvas."

Charles held the remnant of the canvas up to Eve's face. At first, she paid no attention, but quickly sprang up, took two steps, then ran to the equipment room. Charles glanced quizzically at Taylor.

"She caught whiff of something. Let her go," Taylor suggested.

Charles ran to the equipment room in pursuit of Eve, but she had already followed her original escape route and once again tore the grille off the exhaust vent. Taylor joined Charles in the room.

"She's gone," Charles announced. "What do we do now?"

Taylor took his cell phone out and pressed a few buttons, then showed it to Charles. A flashing green dot was moving across a digital terrain onscreen.

"We do nothing. Until she stops."

3:00 p.m.

Detective John Fox sat bedside in the guest room as Heidi slept and SuZee treated her. The shadows in the room darkened as the sky grew increasingly dark and a rainstorm threatened. His mood matched the sky as he watched every move Heidi made. She slumbered fitfully for the first hour, then had slowly settled into a deep unmoving slumber. Not knowing what to expect, he would occasionally feel for a heartbeat or perform a temperature check – each time assured she was, yes, still alive. Dana checked in throughout the day and brought the detective coffee and sandwiches. Four hours had passed and neither knew how long this process would take but Fox was not going to leave her side.

In the kitchen, the second vigil was being held by Charles and Taylor. Eve was on the move. The GPS showed a slow steady pace through the hills surrounding the Reynolds home, then an expanded trek that brought her south through the Franklin Canyon Park mountains, further south through

Holmby Hills then west to Bel Air. Fortunately, there were no freeways to cross and the streets would be easy to pass over, especially in her hidden translucent state. Raindrops spotted the pool outside. A late winter storm had been brewing for most of the day and by five o'clock a steady drumming of light rain on the aluminum patio pergola was heard, punctuated by the occasional cymbal crash of thunder. In a state of perpetual drought, the rain was a needed amendment to the dry brush of the hills in Southern California. Taylor assured Charles that a little rain would not deter Eve from her quest.

Taylor broached the conversation of his return to Cambodia.

"Have you given any more thought to what I suggested for the girls?"

"You're referring to taking Eve?"

"Yes. Of course. I know she means a lot to you both but to be with her family, away from prying eyes, in a protected environment. I really think it would be for the best."

"I really haven't given it a lot of thought."

"You know she'd be well cared for."

"Oh, I know that, it's just—"

Taylor interrupted. "Hold on. She's stopped. Wait a bit. It may be just a momentary halt."

Minutes passed as Dana walked in on the two, hunched over Taylor's GPS.

"Anything new?" she asked.

"Taylor thinks she's stopped. How's Heidi?"

"No change. Do we know where she is?"

Taylor piped in. "I've got an address. It's in Bel Air."

As Taylor announced that, the detective walked in.

"What's in Bel Air?"

"We think Eve found the Van Gogh," Taylor announced as he held out his phone with the GPS location pinging Eve. Fox studied it.

"Shit! That's Randall Heard's place."

The three men stared at each other.

"Wasn't his place searched?" Charles asked.

"Yeah. The house. But he lives on two acres of sloping woodland."

Taylor snapped off his phone and asked Fox, "Do you have any rain gear?"

"Yes, I do."

4:00 p.m.

Dana volunteered to keep watch on Heidi as the men gathered raingear, outfitted themselves the best they could, and set off to make the trip to Bel Air. The steady rain had grown into a full-fledged thunderstorm that had reportedly already clogged drains and washed out a number of intersections on Mulholland Drive. What was an uneventful run-of-the-mill storm in a place like Seattle was a major headline news story in Los Angeles. It was not going to be an easy trip.

Mulholland east to Beverly Glen was the quickest route but the winding roads that skirted the steep valleys were already slick from accumulated oils and already some crumbling retaining walls had dumped debris in the roadway. They approached Beverly Glen as the last light of day bid goodbye and darkness abounded – streetlamps flickered as a nearby transformer blew, spewing sparks and smoke, then died out. The headlamps of the black LTD barely cut through the curtain of rain that fell, then danced madly on the roadway as if they were sizzling oil drops on a flaming hot frying pan. At Beverly Glen, they were stopped by a line of cars blocking the intersection. Two Highway Patrol officers were directing the cars in various directions. Fox rolled down his window as an officer approached.

"You going down Beverly?" he bellowed over the rain.

"Yes, we are, Officer. I am Detective John Fox, Beverly Hills PD. We need to get down there ASAP."

"Ain't gonna happen, Detective. Washed out at the Glen Center. If you go back to Deep Canyon, it'll take you to Benedict, take that and then watch for Angelo Drive. From there you can get back to Bev Glen. Be careful on Angelo though, it'll be just you and canyons on both sides."

"Will do. Thanks."

Fox cursed, turned around, and went back as directed – passing a growing line of cars.

The trio made fair time as they approached Angelo and turned onto it, but after a few hundred yards they were stopped by a red PT Cruiser that had overturned onto its side and was up against the railing overlooking a forty-foot drop. Fox had enough room to drive past the wreck and park the cruiser upstream of the rushing waters. He left the car and immediately went to check on the occupants. Charles and Taylor waited in the cruiser as instructed by the detective. Taylor checked his cell.

"Eve's still in place. Hasn't moved."

Fox rushed back and opened the trunk of the LTD and started retrieving emergency gear – a first aid kit, blankets, two miscellaneous bags. The two got out to help. Fox handed a small kit containing flares to Taylor.

"Taylor, can you light these?" Fox yelled over the downpour.

"Yes."

"Good. Set up a gradual perimeter starting about two-hundred feet away to warn any oncoming vehicles. Then get back to me. We have two adults and a child in the car. We need to try to right the car and triage them until the ambulance arrives. They were able to call 911. In this rain, it's going to be awhile."

"What can I do?" Charles shouted.

Fox grabbed Charles by his shoulders and brought his face close to his. "You take the car. You go up to Randall Heard's and you go get your Eve and whatever she found."

"Are you sure? I can help here."

"No need to. This is what I do, buddy. There are tools in the trunk if you need anything. You go get your girl."

Charles nodded, opened the driver's door, and got in. Fox pounded on the trunk twice and the LTD sped off.

8:45 p.m.

Dana sat bedside as Heidi fluttered her eyes open. She blinked several times, trying to remember where she was and what she was doing. It came back in a rush. She took a deep cleansing breath, held it, then exhaled slowly. She lifted herself up and looked at the N'Khal beside her. SuZee rested peacefully as a yawn followed by a slight whine escaped her mouth. Heidi pushed back against her.

"Her breath stinks," she said. "Can I get a water?"

Dana smiled and poured her a glass from a crystal pitcher nearby.

"How do you feel?" she inquired.

Heidi took the glass and drank half in one gulp. She handed the glass back to Dana, then proceeded to perform a brief self-exam – feeling her neck, chest, and stomach.

"I feel nothing. Is that good?"

Dana noticed the color had returned to her face, her hair looked freshly conditioned, and the clouded eyes had cleared. She took Heidi's hand and felt her – she was cool, and her skin was smooth and supple. This was a different woman than the one who had entered this house six hours earlier.

"I think it's very good."

#

Almost an hour after leaving Fox and Taylor, Charles finally wheeled the cruiser onto the winding road to Heard's place, entered his steep driveway, and parked over the rise that ended in front of the house. The residence was dark and presumably empty. He grabbed an olive-drab knapsack from the trunk that held a flashlight and some additional raingear and tools. Remnants of yellow police caution tape from the early morning's incident whipped violently in the wind driven rain. Charles walked around the side of the house, calling for Eve.

The wooded area behind the house was steeply graded and not tended by any landscaper other than Mother Nature. The rain pelted him, making for a slow marathon. Charles first worked his way across the breadth of the property, crisscrossing down in a grid search for Eve. It was a jungle of overgrowth, and the pounding rain kept his visibility limited but he vowed to cover every square inch. If Eve had found what she was looking for, she would stay with it through the rain to protect it.

It dawned on Charles that's what the N'Khal were – they were protectors. It was the reason they held a special place in their home world. It was the reason Eve had acted those weeks ago when Dana's safety was jeopardized, and the reason yet again just the day before. Now, in searching for the Van Gogh, she was in her way, protecting the last member of our family – he thought – attempting to bring him home. Charles selfishly wanted to keep Eve as part of the family, but even Dana recognized that it would not be in Eve's self-interest, it would be in theirs. Perhaps Taylor was right – she truly needed the community of family and her own species.

Charles and Dana were simply her caretakers for a short while – a short wonderfully miraculous while – one that had changed their lives. How much more could a person ask?

He saw her brilliant coat off in the distance under a large Coast live oak. The canopy of the sixty-foot-tall monster provided for some respite from the rain for Eve, but she seemed impervious to it. As Charles approached, she ran to him and circled around him madly in greeting, edging towards the dig she had started. She hopped into the shallow hole and resumed her dig. Charles laughed at the sight of this beautiful creation, now covered in mud, flailing rapidly at dirt that just as rapidly fell back in on her. He mused that dogs dig; cats simply prefer to move dirt around.

"Looks like you need some help there, girl," Charles bellowed out. He squeezed himself into her work, and she just as quickly jumped out to let him take charge. From the knapsack, he pulled out a small military trenching tool, and dug. The rain washed down the sides, filling the channel with muddy water, but he kept at it. Eve looked on nervously, pacing around the hole, occasionally pawing away dirt that did little to help the cause, but made her feel part of the process. As the water steadily rose, soaking his boots and pants, he glanced at Eve, now sitting perfectly still, observing him, softly glowing and illuminating his labor. What power had she unleashed in him and Dana and all who came into contact? This once small and helpless creature had bonded with his family and extended their love and caring. Charles knew he was making the right decision; however painful a goodbye would be. He resumed his digging, hands now cold and raw, but his heart warmed by the soft purr and display Eve presented with a newly added swirl of changing colors and burning intensity.

Just as it seemed this excavation would yield nothing but blisters and the onset of pneumonia, Charles' shovel felt hard steel. At the same moment, another bobbing light from the hillside caught his attention. Shielding his eyes, he could make out a figure starting to close in on him – and smiled – it was a figure he had burned into his memory. Eve's brilliant color display increased in luminosity and into this bright light walked Dana. Her hair was matted, soaked, and plastered against her face, her eyeliner steaked from cheeks to chin, and her lipstick smeared from wiping away the insistent rain – and yet she was the most beautiful sight Charles had ever imagined.

Panting from his labors, Charles crawled up to greet her. He could only manage a "What… are you doing he—?"

Dana cut him off. "I got worried. You didn't answer your phone. I finally got a hold of Taylor and he told me where you were. Did you find it?"

"Eve found it. I think"

"You need help?"

"Would you just stand by if I said no?"

"Try me," she said.

With the prize now in reach, Charles helped her down into the excavation and doubled his efforts – Dana helped him scoop mounds of muddy earth away from the sides of the box with their bare hands until he had enough of a grip to pull it up partially. Dana joined in and they both lifted the metal box to the side and momentarily rested as Eve pawed at the hasp. They crawled out and pulled the box towards the base of the great oak that provided a slight reprieve from the deluge and the streams of rainwater that cascaded down the hill towards the valley below. Eve lay down next to Dana and snuggled under her arm as Charles opened the hinged top. Inside the box he extracted a round tube mailer. He opened the end and pulled out the contents.

Charles had expected it to be the painting, but the exhilaration of fulfilling his expectations overwhelmed him. As he unfurled the canvas, he could feel a vibration from Eve that was in perfect sync with his emotions. The Van Gogh was going home. Eve let out a triumphant cry that echoed across the canyon. Charles knew deep down that SuZee and Sheila felt her victorious howl.

Through the pelting rain, Charles heard their names being called once more from above. He looked up to see two figures, flashlights in hand, scouring the area with arcs of light. He recognized Detective Fox and Taylor. Eve bounded up the hill, greeted them, and romped back down with them in tow.

Charles hollered out as they got close. "I didn't expect to see you two here."

"That CHP officer came to check on us and offered a ride after the ambulance left. That family's okay," Fox said.

"Thanks to this guy," Taylor added, pointing to Fox.

"You sure got here fast!" Charles added.

Taylor cocked his head and looked at Fox, confused. "Fast? You left us four hours ago!"

Charles looked back at the hole he had dug, now serving as a swimming hole. He grinned.

"Well, I guess it's true." He looked at Dana. "Time flies when you're having fun."

Fox and Taylor looked at each other again, even more confused.

"Did she find the Van Gogh?" Fox asked.

"Yes, she sure did!"

"Then let's get you all home."

11:00 p.m.

Charles Reynolds unfurled the canvas on top of his desk. It had been rolled, folded, creased, water stained, had what appeared to be pinholes in it, and the fibers on its edges were starting to unravel in more than a few places. But – his experience assured him – it could be repaired and made as good as new. The similarities to this past month did not escape him.

Upon arriving home earlier, he was pleasantly surprised to see Heidi join the welcoming party. She looked amazing – thanks to Sheila and a dab of makeup courtesy of Dana. Detective John Fox swept her off her feet and gave her the biggest kiss Charles had ever witnessed. Dana whipped up some simple bacon and tomato sandwiches and a thick homemade potato soup to warm up the group and Charles opened a couple bottles of Fess Parker Chardonnay to share with all. Eve stayed close to both Charles and Dana throughout the late supper, as if she knew her time here was coming to a close.

Eve peeked over the edge of Charles' desk to see him work as he dried and cleaned the Man on the Wall the best he could before placing it in the hands of a restorer. A warm glow emanated from her along with a faint purr that did its job of comforting Charles from the day's challenges. It truly was a good day.

EPILOGUE

Charles and Dana Reynolds allowed Taylor Scott to adopt Eve. They make a twice-yearly trip to Cambodia to visit the girls and Taylor. Charles gifted the Van Gogh painting to Taylor's foundation and named Eve Reynolds as its caretaker.

They are great friends of Detective John Fox and Heidi Richards and spend Christmases together. Charles winnowed down his gallery collection to a few personal pieces and with the monies, started a non-profit job training center serving homeless veterans.

The couple continue having afternoon cocktails at their Beverley Hills home but do not answer the door to many strangers any more. Chloe has free reign of the entire estate.

Detective John Fox retired from the BHPD. Heidi Richards was healed completely from her cancer, much to the surprise of Doc Hedderman. The two got married and moved to Santa Barbara where Fox surfs and Heidi teaches forensic sciences at a local college. Heidi and John both compete in amateur bodybuilding and powerlifting competitions across the United States.

Taylor Scott brought all three N'Khal back with him to Cambodia to live together as a family. A family that will grow as Taylor's wife is expecting their first child. Taylor successfully removed the chip from Xerxes and he became a faithful protector and companion to the N'Khals. The Aussie continues his yearly trek to Koh Ker to enter the remains of the N'Ghap spacecraft where he claims to have uncovered additional DNA and hopes to identify it – and recreate whatever it may be.

THE END